If Valerie Frankel weren't a writer, she'd probably be a bad lady. Fortunately, she's found her niche, writing novels and magazine articles for women who share her somewhat dirty sense of humour. Her previous books include *The Accidental Virgin* and the Quills Award-nominated *The Girlfriend Curse* which *People* magazine described as 'wickedly entertaining'. Frankel writes about sex and dieting for *Cosmo*, *Glamour*, *Self*, *Allure*, the *New York Times* and *Marie Claire*, among other publications. She lives in Brooklyn, New York, with her two daughters and her husband.

D0610123

Hex and the Single Girl

Valerie Frankel

little
black
dress

First published in 2006
by HARPERCOLLINS PUBLISHERS INC.

First published in this paperback edition in Great Britain in 2006
by LITTLE BLACK DRESS
An imprint of HEADLINE PUBLISHING GROUP

A LITTLE BLACK DRESS paperback

1

ISBN 978 0 7553 3674 6

Typeset in Transit511BT by Avon DataSet Ltd,
Bidford-on-Avon, Warwickshire

Printed and bound in Great Britain by Clays Ltd, St Ives plc

Headline's policy is to use papers that are natural, renewable and
recyclable products and made from wood grown in sustainable
forests. The logging and manufacturing processes are expected to
conform to the environmental regulations of the country of origin.

HEADLINE PUBLISHING GROUP
A division of Hodder Headline
338 Euston Road
London NW1 3BH

www.littleblackdressbooks.co.uk
www.hodderheadline.com

Dedicated to Elizabeth Crow,
who, in my memory,
is always laughing.

On a clear day, Emma Hutch, thirty-three, could see forever – give or take a few yards. Technically, she had 20/20 vision in both eyes. If a normal-sighted person could spot a dog in the street from half a block away, Emma could read the license plate number on the truck that swerved to avoid hitting it. Emma's hearing was also sharp. With the clarity of a diamond, she could eavesdrop on her neighbors talking, singing in the shower, or going at it. At her will, having learned over the years to filter out extraneous noise, she ignored them. Sometimes, though, she listened. Even more dynamic, Emma's sense of smell had both strength and acuity. She could detect a pinch of cilantro in a stew or a waning blossom in the wind. Upon meeting new people, her nostrils could sniff out their essential goodness – or badness.

At six o'clock (on the nose), Emma opened the door of her apartment to Daphne Wittfield, a new client.

Instantly, her nasal membranes sprang to attention.

Daphne Wittfield smelled like money. Great green piles of it.

'I am *so* glad to meet you,' said Emma with a big smile, hopefully not too desperate. 'Please, come in.'

The tall blond gave Emma the once-over twice. 'You don't look like a witch,' said Daphne. Her eyes narrowed. Like every other part of her, they were narrow to begin with.

Emma was dressed in a black turtleneck, jeans, black high-heeled boots, and blue-tinted sunglasses. She said, 'We gave up the pointy hats back in 1567.'

'But you look harmless. Bloodless.' Daphne paused. 'That concerns me. And this apartment. It's all white.'

Emma said, 'Makes it easier to find myself.' She waited for Daphne to laugh. Nothing. 'Why don't we sit? Get to know each other better.'

The two women walked across a white shag carpet to the plump white couch piled with white fluffy pillows. The blond shoved the pillows to the side and sat, crossing her long legs at the knee. Emma guessed Daphne was in her late twenties with skin as tight as an apple peel, puffy lips, a pert nose. Her buttery hair was expertly streaked. The client seemed custom designed from the top down. Then again, for all Emma knew, Daphne and her high, hard breasts were one hundred percent authentic. Emma didn't have EPSP (Extra Plastic Surgery Perception).

She sat next to her client on the couch, smiled brightly, and rubbed her palms on her jeans. For some reason, Daphne made her nervous. Emma took a deep breath, inhaling the client's odor of crisp bills. It calmed her down, but not enough.

'What's with the sunglasses?' Daphne asked. 'It's been dark out for an hour.'

Emma instinctively touched her blue shades. 'Most people find the color of my eyes to be a bit distracting.'

'Do they?' asked Daphne, amused (apparently, she was not *most people*). 'Let's see.'

Emma took off her glasses with a theatrical flourish. She almost said, 'Ta-da!'

The blond gasped when she set her eyes on Emma's. She recovered quickly and said, 'Yes, quite dramatic. Put the glasses back on now.'

Replacing them, Emma said, 'Before we get into the nitty-gritty, I have to object about the pace you want. I prefer to go slow. Do the research. Observe from a distance and then make contact.'

'On the phone you said you'd start immediately.'

'Pressure makes me nervous, and, frankly, I've felt queasy from the moment you walked in the door. But then again,' Emma reflected, 'it could be hunger.'

Daphne asked, 'Are you trying to jack up the fee?'

Emma hadn't thought of that. 'What if I am?'

'I offered double your usual rate.'

'But that was before we met.'

'It's been three minutes!' said Daphne. 'Are you the Good Witch or a judgmental bitch?'

'Can't I be both?' asked Emma.

Daphne checked her watch. Frowning impatiently, she reached into her black leather tote, extracting a manila envelope with the Crusher Advertising logo. From that she removed a stack of one hundred dollar bills and fanned it like a deck of cards.

'That explains the smell,' said Emma.

With the authority and condescension of a Fortune 500 company vice president, which she was, Daphne said, 'Five thousand now. Five thousand when the job is done. You will agree to work my case exclusively for two weeks. I want three hits a day, seven days a week. If you fail to secure me a first date in that time, you won't get a second payment and I'll trash your reputation all over town.'

Emma considered her options. She said, 'I don't work on Sundays.'

'Three hits a day, six days a week,' corrected Daphne. 'I'll get you access – invitations to parties and events, reservations at restaurants. It's an aggressive approach. But I hate wasting time.'

Emma longed to grab the bills and rub them all over her naked body. Only an hour ago, just as the October sun set, she'd gone through her mail and found a third ('final') foreclosure warning from Citibank. But Emma hesitated. She had rules about new clients. They had to (1) have good referrals, (2) seem deserving of her help, and (3) be motivated purely by love. If Emma were to take the cash from Daphne, she'd be breaking at least two of her rules, and possibly three. Violating her principles would hurt Emma's sense of ethics. But losing her beloved Greenwich Village one-bedroom would hurt much, much more.

She took the money, of course. Who wouldn't? She took the money, and maybe she'd regret it later, but right now, Emma thought, holding the stack in her hand, she felt immense relief. And humble gratitude.

'Thank you, Daphne,' she gushed, squirreling the bills in her side table drawer. 'I want you to know that this isn't just a business transaction. We're initiating a personal relationship, too. I provide my clients – my *friends* – with emotional services as well. A hand to hold. A shoulder to cry on. We can talk every day, a few times a day, if you need emotional support. I'm available. I listen.'

'That's nice,' said Daphne. 'Can we move this along?'

'O-*kay*,' said Emma. 'Tell me about the man in question.' She leaned forward, grinning. This was her favorite part of the interview, watching her clients' faces light up when they spoke of love. Their excitement, the passion, the pure undiluted joy of mad attraction. Emma soaked it up with genuine empathy. She felt their excitement in her own blood. Vicarious thrill had been sustaining Emma for quite a while.

'I've compiled some information about him,' said Daphne. As she spoke, she pulled a blue plastic folder from her leather tote and passed it to Emma.

A plastic folder? This was the passion, the excitement? 'Most women can't shut up when I ask about the man.'

Daphne groaned. 'I met him a month ago. He hired me to work on an advertising campaign for his new product. And that's all I need to say. Five thousand dollars can do the talking for me.'

'It's definitely speaking my language,' said Emma. 'But, you see, I need to get a sense of the back story, the building of desire, the emotional longing.'

The client gave her a fishy look. 'You get off on this, don't you?'

Emma may have blushed. 'What's the big hurry? Why

two weeks or nothing? What happens if you don't get him by then? You'll dry up and blow away?'

'I'm impatient. I don't want to drag this out,' said Daphne (impatiently).

Emma knew she was striking her head against a brick wall to argue with Daphne. And the blond was a client, after all. Emma was in no position to piss off a paying customer. 'All right. Enough chat,' she said. 'Would you like to see a demonstration?'

Daphne said, 'I didn't come downtown because I like filth.'

'I have to touch you,' said Emma. 'Most clients prefer to hold hands. While we're doing that, try to clear your mind.'

'Do I have to close my eyes?' asked Daphne.

'You don't, no.' But Emma would have to close hers to concentrate. She fizzled when she tried to do it with her eyes open.

'Will the picture come in slowly, like adjusting a camera lens?' asked Daphne.

'It'll be sudden,' said Emma. 'People describe it as a pop.'

Daphne offered her right hand. She wore three rings, all of them heavily jeweled and expensive.

Emma never wore rings. They could catch on clothing and she needed fast hands. Plus, distinctive jewelry was identifiable and therefore reckless. Emma hid her memorable hair – bronze, long, wavy – under wigs. Her eyes were hidden behind tinted shades. Emma had tried colored contacts, tried desperately, prying her eyelid open, jabbing the lens in, blinking, tearing, cursing, sweating, and giving up in frustration. So glasses would have to do. Her ample breasts also drew unwanted attention. Since it was her job to follow and surreptitiously fondle strange men in New York City, she often flattened her rack with Ace bandages.

Emma clasped Daphne's hand and considered what image to send. Daphne was in advertising, so commercial and corporate images were out. The blond probably wouldn't be amused by Mona Lisa with a mustache or the David with a tube sock. A wildlife scene? Emma closed her eyes.

Daphne said, 'Nothing's happening.'

'Just wait.'

'Okay, yes. I got it,' said Daphne.

Emma released Daphne's hand. She said, 'Was the image black and white or in color?'

'Black and white and red all over,' said Daphne.

Emma laughed.

'Tell me what I saw,' said Daphne.

'A lion eating a zebra.'

'Incredible,' said Daphne. 'Do it again.'

'What sort of image?' asked Emma. 'Funny, historical, sexy?'

'Sexy,' said Daphne.

Once again, Emma took her client's hand and closed her eyes.

'It's cloudy,' said Daphne. 'No, it's *steamy*.'

'Shhh,' said Emma.

The two women sat holding hands on the couch, both with their eyes closed, breathing shallowly. After a minute, Emma released her client's hand.

Daphne said, 'Tell me.'

'A man and woman in the shower. Her breasts are pressed against the wet, slippery glass shower door. One of his arms is tight around her waist, his other hand is cupping her . . .'

'That's enough,' interrupted Daphne. 'I'm convinced.' She stood up, too excited by what she'd experienced to sit. She toured Emma's living room office. 'Your power,' she asked. 'What do you call it?'

'I don't like the word "power",' said Emma. 'Makes me sound like a mutant.'

'You are a mutant,' said Daphne. 'I've never seen orange eyes before. Except on a cat.'

'They're *amber*,' corrected Emma. 'And my *skill* is called telegraphopathy.'

'Like a telegraph?'

Emma nodded. 'I transmit images over a short distance – the distance between my brain and yours. I can't receive. And I can't send thoughts or words or movies. Only still pictures. Images can be powerful, though. And dangerous. Which is why I use my skill to help people. For the greatest good.'

'Romantic love,' said Daphne.

'It's all you need,' said Emma, although she managed to muddle through without it.

'Is that what you really believe, or the rap you give to clients?' Daphne asked. She paused in front of a framed diploma on the white wall behind Emma's desk. 'Certificate of authenticity from the Berkeley School of Extrasensory Perception.'

'According to my testers, I'm one of a kind,' said Emma.

'The only confirmed telegraphopathist in the world.'

Daphne asked, 'Do you ever send the wrong picture?'

Emma shook her head. 'I have complete control over what I send and when. Don't worry about accidents. They never happen.'

'You mentioned a contract?' Daphne checked her watch again.

Emma went to her desk and found a standard contract printed on The Good Witch, Inc. stationery. She filled in the name, date, payment schedule, and handed the sheet to Daphne.

The blond read the contract on the spot and signed. Most women took a day. But Daphne did so hate to waste time.

'Call me tomorrow after you've looked through the folder,' said Daphne. 'I have meetings all morning with the SlimBurn people, but I can get to your photographer's studio in the early afternoon.'

Emma's jaw dropped. 'You do the ads for SlimBurn diet pills?'

The blond nodded. 'You like them?'

'I've seen them.'

'We're in the same kind of business, Emma,' said Daphne, smugly. 'We both use the power of image. I do it to sell a product. You do it for the greater good.' She said the last two words with sirloin-thick sarcasm.

'The *greatest* good,' said Emma.

'If you say so,' mocked the blond.

'I want you to swear right now that your intentions are honorable and that you are genuinely, humbly, painfully in love with this man,' said Emma, pointing to the folder on the couch. 'I won't take the case otherwise.'

'I am. In love with him,' said Daphne.

Emma stared at her, wanting to believe. She inhaled deeply, looking for the odor of a lie, but could still only pick up the lingering scent of greenbacks. 'The photographer's studio is also on Waverly Place, right across the street,' she said. 'He's got racks of costumes and props there, so you don't need to bring anything.' Emma handed Daphne a card with the address. 'He'll bill you separately.'

'I'm looking forward to it,' said Daphne. She picked up her tote and headed for the door. 'One more question, before I go.'

'Yes?'

'Do you use your power – *skill*, whatever – to make men fall in love with you?'

'Am I self-serving? Just the opposite, Daphne,' said Emma. 'I put all my energy and concentration into my job. I'm devoted to my clients and work around the clock on their cases. The truth is, I simply don't have time for a love life of my own. Besides, I derive huge satisfaction from helping other women find happiness.'

The blond blinked. Then, with a loud snort, she started laughing and kept at it for way longer than necessary.

When she pulled herself together, Daphne asked, 'Has that little speech fooled anyone? Ever?'

2

Brain fuzz. That's what Emma called the post-transmission cranial snowstorm. Along with that, she sometimes felt ravenously hungry (like now). Or desperately horny (like always).

She pulled off her boots, padded to the center of the room, placed a supportive hand over each tit, and jogged in place. Exercise was the only way to clear away the fuzz, something about blood flow to the brain.

'Wish I had my camera,' said a voice at the doorway.

Emma turned to see her best friend, the photographer Victor Armour. He'd let himself into her apartment (he had a key) with the stealth of a mouse.

He asked, 'Did I surprise you?'

With her super ears, Emma had heard the elevator doors opening on her floor, the footsteps in the hallway, the key tumbling into the lock, and the door creaking open.

'You got me that time,' she lied, still jogging in place. 'Did you see a cool, leggy blond in a tight gray suit in the lobby?'

'You pass the "talk test",' said Victor. 'Just read about it in the *Times*. If you can exercise and talk at the same time, you are not a fat slob loser.'

'I'll cross that off my list,' she said, stopping. 'She's coming to your studio tomorrow.'

'The cool blond?' he asked, flopping onto the couch. 'Is she going to give me a hard time?'

'Hard in all the right places,' said Emma.

'Really?' he asked lasciviously. 'Show me.'

He held out his hand, wanting Emma to put Daphne's likeness into his head. She swatted it away and took a seat next to him. 'I don't transmit on command.'

Victor was both Emma's confidant and her colleague. She funneled her clients to him. He snapped sexy photographs of the women, which Emma memorized and then implanted into the minds of the men they desired. Victor liked his job a little too much.

'I thought you had a date tonight,' he said.

'It's not a date,' Emma corrected. 'It's drinks with a friend who happens to be male.'

'Drinks?' said Victor with disgust. 'Who is this jerkoff? He can't feed you?'

'Hoffman Centry. Book editor at Ransom House. You met him.' Victor gave her the blank look. 'Two days ago. In front of the building?'

'Oh, that guy.' Victor grinned. 'Totally your type. A sexless smurf you'll never be attracted to, so you're safe. Ah, yes, the picture is coming in clearly now. *He's* not the one withholding dinner. You're keeping it liquid. I'm sure he'd love to feed you.'

'A tube steak with relish?' she asked.

'A ham boner,' said Victor.

Emma said, 'Why does it always have to be about sex with you? Hoff and I are friends. I like spending time with him. He's smart and sweet. He smells like Elmer's glue.'

'What do I smell like tonight?'

She put her nose against Victor's neck and inhaled. 'You smell like . . . a stallion . . . cantering across an open prairie . . . a potent musk rising from your mighty flanks . . .'

'All that and a hint of Irish Spring,' he said. 'It's been six months since the last time you tried to have sex. You should give the smurf a chance. Maybe it'll be good with him.'

'I'm not up for another humiliation,' said Emma. 'It batters the soul. I'm a deeply sensitive person, as you know, Victor.'

'So you say, over and over again. Get in the shower,' he said. 'I'm choosing your outfit tonight.' He stood up, helping Emma to her feet. They went into her (white) bedroom in the back of the apartment. She ducked into the (white) bathroom while he threw open her closet doors.

Victor had an eye for frame, color, and content, which made him a talented photographer. But style was his sixth sense. He could reach into Emma's cluttered closet and pull out pieces that fit together into a cohesive, kooky whole. Left on her own, Emma would wear the same black dress and boots every time she went out.

Emma emerged from the shower to find half her clothes on the bed. Victor had not yet found an outfit to his liking. She watched from the uncovered corner of the bed as he appraised her meager selection.

'Black, black, faded black, graying black, pilling black,' he said, pushing one hanger aside at a time. 'Witches don't have to wear black. You won't be excommunicated from the coven if you wore, say, red or purple.'

Emma said, 'I'm not in a coven. I'm the lone witch. And speaking of other, lesser witches, what's the Monica update?'

He shrugged and said, 'Her tits are small, she laughs like a donkey, and she doesn't swallow.'

'She should be shot,' said Emma.

'And get this: Monica said she didn't believe a Greenwich Village photographer with a two hundred dollar haircut and low-rise jeans could be straight.'

'Small-minded publicist,' said Emma. 'Anyone can see that you're straight but not narrow.'

'Well, I straightened her out,' he said. 'Monica will never come below 14th Street again. A-ha!'

Victor had found a red wrap dress under a pile of sweaters on a high shelf.

'What is that?' she asked.

'You don't know?' He held it up to his chest. 'Needs ironing.'

'It's one of my mother's dresses,' said Emma. When Emma's mother died eight years ago, her dad had given her a bag with some of Anise's clothes. The pieces had floated in and out (mainly out) of her awareness, unworn, overlooked. Until now.

'It's so red,' said Emma. 'And the material is too thin for October.'

'Wear a coat,' said Victor. 'You do have an iron?'

'Under the sink.'

He dropped the dress on the bed and went to get the iron. Emma touched the soft rayon, the scent of cinnamon rising from it, as if her mom were in the room. Emma's heart clenched. She'd been grappling with her mother's legacy for nearly a decade already. She preferred not to think about it, especially on not-dates. But she couldn't easily push those thoughts to the back of her mind if she were wearing Mom's clothes.

'I'm not putting that on,' she announced when Victor returned to the bedroom, a hot iron in his hand.

He said, 'You're wearing it.' He put a towel on her dresser and the rayon frock upon it. In a few swift strokes, he made the dress look new. He wrapped it around her and tied the bow expertly just above her hip. A quarter inch of her lacy black bra showed. She started to pull up the neckline to cover it, but Victor said, 'NO! Do not touch. Leave it exactly like that.'

Victor picked black patent pumps and red, sucking-on-cherries lipstick. He stroked the makeup on thick and blow-dried her bronze waves straight, training strands to dip into her décolletage.

He steered her toward the full-length mirror on the inside closet door.

'Yes, this is a hell of a dress,' she said, gazing at herself. 'Yes, I am a hell of a woman.'

'This Hoff won't be able to keep his smurf mitts off you,' said Victor. Seeing her expression, he added, 'Keep thinking about how hot you look. Maybe you'll excite yourself.'

'You talk as if I don't want a relationship, as if I purposefully date men I'm not attracted to. And it's not a date. It's drinks with a friend who is male.'

'I thank God every day that you never jerked me around like this poor preppy,' said Victor, turning on the TV. 'My cable's out. Don't worry. I'll be long gone by the time you bring home the smurf. And I'll hang up these clothes so you can use the bed.'

She left him to his channel surfing. With a few free minutes before she had to leave, Emma went into the living room and opened the folder Daphne left for her.

The top sheet was an 8×10 glossy black and white publicity photo of the man she'd be stalking for the next two weeks. He wore a dark jacket, white shirt, and a skinny tie. No ring. Good. (Emma refused to work on married men.) She guessed he was in his mid to late thirties. His hair was dark brown or black, foppish, bangs hanging in his blue or green eyes. He was slender with fine bone structure. His expression was confident, but not effete, a mischievous schoolboy all grown up. In his eyes, she detected a mix of intelligence and ego.

It was an undeniably handsome face. Emma would come to know it as well as her own. She'd follow him. When opportunity presented itself, she'd touch him and transmit a sexy image of Daphne into his head. Emma had committed to three hits a day, except Sundays, for two weeks – or until he asked Daphne on a date, whichever came first.

If he were like sixty percent of the men Emma had worked on before, he would call Daphne within ten days. If a guy found himself picturing the same woman nearly naked multiple times a day, day after day, he'd reach the logical conclusion that *he must be in love with her*. Or, at the very least, in lust. And it would follow that the man would ask his love/lust object on a date. Emma would receive a second payment. Then she'd wish her client the best of luck and bow out. As she explained before accepting any case, her job was to create the spark that the client would then fan into a flame. Once the relationship began, Emma's involvement ended. It was in the contract.

She looked up from the photo and around her cherished white sanctuary. Women in love had paid for every stick of furniture in it. Her income, like most freelancers', was cyclical. She'd been on a down swing for a while now. With her nest egg evaporated (another story), Emma hovered on the brink of losing what she loved most. She needed Daphne's money badly. This case had to go smoothly.

Victor wandered into the living room and into the galley kitchen. She watched him pull a Diet Coke out of the fridge.

Emma held up the glossy for him to see. 'My new target.'

Victor took a sip and glanced over. He then spit a mouthful of soda on the kitchen floor.

'Hey! I just Swiffered that!' she said.

He rushed over and snatched the photo from Emma's hand. Shaking it, he asked, 'You don't know who this is?'

She scanned the photo. No recognition. She looked down at the dossier stuffed with press clippings and an address list, including his home(s), office(s), favorite restaurants, dry cleaner, coffee shop, bank, movie theaters. She read the name on his bio.

'William Dearborn,' she said. 'Oh.'

'You've heard of him?'

'Of course. I don't live under a rock. I live on top of one.'

'He's an artist and designer. He invented the best-selling software for editing digital photographs. I use it every day! I collect postcards of his paintings! He's a legend, a fucking genius, stinking rich. He's slept with more beautiful women in the past week than I will in my lifetime.' Victor got quiet. 'He's my idol,' he whispered reverently. 'I worship the shit on his shoes.'

'This is bad,' said Emma.

'This is great! The cool blond – she's after Dearborn?' He was practically peeing his pants with excitement.

'No wonder she's paying me so well,' said Emma. 'How am I going to get near him? He's probably got body-guards.' She remembered that Daphne said she'd help her get access to him. But what of his revolving bedroom door? Would his head be so crammed with libidinous memories that the Daphne pictures – however risqué – wouldn't register? Emma didn't have much experience meddling in the minds of visual artists. Dearborn's logic was bound to be more circuitous.

Victor was thinking the same thing. 'William Dearborn might be the one man on the planet who's immune to your mental manipulation,' he said.

'Don't underestimate me,' she said.

He shook his head. 'I'd never do that. But don't underestimate him either.'

Hoffman Centry sipped his wine. 'Are you sure you don't want to order an entrée?'

Emma had engulfed most of the plate of appetizers Hoff ordered for them to share. He barely got his fork in.

'I can't believe I ate the whole thing,' she said, backing away from the food. 'I was hoping to come off as classy.'

'You do look classy,' he assured her. 'Like a high-priced gun moll.'

She laughed and then smiled prettily at him.

He stopped talking and stared. This happened sometimes. She'd gone without shades tonight, and Hoff was stuck in her eyes, his own glazed over, his mouth slightly open.

'Ahem,' she said. 'Would you get me another beer?'

He snapped back to reality. 'Right away,' he said, squeezing her hand. 'Do not move from this spot.'

Emma checked out the joint from their booth. Hoff had

taken her to Ciao Roma, an Italian lounge/restaurant nestled between Chinatown and the Financial District, blocks away from the border of Little Italy. According to Hoff, Ciao Roma was one of the best-kept secrets in Manhattan. Judging from the empty tables and lonely barstools, the secret might be too well kept. She watched Hoff talk to the ancient white-haired bartender who looked like he'd uncorked many thousands of bottles of Chianti in his lifetime. As if on cue, he and Hoff looked at Emma at the same time.

Emma busied herself by eating. She popped a tentacle of calamari between her cherry-colored lips just as Hoff returned with her beer and another glass of wine for himself. Instead of sitting opposite her, though, Hoff slid in next to her. His thigh touched hers under the table.

She said, 'It's stuffy in here.'

'We can leave,' he said. 'Go to your place.'

'No!' she said, way too quickly. 'I'm still eating.' She ate another tentacle.

Hoff was patient. Hoff was polite. Hoff was raised to be respectful of women. He looked good in a black cashmere jacket, lavender shirt and flat-front khakis. Emma had enjoyed their friendly not-dates and wanted to keep him in her life. But the only way to make sure of that was never to be alone with him.

The bartender left the room.

Hoff said, 'Finally, we're alone.'

She tried diversion. 'Tell me about this top-secret project. The one you're so busy with at work.'

He said, 'It's a non-fiction book called *Smoke and Mirrors*. The author is Seymour Lankey, the former CEO of Riptron Electronics. You must have read his name in the newspapers. Huge corporate scandal. Cooked accounting books. Criminal investing practices. An executive cover-up, embezzlement, six hundred million dollars missing from the pension fund.'

'I'm familiar with the case,' said Emma in a small voice.

'You look sick all of a sudden,' said Hoff. 'Is it the calamari?'

'I'm fine.'

He continued, 'In the book, Lankey claims he's been railroaded by a junta of second-tier execs that'd accused him of stealing and hiding the missing money. All of them, including Lankey, are in prison, convicted on criminal charges. There's a class action lawsuit pending – brought by Riptron employees and small investors. But even if they win, the plaintiffs won't see a penny unless the missing money is found.'

'Is this a hardcover book? Retails for twenty-five dollars?' she asked. He nodded. 'With my share of the settlement, if I ever get it, I'll buy a copy.'

'Oh, Emma!' said Hoff. 'Not you!'

'I was one of the so-called small investors,' she said. 'To the tune of one hundred thousand dollars. I lost my life savings.'

Hoff whistled. 'Sorry to hear that. A hundred grand. You make that much excess cash consulting? I'm still not clear on what exactly you consult about. You always change the subject.'

She hadn't told him much about The Good Witch, Inc. She was loath to launch a conversation about her special ability. So she went vague. 'It's a matchmaking service,' she explained. 'I help women and men take the first step.'

'How can we take the first step?' he asked.

She said, 'We've gone out six times.'

'Whenever I touch you,' he said, 'you tense up.'

'Hoff, we're friends.'

'You're not attracted to me.'

'You're adorable, Hoff. I just don't want to risk our friendship.'

'I haven't been thinking of you as a friend, Emma,' he said. 'My feelings for you are unfriendly.'

And now he was going to say, 'Have sex with me or forget the whole thing.' She'd lost more potential friends this way. But she'd rather lose a man to an ultimatum than a botched sexual encounter. She decided to give him her usual excuse for sexual aversion, which served the dual purpose of turning him off and placing the blame solely in her own lap (as it were).

'The truth is, Hoff,' she said gravely, 'I'm anorgasmic. I can't come. Freud would have called a woman like me frigid.'

'You can't come?' he said, incredulous. 'Never?'

'Can we drop the subject?'

'Of course,' he said. 'But I want you to know, Emma, that your inorgasmia—'

'Anorgasmia.'

'Your *anorgasmia* is not deterring me. In fact,' said Hoff with seriousness, 'I think I can help you. I know I can. Give me a chance.'

'Not a good idea,' she said.

'Why?' he said.

'Trust me,' she said. 'Sex with me will not be fun for you.'

'I'll have an excellent time,' he said. 'And so will you. I promise.'

'What if you break your promise?' she asked.

'You can spank me,' he said.

Emma laughed. Well, he hadn't flinched. He was made of tough stuff. Perhaps Victor was right. She was due for another attempt. Maybe sex with sincere, sweet Hoff wouldn't be a disaster. A shot of optimism buoyed her hopes. Or maybe it was that the three beers were now making themselves known to her bladder.

'Would you excuse me for a minute?' she asked.

He slid out of the booth to let her get by.

Just then, a group of around ten people banged through the restaurant doors. They were loud and probably drunk. The men were dressed down, except one guy in a skinny brown suit. The women, laughing and stumbling on platform sandals, jiggled in halter dresses under faux-fur coats. A pair of the high-haired women peeled off from the cluster and stumbled sloppily, yet fetchingly, to the bar.

Hoff said, 'So much for being alone.'

'I'll be right back,' she said, and walked through a large, dark, deserted banquet room in the rear of the restaurant toward the neon sign that hummed, 'Ladies.' She entered the dim room and locked the door behind her.

After using the facilities, Emma washed her hands and examined herself in the mirror. She did resemble a gun moll, with the big eyelashes and red lips. She liked how she looked and wanted desperately to be admired, appreciated, loved. The things all women craved.

Emma decided then and there to give Hoff a shot. She might wind up with another mess to clean up, but she was tipsy enough – and he was smitten enough – to push fear aside.

A knock. She said, 'One second.'

Emma swung the door inward and stepped into the dark banquet room. Suddenly, strong arms circled her waist from behind, lifting her off her feet. They carried her into the darkest corner of the deserted room. She couldn't see a thing (Emma's vision could go great distances, but nowhere in the dark). Before she could react or speak, soft lips pressed against her throat, moving quickly up the side of her neck until they found her cherry-colored lips.

Hoff was much more daring than she realized, Emma thought. She struggled a bit against the force of his kiss and the arms around her waist, her ribs crunched, lungs compressed. He pulled back momentarily, giving her a chance to breathe, and then plunged in again, lifting her higher off her feet, sealing her mouth with a dizzying smack.

She sank into it, against him. Her entire lower half ignited as if she'd waded into a pool of fire. Hands on her lower back, pressing her tighter against his body. A hand on her ass, lifting her higher. How had she not noticed that Hoff was so tall? Or that he'd stopped smelling like glue and had taken on the scent of toasted marshmallow? She held on, her arms around his neck. Behind closed eyes, she saw red flames that licked and swirled into white tips. Each passing moment sent the flames higher.

And then a shrill scream. 'Get your hands off him!'

Emma felt herself falling out of his arms, landing on her

feet, but not squarely. She could make out the shape of a woman in front of her. For once, Emma hadn't heard her coming.

'Liam! What the fuck is going on here?' demanded the female silhouette.

The lights came on. Emma blinked and registered that a dozen people were streaming into the banquet room. A platinum blond was standing in front of her, huffing, puffing. She was gorgeous, skinny, tall, and furious. She stamped heels sharp enough to pick teeth with, her mouth twisted and her sea-blue eyes roiling in fury. Despite the malevolence, the woman's powdered skin and pink lips made Emma think of a strawberry Pop Tart, right down to the red sprinkles of her sequined mini-dress. Emma doubted, however, that this woman had a fruity, gooey center.

A tall man in a brown suit was standing next to Emma. His lips were smeared with cherry lipstick. Hoffman Centry, weirdly, was only just now coming into the back room from the bar. Emma realized with a start that the tall guy, this Liam, was who she'd been kissing. He gaped at her, his eyes and mouth round Os.

Feeling embarrassed, exposed, and freezing cold, Emma hugged herself. The front of her dress felt clammy and damp. She looked down, horrified to see that, from neckline to hem, the fabric was soaked.

'Liam, you're all wet!' said the Pop Tart.

True enough, his jacket was covered in dark blotches and his shirt was ringed with sweat. His shaggy hair was damp, and his forehead dripping.

Hoff was pushing through the crowd, gawking at

Emma's wet dress, and then looking at the equally soaked man next to her. He asked, 'Are you all right?'

She croaked out, 'I'm okay.'

The crowd of people, giggling nervously, did laps with their eyes at the principal players in this mini-drama. Emma dared to glance at the Pop Tart's angry scowl, at Hoff's frown of concern, at the man who'd mauled her. He was still staring at her with jade green eyes, seemingly unaware of everyone else in the room, or that beads of sweat were streaming down his neck.

With a faint English accent, he said, 'I was a fireball rolling down a smoking mountain.'

No one else spoke for a few seconds. Then Hoff placed his jacket around Emma's shoulders and said, 'I'll take you home.'

'I thought he was you,' she said feebly.

Liam said to the Pop Tart, 'And I thought she was you. You did tell me you were going to the bathroom.'

'I had to get my purse out of the limo first,' she said. 'And how do you expect me to believe that you could mistake *me*' – she placed her pink shell of a hand on her skinny collarbone – 'for *her*' – pointing an accusatory finger at Emma's plump chest – 'even in the dark?'

Good question. Emma would have loved to listen to his answer. But Hoff tugged her back into the front room of the restaurant, grabbed her coat, draped it over his jacket on her shoulders, dropped a hundred on their table and propelled her through the door of the restaurant. She could hear the tall man stammering for an explanation all the way out.

Sure enough, a limo idled at the curb. They walked

quickly past, Emma still shivering, even with two coats on.

Hoff said, 'If you were going to mistake another man for me, you couldn't have chosen a more impressive substitute.'

'You know that guy?' she asked.

He seemed surprised by her question. 'You don't?'

He had looked familiar, but he'd been wet and unhinged. Plus, she'd been so embarrassed, she could barely look at him.

'I'm not sure,' she said.

Hoff said, 'That was William Dearborn!'

Oh, no. 'That woman called him Liam.'

'Short for William,' said Hoff. 'He must have some kind of glandular problem. Sweating like that.'

She groaned. 'You think he got a good look at me?' she asked.

Hoff laughed. 'I'm sure the sight of you with a soaking wet dress plastered to your very female form is now and forever burned into his brain.'

Shit. So much for anonymity. She'd have to use her most exotic disguises with him.

Hoff hailed a cab, and they got in. He gave the driver her address and said, 'So you really thought William Dearborn was me.'

'I sure didn't think he was him!' Dearborn was the very last man on Earth Emma wanted to be noticed by.

'And you liked kissing him?' asked Hoff.

'It was okay.' It was the best kiss she'd ever had.

'So you'll probably like kissing me,' said Hoff.

Without waiting for the go-ahead, Hoff planted one on

her, a squishy, gurgly kiss that made Emma think of Liquid Plumber unclogging the kitchen sink.

She pushed him away – gently, with the strength of ten butterflies, not wanting to offend – and said, 'I need another drink.'

As soon as they'd reached her apartment, Emma changed out of her wet dress. She put on a two-piece pajama set, tops and bottoms, navy blue fleece with a snowflake pattern. Not sexy stuff at all. Nonetheless, when she padded in her PJs into the living room, Hoff said, 'Let me give you a back rub.'

'Okay,' she said.

Hoff started rubbing, massaging, kneading. The muscles in Emma's back yielded. She softened. A sigh slipped from her lips.

'Better than a drink, right?' he asked. She nodded. He *was* good. Emma wondered how many back rubs he'd given to seduce women before. Not just seduce. He could make a woman fall madly in love with him because of this. Emma wondered if it was wrong to fuck a man for his thumbs. Not that she would.

Hoff's hand slipped under her pajama top. Emma

instantly tensed. Hoff felt her reaction, but he kept working his wonders, making her spine bend with relief.

She said, 'Do you believe that everyone has a special gift? A special "power", if you will?'

'Absolutely,' he said.

'I think I know what yours is.'

Hoff laughed. 'You ain't seen nothing yet.'

He forged on, squeezing, pulling, hurting her the right way. Emma let herself float along, on a raft of relaxation, on a slow and winding river, pine trees on the bank like in Maine, the scent of clean air, the sound of running water.

Emma was still on that raft when Hoff raised her arms to remove her pajama top. She stayed on it as he laid her down on the couch, belly up. He began massaging her again, turning his attention to her large floaters.

Hoff was as good with the front rub as he was on the back. Better, even. He slipped off her pajama bottoms. And then nothing. Emma opened her eyes a crack and saw that he was undressing himself.

He caught her looking and said, 'Is this all right?'

'So far so good,' she said. After that volcanic kiss at the restaurant and a float down the river thanks to Hoff's magic fingers, Emma had high hopes. If she were ever going to have successful sex, it'd be tonight.

He removed his clothes in a hurry. 'You have a nice body,' she said. Hoff was medium weight, not very toned, but not flabby either. His bare chest was freckled and pale, his belly cutely rounded. The legs were sturdy. He left on his boxers, and she wished he'd take them off. She hadn't seen a naked man in at least eight months. And all she remembered of that night was the guy's bare ass as he stumbled into the hallway, his clothes a bundle under his arm.

Hoff knelt in front of Emma, who was still on her back on the couch. He put his hand on her belly. She cringed.

Hoff said, 'Relax.'

'Sorry,' she said.

'Don't apologize.'

'Sorry for apologizing.' Emma took a few deep breaths and tried to calm down.

'You're all stiff,' he said.

'As are you,' she replied. His hard-on stretched the purple polka dot shorts before forcing itself through the gap, jerking and twitching like a puppet on a string.

Now or never, she said to herself. Emma patted the couch and Hoff sat. She took his place, kneeling on the floor in front of him. She opened her mouth and closed her eyes. Emma began moving her head slowly, her hands resting on his legs.

Emma had to be doing something right. Hoff moaned and put his hands in her hair. He was throbbing, puffing bigger in her mouth with each movement. William Dearborn, from what she could tell, had a bigger dick than Hoff. During their kiss, he'd pressed himself, rocked himself, against her hips. Emma imagined William now, on her couch, naked, legs spread, cock big and red as a fire hydrant, jerking himself off with one hand while the other hand rested on his stomach like a wounded bird.

Hoff made a strangled, caged sound. Then he went limp as a shoestring in her mouth.

Emma released him and thought, 'Here we go again.'

Hoff sprang to his feet, tucked himself back into his

boxers, and reeled away from her as if he'd discovered a pair of horns under her hair. He stammered, 'I . . . I . . . I've got to go.'

He turned his back to her and searched crazily for his clothes. His face was bright red. When he put one leg in his pants, he tripped forward and fell on the floor. Rolling onto his back like a beetle, he tried to put his other foot in, the empty pant leg flapping above him.

Emma slipped on her pajama top and said, 'I'm not letting you leave until you tell me what just happened.' She'd said the same thing to over a dozen men in the past. None had given her satisfaction.

Hoff got his khakis on and was buttoning his shirt. He said, 'This has nothing to do with you.'

'My sex life has nothing do to with me?' she asked. 'I'm repellent. I disgust you.'

'No, you're gorgeous. Your body is fantasy material. It's not you. Something's wrong with me. I need to think about it alone. It's private. I can't talk about it.' When he said the last part, his voice caught like he might start crying.

Most of the men cried. Some wept. Some cursed, groaned in psychic pain, squeaked with fear. 'I'm not anorgasmic,' she confessed. 'I only said that so we wouldn't end up exactly where we are now.'

'I was on the verge of a massive orgasm, and then . . .' Hoff looked terrified.

'Please sit down,' said Emma, managing to lower him to the couch.

He moved slowly, as if in shock. He said, 'It's not you, I swear it. You are amazing. What you were doing, I was in ecstasy. I was impressing myself with how hard I was, how big, and . . . then . . .'

'Go ahead,' she urged.

'At a very critical moment, I thought of something . . . it was horrible.'

'What was it?'

'I can't,' he said, shaking his head, the heels of his hands pressed against his eyes.

'You'll feel better if you just tell me,' she said softly.

'It was William Dearborn,' he blurted, voice jagged. 'I saw William Dearborn, completely naked. He was . . . I can't say it. He was performing a sex act.'

Emma's heart skipped a beat. Was it possible? Had she sent an image by accident, without flicking the mental switch to transfer mode?

Hoff said, 'I've always admired William Dearborn. I thought it was based on respect and envy. But now I see that I haven't wanted to *be* William Dearborn. I've wanted to be *with* him.'

Emma's head spun with revelation. She replayed botched sexual encounters in her past. To compensate for her ambivalence, for her lack of attraction, for the man's incompetence, she'd fantasized about other men, during.

'Seeing him in person at the restaurant tonight must have been some kind of trigger,' said Hoff. 'I want William Dearborn! He's a man. I'm a man. This means I'm gay.' He looked accusingly at Emma. 'All because of your blow job. I don't know whether to thank you, kill you, or throw up.'

'Are those the only options?' she asked.

Hoff stood. 'I've never had the faintest interest in men. The idea of sex with a man has always made me gag. I've loved girls since I was five. I must have suppressed my homosexuality so deeply that I've overcompensated with unrelenting lust for women.'

'There could be another explanation,' said Emma tentatively.

'Such as?'

'Such as, I was thinking about William while blowing you and you somehow knew.'

He considered it. 'Not possible. You were so into it. You were honest and loving. Right now, looking at your bare legs, I'm getting hard. I'm twitching in my pants. You'd think I was straight as a missile.'

On that tantalizing note, Hoff fled her apartment, leaving Emma alone with her revelation and frustration.

All this time, at the height of her excitement, Emma had been unwittingly sending a gay porn slideshow into the minds of her lovers.

No wonder they ran away screaming.

5

'Boudoir?' asked Victor. 'Hay loft? Beach? Classroom? Forest of nymphs? Planet Strumpet?'

'How about the dungeon?' Emma sat on a beanbag chair on the floor of Victor's studio, lazily flipping through the portfolio of photos he'd taken for previous The Good Witch, Inc. clients. The sun was brutally bright that late October morning, its rays burrowing into Emma's hung-over brain. Even though Victor's studio windows were covered with blackout curtains, Emma couldn't bear to take off her shades. When bloodshot, her eyes looked particularly bizarre. After Hoff deserted her, she'd dipped into the Bailey's. Big mistake.

'On second thoughts, don't wheel out the racks yet,' said Emma. 'Daphne is the type to bring her own props.'

'Do I get paid extra if she annoys me?'

'Charge her double. Triple. She can afford it.'

'Tell me again how you licked William Dearborn's uvula.'

Emma shushed him. 'Daphne will be here any minute. She can't know about that.'

'She should know he has a girlfriend.'

Emma closed the portfolio. 'I make men think they're gay,' she whined. 'This is just further proof that I am not destined for love. I'm stuck, I tell you. Stuck in a halfway world where I can see everything, hear a pin drop on the subway, taste a single grain of nutmeg in a muffin, smell the molded cheese in your fridge – please throw that away – but I'll never be touched. I'll never have love. I'm broke and alone. Bamboozled out of my life savings; cheated out of having a life.'

Victor said, 'Do I get paid extra if *you* annoy me?'

'Admit that this is a hell of a conundrum,' she said. 'Sending images by accident, that's scary.' Until last night, Emma believed she had complete control.

'From what you tell me,' said Victor, 'William Dearborn didn't shrivel at your touch.'

'I reflected on that fact for some time last night between obsessively plucking my eyebrows and alpha-betizing my pantry,' she said. 'He was like a throwback to the stupid, thoughtless sex of my teens and early twenties. Before the trouble began. When Dearborn kissed me, I could barely breathe, let alone think about other men.'

'You may have gone overboard on the eyebrows.'

'Too thin?' she asked, touching them.

'Makeup table's free,' he said, taking her by the wrist and escorting her to the vanity. 'Do all women fantasize about other men during sex?'

Emma sat down and cringed at the sight of her

eyebrows. 'I have no idea,' she said. 'I bet Monica fantasized about a straighter straight man.'

'You should ditch the case, and go out with Dearborn yourself,' he said. 'And then I can be his best friend by proxy.'

Victor picked a medium brown eyebrow pencil and went to work, fattening, lengthening her eyebrow. 'He's so out of my league,' said Emma. 'Besides which, he's a slut. And my job – my housing – hinges on making him fall for Daphne Wittfield.' She studied her reflection in the mirror. 'Dearborn got a good look at my face. And my body. I need a disguise that'll make me invisible.'

'Cop. Men never look at women cops. The uniform is as sexy as soap scum,' said Victor. 'Homeless person. Religion nut.'

The buzzer. 'Must be Daphne,' said Emma.

He buzzed her in and opened the loft's inside elevator door. While the car lifted Daphne to the third floor, Victor and Emma scurried around the vast space, tidying. They threw dirty clothes under his bed, hid dirty plates in the cabinets. Emma made sure the bathroom door was closed.

The elevator clanged and whirred upward. As the platform rose, Daphne appeared behind the metal gate. First the buttery hair, her taut, tense face. Then the lean arms, a slim torso and long legs that kept getting longer and longer, shod at the bottom in high heeled boots. Head to toe, Daphne wore leather, tight and black.

'Definitely the dungeon,' said Victor.

Daphne stood in the elevator, thwacking a rolled up *New York Post* against her thigh.

I am that newspaper, thought Emma.

Victor pulled open the gate, bidding her welcome. Daphne said, 'You're Victor Armour?'

He said, 'That's me.'

'Am I paying you by the hour, or by the shot?'

'Both,' he said brightly.

'Then we'd better not waste any time – or film,' she said.

He said, 'I'll be using a digital camera.'

'Then why am I paying by the shot?'

'For the prints.'

Daphne chewed on that one.

Victor said, 'No need to waste time thinking about it. I'm worth every dollar.'

Emma held her breath, fearing Victor had overstepped there. But Daphne seemed to like his confidence. She said, 'Let's get on with it.' She unzipped her leather jacket, revealing nothing under it but a black bra.

Emma said, 'Whoa, Daphne! Don't you want to look at the book first?' She retrieved the previous client portfolio from the beanbag chair. 'Victor has two dozen backdrops, racks and racks of costumes – lingerie, shoes, props.'

Daphne said, 'I won't need any of that. We're doing nude portraits.'

'Just check out the book,' implored Emma, holding it open for Daphne to see. 'It's full of great pictures. Look, this client dressed up like a fairy princess. Okay, maybe that's not you.'

Emma started to flip through the pages. Daphne took the book out of her hands and said, 'I excel at targeted marketing. Emma. I'm not selling my image to a simpleton wanker who blows his wad at the sight of a garter belt. My target is sophisticated and intelligent. I need images that will not only titillate William but intrigue him.'

Victor said, 'I love garter belts.'

Emma said, 'But I'm used to working with a certain kind of image.'

'You'll have to get used to working with something else,' said Daphne crossly.

Emma sulked in the corner while Daphne and Victor discussed backdrops, filters, lighting. They spoke quickly, in shorthand, seemingly meeting minds on what was to happen.

Victor started arranging a white backdrop and lighting equipment. He said to Daphne, 'I've done some advertising work. Maybe I can show you my book.'

'Consider our shoot a tryout,' said Daphne amicably. So this was how Daphne treated someone she *liked*.

Emma was not usually a jealous person. But she could smell her own slow burn, watching Daphne get chummy with Victor, her best friend, the one man in her life who'd never run away from her. Wasn't it enough that Daphne had the big job, the upturned nipples, huge discretionary funds, and enough self-confidence to go after a man like William Dearborn? The same man Emma'd thought about, much to her quivering satisfaction, in the ten minutes between going to bed and going to sleep last night.

Maybe Daphne hated women, thought Emma.

'Speaking of advertising,' said Emma. 'Victor, were you aware that Daphne is responsible for the SlimBurn diet pill ads?'

Victor froze. 'The ones with Marcie Skimmer?' he asked.

Marcie Skimmer was an old acquaintance of Victor's, a model he'd worked with long ago, before Marcie got big – figuratively and literally. As the gossip pages reported it, the model fell into a depression a year ago, gained a ton of weight. Then she did the SlimBurn ads, after which point she had a nervous breakdown and attempted suicide by consuming ten pounds of Death-by-Chocolate cake. Marcie believed one could eat ones way into a diabetic coma. Miraculously, she survived and went to some kind of rehab sanitarium upstate. Emma found the whole story sad but predictable. When one's worth is based on appearance, depression and self-destruction is a given.

Daphne cheerily asked Victor, 'Oh, do you know Marcie?' He nodded. She said, 'We have a mutual friend.'

'You call her a *friend*?' he asked. 'You had Marcie pose in a bikini, on all fours, among a herd of Holsteins in a muddy field!'

'With the caption, "Time to get off the farm?" ' said Daphne proudly. 'We moved half a million units of Slim Burn pills the week that ad appeared. But that was nothing compared to sales after the follow-up ads.'

The follow-up shots were Marcie flying above Broadway like a float in a parade with the caption, 'Time to come back down to Earth?' The third in the series: Marcie in a blue bikini, photo-shopped among a pod of whales in the ocean with the caption, 'Time to get on dry land?'

Victor said, 'You humiliated her.'

'She was paid millions,' said Daphne. 'And that's a lot of Death-by-Chocolate cake.'

Emma gasped. Daphne's insensitivity was galling. This was a woman capable of love? Her heart was as hard and black as onyx. William deserved better. Or not. He could be just as horrible as Daphne. For all Emma knew, they deserved each other.

Daphne, meanwhile, peeled off her jacket, unhooked her bra, kicked off her boots and pulled off her pants. Standing tall and proud in a black vinyl thong, she asked, 'Are you ready?'

Victor feasted his eyes. He couldn't help himself. He squeaked, 'Ready.'

'Everything that happens here is confidential,' she said to him.

'Emma and I have been working together for ten years,' he said. 'She can vouch for me.'

'I vouch,' said Emma, her own jaw in the dropped position at the sight of Daphne's lean body.

The client said, 'Emma, you can go now.'

What? She was being kicked out? 'You want me to leave?' she asked. 'But what about my emotional services? Clients in the past have always relied on me heavily during the shoots. To help them pick outfits and backdrops. Being photographed in lingerie makes most women feel vulnerable. They wanted the handholding. The soft shoulder. Encouragement.'

'Do I look vulnerable to you?' asked Daphne, her arms akimbo.

She looked like she could chew metal, thought Emma. 'I'm sure you'll be wonderful,' relented Emma. Daphne was a client, after all. And she was in the client pleasing business. 'I'll take off then.'

'Thanks for stopping by.'

So she had the day off. Emma should be glad for the

free time to rest her hangover. She should be relieved not to have to button a corset or say 'you don't look fat' ten thousand times. She should be happy. But she felt excluded. Unwanted. Again.

'This is good. It's perfect. I'll have extra time to study up on William Dearborn,' said Emma with forced brightness. 'I want to be as prepared as I can possibly be. My cases are my life! I live to serve! One bit of advice, before I go.'

'What?' asked the client (impatiently).

'Don't forget to smile.'

The bank manager, seated behind his desk in his glass-walled cubicle, wore a bow tie. Emma hadn't dealt with this guy before. She was passed around among the managers. None of them wanted to deal with her twice. She sat across the desk, in the hot seat, at Citibank, conveniently located across Sixth Avenue from her apartment building. Emma had cried here. And pleaded shamelessly for extensions. Ah, the memories, she reflected nostalgically.

'Ms Hutch,' said the talking bow tie. 'I've heard about you from my colleagues.' He reached a hand across the desk. 'I'm Mr Cannery. Let's get down to business, shall we?'

While he click-clacked on the keyboard, Emma sized him up. Would he be nice or use her to take out his anger at every person who'd done him wrong? Bank managers, as a whole, seemed particularly spiteful.

'According to my screen,' Mr Cannery said, adjusting his horn-rimmed glasses, 'you've been in arrears for two months. Unless you pay what you owe, in full, plus fines, within ten days, we will be forced to . . .'

'I've got five thousand dollars,' she said. 'In cash.'

Mr Cannery said, 'In cash?' He got a bit twitchy, edged forward on his chair, face flushed. Emma removed the bills from her purse slowly, tantalizingly. Mr Cannery started to glow, a thin layer of expectation on his face. Emma could smell his salty excitement. Apparently, she thought, one woman's mortgage payment was another man's porn.

She held out the wad of bills. Mr Cannery, fingers shaking, breath short, reached for it. Emma snatched it back.

'Not so fast,' she said. 'This covers what I owe on the mortgage – and then some.'

'Not exactly,' he said. 'You're short on the minimum balance in your checking account.'

She said, 'That can't be right. Let me see.' She leaned across his desk.

He said, 'You're not permitted to look at the computer!'

She sat back down, wondering if he had her account info on screen or sexy photos of dollar bills in lingerie. 'I need some walking around money.'

'You have three hundred to spare,' he said. 'I advise you to spend it wisely.'

Emma said, 'I was going to blow it on luxury items, like food and heat.' Then she counted out hundreds and forked over forty-seven hundred dollars.

He wrote her a deposit slip, and printed out an updated mortgage statement. She stood up to leave. Mr Cannery said, 'Remember, you have another payment to make on November first. According to my screen, you've used up your last extension. If you can't pay on the first, the bank will take possession of your property. You do not want to be in arrears again, Ms Hutch.'

'You bet I don't,' she said. 'Way too cramped.'

Daphne had given her two weeks; Mr Cannery had given her just over one. No matter how she sliced it, Emma was cut to the financial bare bones. To make herself feel a little bit less anxious, Emma ducked into the 14th Street Barnes & Noble and bought the Wilco CD, *A Ghost Is Born*. Halloween was fast approaching – her favorite holiday. She could buy herself a little seasonal ghostly cheer. Back on Sixth, she inhaled the afternoon air, crisp as a cracker. On a whim, she headed east, toward Washington Square Park. She could buy some pot there. That might help her free-floating dread. Plus, Emma had always found comfort in the park's concentric rings around the center fountain, like Dante's circles of hell.

Washington Square Park (and hell?) was dotted with junkies, dealers, sleeping homeless people, street musicians, rollerbladers, artists, prophets, and hot dog stands. To Emma, it smelled and looked like home. She'd spent much of her high school years in this asphalt 'park', finding kinship among the outcasts and freaks of Greenwich Village. Emma stayed local for college, graduating from NYU. As soon as she could, she bought an apartment in the neighborhood – the Waverly Place one-bedroom she was holding on to by a thread.

Her parents were supportive of the purchase (they'd lived just a few blocks away). Her mother *felt* the apartment would be a good emotional and financial investment. And when Emma's mother *felt* something, she was always right. She died two years after making that prediction. Emma often wondered – especially now, on the brink of ruin – if her mom's forecast had been long term, or only as far as she would live to see.

Emma walked quickly and purposefully, hugging the lip of the park's innermost circle, the round fountain in the middle. Loiterers were perched on the edge of the fountain in pairs, trios, quartets. She nodded at anyone who caught her eye, hoping someone would try to sell her pot. But then she got another offer.

'Palm reading, five dollars,' said a woman perched on the northern curve of the fountain. She was a tiny middle-aged black woman in blue jeans and a blue hoodie that had the words 'Above Average' stenciled on the sleeves. Hair in cornrows, her face was intricately wrinkled.

Emma slowed, vaguely intrigued by the offer. For all her heightened senses and telegraphopathy, Emma had no intuition or precognition. She didn't *feel* things the way her mother had. She'd never studied palmistry or Tarot, preferring to keep her focus Earthbound, as she was.

The woman said quickly, 'For you, three dollars.'

'Deal,' said Emma, sitting on the fountain edge and holding out her right hand. The woman stretched the skin to make the white lines turn red.

Running a finger across the middle of her palm, the woman said, 'This is the life line. It's very long.

You'll live to be eighty-nine years old.'

'It says eighty-nine?'

'Yes,' she said. 'This is your creativity line. You are a creative person with a big imagination.'

'Really,' said Emma.

'This is your head line. You are highly intelligent.'

'Won't argue there,' nodded Emma, who was willing to bet (more than three dollars) that every sucker who submitted to a reading would live to be eighty-nine, was creative, and intelligent.

'This is your heart line,' said Above Average.

Now she'll tell me I'm destined to find my true love very soon, thought Emma.

'Your heart line is all criss-crossed,' she said, peering into Emma's palm, 'like it's X-ed out.'

Emma's romantic misery was plainly evident, even to street hustlers. The word 'alone' might as well be tattooed on her forehead. She'd never find a man to love her. He didn't exist. The idea of him was just one more fantasy rolling around in her warped brain.

'Whoa!' said Above Average suddenly.

'What?' asked Emma.

'I pressed on your heart line, and a picture popped into my head. I saw a man. A famous man,' said Above Average, excitedly. 'Hold on to your sunglasses, sister. It was William Dearborn! You lucky bitch. He's hot!'

Emma swallowed hard. Not again. Dearborn's image was oozing out of her like slime.

Besides which, was there anyone in New York who *didn't* love William Dearborn?

The palm reader shouted, 'I have the sight!'

'Oh, God,' said Emma, cringing. Other people around the fountain were looking.

'You and William Dearborn! I've got to tell everyone, so when it happens, I'm on the record. What's your name?' demanded Above Average.

'Her name is Emma Hutch,' said a female voice over her shoulder. Emma spun round to see who'd spoken.

'Susan Knight,' said Emma warmly. A former client. They hadn't talked in months.

'I've got the sight!' said Above Average to the universe. To Susan, she asked, 'Read your palm? Twenty bucks.'

'I thought it was three,' said Emma.

'My price just went up.'

Susan said, 'No thank you,' and then, to Emma, 'I need to speak to you. It's important.'

'Are you okay?' She didn't look okay. Susan had been Emma's least demanding client. If one could call her a client. The man in question asked Susan out before Emma got the chance to work on him.

'I was cutting through the park toward your place when I saw you here.'

'Kismet,' said Emma, standing, putting her arm around Susan's petite shoulder.

'Where's my money?' said Above Average.

Emma took out her wallet. Her smallest bill was a twenty. 'Can you make change?' she asked.

'Do I look like a cashier?'

Emma gave her a twenty. Mr Cannery would disapprove. She and Susan headed west to Waverly Place.

'It's so good to see you, and I'm sorry I haven't been in touch,' said Emma. 'I've been lying low.'

'Why?' she asked. 'What's the matter?'

Money. Men. Fear of imminent death. 'Nothing I can't handle,' said Emma. 'You look good, by the way.'

Susan was dressed, as usual, conservatively, in a blue pleated skirt and a similar (but not matching) blazer. She wore nude stockings and low-heeled pumps that accentuated the tight balls of muscle in her tiny calves. No makeup. Her light brown hair was pulled into a swingy ponytail. With her cute little figure and patrician skin and teeth, Susan could do natural.

'Jeff left me,' blurted Susan, chin suddenly aquiver. 'He came over last night and said he quit his job and wanted to quit seeing me, too.'

'Good riddance,' said Emma.

Even though she never got close enough to touch him, Emma had done preliminary research on Jeff Bragg, including long-distance observation. Emma didn't need superior farsightedness to see, at twenty feet or two inches, that Jeff was a jerk.

'He's the best boyfriend I've ever had,' choked out Susan.

'The best boyfriend you ever had liked to spit on the sidewalk,' said Emma. 'He was a bad tipper.'

Susan said, 'When he touches me, it feels like every cell in my body opens to him. As if he enters me on a molecular level. He told me' – she drew a ragged breath – 'he told me that my neck smells like vanilla ice cream.'

Susan started sobbing on the corner of Waverly and Sixth, right in front of Citibank. Emma hugged her, patted her back, and stroked her hair. She was secretly glad to be needed by someone, to be sought out for help. This felt familiar, comfortable. She was a hand to hold. A shoulder to lean on. Emma inhaled with pleasure, picking up Susan's scent. Jeff was right about one thing. Susan did smell like vanilla ice cream.

Interrupting their moment, a man on the sidewalk said, 'Jesus might bring you comfort.'

Emma glanced at him. Dark hair, wiry two-day stubble. Yellow T-shirt stretched over a chubby gut, short legs in jeans, around forty, droopy nose and chin. She said, 'Bug off.'

'Have a blessed day!' he said earnestly in return, and redirected his attention to other sinners on the street. Over Susan's shoulder, Emma watched him pass pamphlets. His yellow T-shirt had a Star of David with the words 'Jews for Jesus' stenciled across it.

Victor was right. No one paid attention to religion pamphleteers. Emma gave Susan a squeeze and let her go. She approached the Jew for Jesus. 'I'd like to buy a T-shirt,' she said.

The man said, 'Sorry. I don't have any here. But I'm having a thousand made. Come back in a few days and I'd be happy to sell you one.'

'I'll give you twenty bucks for the shirt you're wearing. And a stack of flyers.'

'I'm planning to sell the shirts for ten. It'd be making a hefty profit if I sold this one for twenty. Jesus wouldn't want me to take advantage. That wouldn't be very Christian of me.'

'Fifty bucks for the shirt, right now, take it or leave it.' Emma reached into her pocket for her wad, and peeled a fifty off the top.

Just as she was showing it to the Jew for Jesus, Mr Cannery happened to walk out of the bank, catching her green handed.

The banker tisked. 'Is this a wise expenditure, Ms Hutch?'

'Jesus loves you!' said the religious nut, trying to hand Mr Cannery a pamphlet. The banker blanched and dashed uptown. 'And you,' the nut said, turning to Emma. 'You must learn patience. You'll have to wait for a shirt. Come back in a few days.'

Emma and Susan went across Sixth Avenue. Susan asked, 'Thinking of converting?'

Emma said, 'It's for a disguise. I'll need a Jewfro wig.'

'If you went to Times Square, you could score a "Muslims for Moses" shirt, too.'

'And a "One Life to Live" Hare Krishna toga,' said Emma.

They were in better spirits when they reached Emma's apartment. With that in mind, the Good Witch said, 'Let's have a drink.'

'It's three o'clock,' protested Susan.

'On a Friday,' said Emma.

'I told my assistant I'd be back by four.' Susan worked at the Verity Foundation, a not-for-profit watchdog group that organized litigants for class action lawsuits, among other dogood work.

'You can't take an afternoon off?' asked Emma. 'You're a VP.'

'I'm a VP because I don't take afternoons off,' she said. 'But I suppose once in four years is allowed.'

Emma went into the kitchen, opened the fridge and

grabbed the bottle of Bailey's (she'd only dented it last night). She returned to the living room with the bottle and two juice glasses. She poured. They drank.

After licking the edge of the glass, Susan said, 'I want to hire you again.'

Emma said, 'That's against policy. Besides, I'm working on a big case exclusively for the next two weeks.'

'I need you, Emma.'

Music to her highly sensitive ears. 'You know I love to help. But I just can't do it. I guarantee the first date only. After that, it's all up to you. It's in the contract.'

Susan sipped her beverage. 'God, that's good.'

'And only a thousand calories per thimbleful,' said Emma.

'I got the first date on my own,' said Susan. 'You insisted on returning my initial payment and that invalidated the contract.' Susan was a lawyer. She should know.

'Implanting your image won't work on him now,' said Emma. 'He's already seen you – in the flesh, not just pictures.'

'If you put me in his head, he'll think he misses me. He'll want me back.'

'It's been only one day. Why don't you wait a week? See if he misses you on his own.'

Susan said, 'I can't wait a week.' She seemed serious.

Emma squirmed uncomfortably on the couch. She wanted to make her friend happy. But she said, 'If it were any other man, I'd consider it. But not Jeff Bragg. I never told you that I saw him frottage a teenage girl on the bus.'

'He cheesed her?' asked Susan.

'Not *fromage*,' corrected Emma. 'Frottage. He stood behind the girl on a packed uptown bus and subtly humped her whenever the bus lurched.' Emma sipped her drink.

'It was by accident,' said Susan. 'A crowded bus, midtown traffic. That's a lot of lurching.'

'And humping.'

'You can't prove he was humping her,' said Susan.

Emma demurred. 'No, but the girl had a terrified look on her face, and she bulldozed her way off the bus at her stop.'

'As disgusted as I am by that story,' said Susan, 'the idea of Jeff rubbing himself against a rusty storm drain turns me on. I want to be that rusty storm drain. Or that fromaged teen.'

'Frottaged,' reminded Emma.

'Haven't you ever been madly in love?' Susan asked, exasperated by Emma's refusal. 'My skin comes alive when we touch, as if it's a separate, independent entity and not connected to my brain or soul.'

Emma had not been madly in love, and Susan damn well knew it. 'Sex isn't everything,' she said.

'That's one way of seeing things. Sex isn't everything. But, without it, you've got nothing.'

'Now you're just being mean.'

'Although we weren't talking about you, Emma,' started her increasingly snippy friend, 'I will say this: your problem is that you live through other people's romances – you *engineer* other people's happiness – but in the year we've known each other, you've given me a million excuses for not pursuing your own. You hardly go out. You hate parties. You're uncomfortable talking to strangers. You're so detached from what you want, *you don't even put yourself in your own sexual fantasies.*' Susan seemed to think of something suddenly. 'Have you ever had a fantasy about Jeff?'

'Yes,' admitted Emma.

'You have?'

'I had a fantasy he had a heart attack seconds before being run over by a bus.'

Susan laughed. 'I shouldn't have asked.'

'You're the only person I know who would come to me for a favor and then assail my quirks,' said Emma. 'You're also the only lawyer I know. Coincidence?'

'These are serious issues, Emma. You should seek help.'

'People seek me for help,' she replied. 'And they get it. Including you.'

'So you'll take my case?' asked Susan with a sudden glimmer.

Emma finished her Bailey's and poured some more. 'Here's what I'm willing to do. Since my usual methods are off the table, I'll talk to him. Find out what I can. But I'm not making any promises about a reunion.'

Susan said, 'I'll take whatever I can get.'

'I have to charge you,' said Emma. 'The Good Witch, Inc. is a for-profit company.'

Susan agreed. 'When can you start?'

'Tonight,' said Emma. She wasn't expecting Daphne's pictures until tomorrow, and she would rather work than drink five thousand calories of Bailey's. 'Where can I find the scumbag?'

'Today was his last day at work,' said Susan. 'So he'll probably go out with his colleagues for a farewell drink.'

'They'll go to that cigar and Scotch bar near his office,' said Emma, remembering the place. 'What's it called again?'

'Bull,' answered Susan.

7

Emma pushed open the door of the Bull Bar on Water Street. Blue smoke swirled across her half-exposed breasts. She stepped inside, fully aware that every man in the joint was looking at her. In her four-inch heels, raisin-colored lips, and black, banged wig, she strutted to the bar. A cluster of men parted to let her by. She dropped her hand on a black leather bar stool and asked, 'Is this seat taken?'

The men didn't or couldn't respond to the simple question. So she lifted her thigh and slid onto the stool. She crossed her legs, adjusted her black movie star shades, and said, 'I sure could use a drink.'

Five men shouted for the bartender. He rushed over. 'What's the most expensive cognac you've got?' she asked.

The bartender, a chubby guy with a fuzzy mustache, said, 'Remy Martin.'

'I'd like a bottle.' Emma looked from man to man and

then pointed at the youngest and best looking. 'This gentleman is happy to pay for it.'

'I am?' he asked.

'It would be your *pleasure*,' she said.

The man grinned and raised his eyebrows. His four buddies cackled and winked at each other. 'What the hell. I'm celebrating,' he said. To the bartender: 'Two glasses.'

His buddies downed the dregs of their beers and pulled on their suit jackets. Along with Friday fatigue, each wore a gold wedding band. The fat one said, 'Heading out.' A chorus of 'me, too' and 'long way to Livingston' followed. They slapped their lucky friend on the back and split.

Once they were gone, Emma held out her hand and said, 'Connie Quivers.'

'Jeff Bragg,' he said.

'What are we celebrating?' she asked.

'To fresh starts and beautiful women.' He raised his glass.

'I'll drink to that,' she said.

'Forgive me in advance for what I'm going to ask you,' he said.

'I'm not a hooker,' said Emma, although she might look like one in her Bettie Paige wig. 'I'm just lonely. So talk to me for a while, all right?'

'Absolutely. What would you like to talk about?'

'Tell me all about your love life,' she drawled.

If Emma thought Jeff would spill his guts the second she asked him to, she was sorely mistaken. Two hours later, insight about what went wrong between Susan and Jeff was not forthcoming. Emma was nursing her cognac. Jeff had been talking non-stop about everything but his love life.

'. . . and that's when I got promoted to senior vice president of accounting at Dooey, Fleecum & Howe. I made a couple of fast deals and now I've got more money than I can spend. Yes, it's been a long climb, but I've finally reached the top.'

'I've reached the bottom,' said Emma, showing Jeff her empty glass.

He poured her another dram. 'Today was my last day at Dooey,' he said. 'I'm taking my winnings off the table, leaving the city, the office, the suit. Going to live on a beach somewhere.'

'Sounds like you're running away,' said Emma.

He said, 'I'm not running. I'm going on vacation. Permanently.'

Emma wondered if Susan knew about his windfall or his travel plans. He'd shared his body with her, but, apparently, little else. And for that kind of relationship, Susan would turn herself inside out. The vicarious thrills in this case were more like chills.

'But the economy is terrible,' Emma said. 'Stocks down, huge deficit. Corporation scandal. Enron, Tyco, Riptron.'

'I've been careful,' said Jeff. 'Kept my nose clean. My firm handled the Riptron accounting. Twenty people went to prison because of that.' He leaned in close. 'Just between you and me, for every person who went to prison, someone else got rich.'

Emma's stomach lurched. 'Can we get back to your emotional history? Your recent romantic past?'

He paused. 'I do have one regret about leaving New York.'

Emma softened. 'A girlfriend in the city?'

'My regret is that I'll be spending my last week here alone,' he said. And then he put his hand on her bare knee.

She flinched. 'Your hand is freezing.' It felt like he'd dropped an icicle on her skin. 'Mind moving it?'

He moved it higher up her thigh.

Emma had long believed her sense of touch was her weakest. But, at times like this, it showed its super strength. An icy spread crept from her knee to her hips. The same man who made Susan melt had frozen Emma's entire leg. She brushed his hand off her and sighed. This was a waste of time, she thought. He wasn't talking. She'd learned nothing. She'd have to chalk it up as a no-win night.

Emma said, 'Well, it's been incredibly dull talking to you, Jeff. I'll be shoving off now.' Emma tried to slide off the stool but her right leg was still defrosting.

Jeff grabbed her elbow, stopping her. 'Where's the fire?'

'Let go,' she warned.

'You walked into this bar and made right for me.' His voice sounded deeper. 'Why?'

'You were the best looking guy here,' she said.

'You can speak the truth and still be a liar.'

'You can be handsome and still turn my stomach.'

He squeezed her elbow tighter and the freeze seeped through the fabric of her dress, numbing her arm. Jeff said, 'I think you were sent here by a man who shall remain nameless to spy on me. You can tell him to back the fuck off.'

While he spoke his gibberish, Emma struggled to

wrench her arm free. The bartender appeared. 'Any trouble?'

'We're just saying goodbye,' said Jeff, giving her a weird warning with his beady eyes.

He was insane. And paranoid. 'I wasn't sent here by a man,' said Emma. 'And I'm not a spy.'

Jeff said, 'Your wig is crooked.'

'These pictures are horrible. No offense, Victor,' said Emma the next morning, in Saturday yoga pants and a red poncho. 'Are you sure this is what she wants?'

Victor was eating grapes from her fridge. 'I don't argue with the client,' he said.

Emma examined the three prints of Daphne Wittfield on her desk. 'I don't get it,' she said of the first one.

The image was black and white. Daphne stood nude, arms at her side, feet shoulder-width apart. A powerful lamp shone from behind her at hip level.

Victor said, 'You see how it looks like a circle of light is floating behind her? That's subliminal.'

'And the hidden message is?' asked Emma.

'As Daphne put it, "That the sun shines out of my ass."'

'It looks more like she passes noxious gas.'

'Daphne thought it was perfect,' said Victor.

Emma shook her head. 'I can't work with this,' she declared. 'Or this.'

She held up the second photo. The shot was black and white, but with a blue wash. Daphne's hair was spiked and her body posture rigid. 'She looks like she stuck her finger in a light socket,' said Emma.

'Exactly,' said Victor nodding and chewing. 'She wanted to send the message that she's electric. A real live wire.'

The next photo in the portfolio was tinted red, showing Daphne, naked again, sitting cross-legged on a mat (thank God for artful shadowing), her arms stretched above her head, bent gracefully at the wrists and elbows. 'Daphne on fire?' asked Emma.

Victor touched his nose. 'She's supposed to be the shape of a camp fire. Her arms are flames.'

'I'm not sure I can do this,' said Emma. She was so used to the innocent theatrics in the staged shots of yester month. She loved her clients as wood nymphs or Cleopatras; the photos reminiscent of lingerie catalogues, female-crafted soft-core porn. It was part of the fantasy Emma created in the minds of men.

But the Daphne portfolio, the stark, conceptual so-called 'art' shots? And the total nudity? Emma was embarrassed to look at them, let alone work with them. She also realized that she was at a disadvantage, missing the shoot. Watching the process helped Emma cement the images in her mind. The finished photos became reference points, reminders of what she'd already seen of her clients' body, heart, and soul.

Daphne hadn't let Emma see anywhere near her soul.

Whether the blond had a heart remained a mystery. Emma dropped the portfolio on her desk. 'I far prefer the usual cheesecake,' she said to Victor.

'You can't have your cheesecake and eat, too,' he replied, taking a seat on the couch and opening up his copy of the *New York Post*.

'I hate this case,' said Emma. 'Daphne shows zero emotion. She's approaching seduction like a marketing plan. And she's weirdly confident. Woman in love are insecure. They're anxious and confused.'

'Sort of how you're acting right now,' said Victor. 'Does that mean you're in love?'

He meant it as a joke, but Emma was not amused. 'Do you remember Susan Knight?' she asked, changing the subject. 'You shot her about a year ago. Petite, brown hair, blue eyes. Headband, nude hose and flats?'

Victor asked, 'Posed as a wild west call girl?'

Emma nodded. 'I'm working with her again.'

'Who's the guy?' asked Victor, flipping the pages of the paper. 'Does she need new pictures?'

'Same guy,' said Emma. 'I made a special exception for her. But I'm done with him. It was one-night only.' She hadn't called Susan yet to report in about Jeff.

'Emma, I'm impressed. You have achieved a feat that is the goal of every New Yorker.'

'Having two clients at once?'

'You made Page Six,' he said. He saw the expression on her face. 'Relax. It's a blind item. Your anonymity is safe.'

Emma sat down next to Victor and read the entry.

JUST ASKING . . .

What Anglo artist got caught canoodling with a buxom brunette in the back room at Ciao Roma by a larger-than-life model who may or may not be his new girlfriend? The brunette's identity is a mystery to us – and to the bewitched Brit who's been searching for her ever since.

'He's searching for me?' she whined. 'How am I supposed to sneak up on him now?' Much as this complicated her case, Emma's pulse was doing the tango. She couldn't help remembering their kiss, and a wave of heat careened south.

'Bewitched Brit,' read Victor. 'Apropos word choice.'

Ring. Landline. It had to be either Daphne or Susan, and Emma didn't want to speak to either one. She let her machine get it.

The message: 'Emma. Daphne Wittfield. I hope you approve of the photos. You'll get to put them to use tonight. William is having a party to preview ArtSpeak, his new software package. It's at Haiku on 14th Street and Ninth Avenue. I'll be working the event. I expect to see you there at eight o'clock sharp. Your name is on the guest list.' Click. Message over.

'She didn't say goodbye,' said Emma.

'I love Haiku,' he said. 'I'll be your date.'

'I love haiku, too,' said the Good Witch. 'Here's one:

I am not
A brunette;
But I do

Concede
Buxom.'

'Any shade of brown – including bronze – falls under the category of brunette,' said Victor. 'And your poem does not follow the haiku format.'

'Daphne's voice rings in my head like warning bells. And, because of my sensitive hearing, the bells are very loud.'

'Don't tell me you're getting a *feeling* about her,' said Vic.

'I'm not *feeling*,' corrected Emma. 'I'm hearing.'

'She's not so bad – for an egomaniacal control freak. I know you like to provide clients with your "emotional services." Just forget that part. This case is all mind, no heart. Daphne hired you to do a job. Do it, take the money, and be done with it.'

'A job. That's really all my matchmaking is,' said Emma. 'The thing is, I've always thought of it as a personal involvement. Like I'm part of something larger than myself.'

'I feel sorry for Dearborn,' said Victor. 'You've got Daphne for two weeks only. If you succeed, he'll have to deal with Daphne for a lot longer. Once she reels him in, she's not going to let him go.'

An image flashed in Emma's mind. William, naked (as usual), with a rope around his waist. Daphne was pulling the rope, drawing him toward her. William struggled, not understanding why he couldn't overpower her. He stared at his captor, eyes wild. Then he turned his head and his eyes seemed to look right at Emma, the audience. He said, 'What are you waiting for?'

Vic chuckled suddenly, bringing her back to the living room. 'I just got an idea for your costume. I can guarantee you he won't look at you.'

Her heart still pounding from imagined eye contact with Dearborn, Emma said, 'Ladies' room attendant?'

He shook his head. 'Considering your history with him, and his history with women, we have only one option.'

'Which is?'

He put down the paper and stood up. 'I'll be back in a few hours with everything we need.'

'Just tell me,' she said impatiently.

'And ruin the surprise?' he asked.

Victor left and Emma was alone with the photos of Daphne. She couldn't bear to look. Instead, Emma reached for the phone to call Susan. But what would she say? Jeff proved himself a scumbag by touching her and a paranoid maniac by accusing her of spying? It was all too weird. And for Emma, who was weird by any conventional standard, that was saying a lot.

Emma's mind kept going back to Dearborn. What would he make of these odd images of Daphne when Emma popped them into his head? Would he think the sun shone out of Daphne's ass, as the client intended? Or would he be mystified by Daphne's apparent cumulous flatulence? What would happen if she put herself in his mind? If she did self-serve? For one thing, she couldn't easily do it. Since she avoided being photographed and hardly ever gazed at herself in mirrors for long languid minutes, she couldn't quickly conjure a still picture of herself to send.

But her job was to send these images of Daphne. She'd been paid, and her professionalism was above reproach.

Emma closed her eyes and visualized making the transfer. A ghostlike wave would travel from her cranium and into William Dearborn's. His green eyes, shiny like stones in a brook, would react to the transmission, a cocky grin erupting on his face, stretching his sideburns, dimpling his cheeks. The same cheeks she had held in her hands when they kissed.

Her eyes snapped open.

This would not do. Emma said aloud, 'Keep focused.' And, 'Remember what's at stake.' And, 'It's just a job.'

She made 'It's just a job' her mantra for the remainder of the afternoon. The phrase came out of her mouth with ease.

But she couldn't get Dearborn out of her head.

'Name?'

'Emma Hutch.'

The officious-yet-cute woman with the loose brown bun and tweed mini-skirt checked her clipboard. She flipped pages on it. She tapped it with her pen. Emma and Victor were standing outside Haiku on the coldest night of the year thus far. 'I see the name. You're Emma Hutch?' Tweedy asked, doubtful.

'You bet I am!' said Emma.

'I don't think so,' replied Tweedy.

'Check for Victor Armour,' said Victor.

'Are you together?' asked the gatekeeper.

He smiled slyly. 'Why do you want to know?' Tweedy gave him a flirtatious smile. 'I have nothing to do with that person,' he said.

She checked her list. 'No Victor Armour. Sorry.'

The crush of people behind them forced Victor and

Emma to the side. They watched as Ms Tweedy approved and rejected the aspiring guests one by one, occasionally reminding the crowd, 'This party is invite only!'

Victor whispered, 'Your costume is presenting a problem. It's too good. Better call Daphne.'

'But she can't be seen with us,' said Emma, watching a cluster of gawking tourists, a passel of local press, a klatch of slutty women, and a pride of hero-worshipful tech geeks, all of them leaning across the velvet rope, desperate to pass through the black-lacquer doors of Haiku.

Emma said, 'You look dashing tonight, Victor.' He really did, in a slim-legged gray suit and blue tie, hair tousled with precision. 'I'm proud to have you for my date.'

'You look good too,' said Victor. 'If I were a woman, I'd fuck you.' He looked down the length of her, stopping at her fly. 'You should have let me pack your panties, though.'

She'd drawn the line there. Emma was more than willing to strap down her breasts, glue on an itchy fake beard, mustache, sideburns, and man wig. She liked her wool suit and the wingtips. But she steadfastly refused to put a stuffed sock in her underwear. She said, 'Say it slid down my pant leg and landed on the floor.'

'That would be awkward,' said Victor. 'I can't believe I'm going to meet William Dearborn! You have to call Daphne.'

Emma dialed Daphne's cell.

Within three minutes, the client sneaked them in a fire exit, Tweedy none the wiser.

The writing was on the wall as they re-entered the club, but Emma had no idea what it said. She didn't read Japanese. Daphne snapped her fingers. Both Victor and

Emma stopped admiring the club's murals of cherry blossoms and Mount Fuji and gave their attention to the client. 'William is in the main room, down the hallway there.' She pointed a finger to the left. 'In half an hour, there'll be a demonstration of the software. After that, William will be working the room. You can hit him then. Excellent disguise, by the way. You are utterly forgettable as a man.'

'Too short,' said Emma, feeling tiny without her heels.

'This is the last time we'll talk tonight. I don't want William to see us together, even in your disguise,' said Daphne, who was exquisitely put together in a red halter dress with gold beading. 'Did you like the pictures?'

'Like isn't the word,' said Emma enthusiastically.

The client nodded. 'Hit him three times tonight, at the very least.' Emma gave her the thumbs up, but Daphne was already gone, dashing down the narrow hallway to the main room.

Victor, meanwhile, had found a seat at the front area's bamboo bar. He ordered two mai-tais and asked the bartender – of Asian descent and American demeanor – what the Japanese characters on the wall meant.

He said, 'It's an ancient Japanese proverb.'

'*Japanese* proverb?' asked Victor.

'You think the Chinese are the only Asian people with proverbs?'

Victor, who was half-Italian, half-Polish and sensitive to ethnic stereotyping, said, 'No! I'm sure the Japanese are pithy as hell.'

Emma asked, 'So what does the writing mean?'

The bartender cleared his throat. 'It reads, "A wise man

drinks quickly, quietly, and leaves a big tip." '

Emma laughed and the bartender smiled at her, his almond skin stretched over gracefully rounded cheek-bones. He was a doll. Cute, funny, employed. Three qualities she could go for. Emma fluttered her lashes at him. The bartender looked spooked and walked to the other end of the bar.

Victor said, 'I guess he's not into facial hair.'

Touching her cheeks, Emma remembered: she was a guy. 'I forgot!' she said. 'Maybe I should've used the sock, just for the bulging reminder.'

Emma and Victor quickly and quietly drank, left a big tip (as instructed), and headed for the main room. Pushing open the screen door, they were engulfed by the smell of sandalwood and jasmine. For Emma's sharp nasal receptors, it was a bit much.

'One lap, then we lock on target Dearborn,' suggested Emma.

Victor nodded and they were off, squeezing their way through the crowd of beautiful people, young, gloriously dressed, laughing, drinking, having a swell time. Emma wondered how long it'd been since she went to a party. Years, probably. She avoided large gatherings. Too much noise. Too many places to look, things to smell. Her senses would become overwhelmed and she'd feel trapped. She usually lasted about half an hour. Then she'd run home for the sensory static of her white sanctuary.

Tonight, though, she felt somewhat calm, thanks to her costume. It served as a protective shield, like an invisibility cloak. Men simply overlooked her (she was only 5'5"), and women would either appraise her in two brutal nanoseconds or overlook her completely to check out dashing Victor at her side.

Emma said, 'Women are looking at you, Vic.'

'What did you think of that girl out front?' he asked. 'The one with the guest list?'

'Cute. For a clipboard Nazi.'

Toward the far end of the room, the crowd loosened. Through the slit of space, Emma saw a naked woman, flat on her back, on a table.

Victor spotted her too. He said, 'This is the best party ever.'

The nude woman – mixed Asian, jet-black hair cascading over the edge of the table – lay supine on a lavishly garnished table. Clusters of sushi were artfully arranged on top of her, dotting the length of her arms, legs, torso, piled on her breast and pudendum. Globs of wasabi and pickled pink ginger connected the sushi dots.

'Quite a spread,' said Victor, grinning.

The human platter looked right at him, which was disconcerting to say the least. 'Before you make a stupid crack about where to find the spicy tuna, you should know that I can kill with a single chopstick.'

He stepped backward, away from the table, a bit shaken. 'I *was* going to ask for the spicy tuna,' he said to Emma.

'Victor Armour? Is that you?' A tall, bony blond with pink frosted lipstick and glued-on eyelashes rushed at him, grabbing Vic by the lapels. Emma only glimpsed her face before she leaned in to kiss him.

Victor seemed puzzled. And then recognition kicked in. 'Marcie?' he asked. 'Wow! I hardly recognized you. Hey,

Emma – I mean, *Emeril* – this is Marcie Skimmer. The model.'

The same model who'd posed as a cow, a parade float and a whale for Daphne's SlimBurn ad campaign. The model who had, allegedly, been living in a sanitarium for the past several months. Wherever she'd been, Marcie had lost a ton of weight. She looked beautiful. She also looked exactly like the strawberry Pop Tart who'd been with William Dearborn at Ciao Roma the other night. In fact, Marcie was the Pop Tart.

'Emeril?' prompted Victor. To Marcie: 'He's very shy.'

'Pleased to meet you,' said Emma with a deep voice.

Marcie glanced at her (him), barely acknowledging that she (he) existed, and turned back to Victor, the natty photographer, a man who might serve her some purpose. She said, 'What a surprise to see you here.'

'I've got friends in Haiku places,' he said.

Marcie laughed harder than the joke called for. Emma wondered if she were drunk, stoned, or just demented. For her part, Emma was relieved to stand there and listen, not to have to talk.

Victor said gently, 'I'm glad that you're feeling better.'

Marcie smiled, showing her famous white teeth. 'Despite what you must have heard, I did not try to eat myself to death, and I was never in a detox hospital in the Adirondacks. I *was* at a private spa in the Catskills for a few months. All part of the SlimBurn campaign. Taking the pills, dieting, exercising. I lost fifty pounds.' The slenderized mannequin did a graceful twirl.

Fifty pounds in three months? Was that possible? Emma had been trying to lose ten pounds for fifteen years.

'Wait until you see my new SlimBurn ad,' said Marcie. 'It's absolutely mind-blowing.'

Emma cringed. She hated that phrase, hated the memories it dredged up even more. On reflex, she reached for her forehead and massaged.

Victor saw her react. He knew how she was at parties. He put his arm around her (him), not caring how it might have looked to Marcie or anyone. Emma smiled at him gratefully. Someone came out of the crowd and embraced Marcie. She was dragged away, waving over her shoulder at Victor. Emma was glad she was gone. Victor whispered, 'Are you okay?'

Emma said, 'Holding firm. Thanks to you.'

He lowered his arm. 'Hard to believe that Dearborn could mistake you for Marcie. She's six inches taller than you. And, forgive me, slimmer.'

She (he) had to agree. 'It does stretch the boundaries of comprehension. I think it was an honest mistake at first, but then we were into it and forgot about who we thought each other was supposed to be.'

The pulsing techno music stopped. Emma felt instant relief about that. A man walked onto the bandstand. He wore his signature Beatles style suit with a skinny tie. William Dearborn smiled at the crowd with honest pleasure at its size and applause.

Victor was clapping and hooting like a fifteen-year-old at a Green Day concert. Emma was silent, still as a statue. Her internal reaction to seeing Dearborn, however, was as chaotic and jubilant as the crowd's. She felt herself pulled toward him, as if he were the magnet and she a helpless sliver of steel.

'I want to thank you for coming out,' he said once he'd quieted the room. His British accent sparkled like champagne in a glass. 'Thanks to the management of Haiku for having us. Thanks to Crusher Advertising for organizing the event.' He gestured toward the wings of the stage. Emma spotted Daphne, her arms crossed, eyes pinned on William.

He continued. 'ArtSpeak has been in development for over a year. But it's been a dream of mine for a decade. I'd rather show you what it can do than tell you.' Dearborn nodded at Daphne, who pushed a button on a hand-held remote. The curtains behind the stage parted, revealing a wall of computer monitors – a dozen flat-panel screens, in two rows of six. The screens were blank. Also, on stage, there was a table with an Apple computer on it, the monitor huge. A murmur rose from the crowd. Emma smelled the odor of anticipation – like acidic red wine – around her.

Dearborn said, 'We all talk to our computers. But it's usually to curse at them when something goes wrong.' The crowd laughed dutifully. 'ArtSpeak lets you talk to your computer to coax something beautiful out of it.

'I want to explain a few things before I start,' he continued. 'The software responds to individual voice commands. The user installs his or her vocal tones into the computer by reciting the alphabet. ArtSpeak can retain three users' tones per package, in English, German, Japanese, and French.' He sat at a chair in front of the Apple. 'I'm going to paint now by using voice commands. I chose an image that's been stuck in my mind. Here goes.'

He took hold of the computer microphone. The lights

were lowered. The Apple monitor flickered to life. The wall of screens behind him remained black. The only sound in the room was Dearborn's voice.

'Caucasian female head. Oval. Cheekbones wide, wide. Wide. Half narrow. Chin round, round, half sharp. Half sharp.'

It went on like this for a minute or two, William speaking into the computer microphone in this rarified code language. The audience watched the monitor as a face took shape. Emma was not impressed. It was the head of a woman, her features rudimentary, with shape but not dimension. The crowd shuffled impatiently, and Emma was worried for William that his program would be a flop.

'I'm going to add color now,' he said. 'Color wheel engage. Hair brown, red, half red. Highlight, gold. Gold, half gold. Eyes orange. Red. Zero red. Orange. Brown. Half brown.' The portrait was getting more interesting, but it still didn't amount to much. 'So that's what you get in five minutes,' he said. 'To make a more complex work of art, on canvas or on screen, it takes time. I spent a couple of hours last night on a detailed portrait of her, which I'll show you now. No one has seen this yet except me.'

He clicked the mouse, and a full-color portrait appeared on screen. The crowd gasped collectively. The portrait was beautiful, detailed, with vibrant color and dimension.

Victor put his hand on the back of Emma's neck and squeezed hard.

Dearborn said, 'She's a stunner. This is what she'd look like on the wall of the Post Office.' He clicked the mouse and one of the twelve monitors behind him flickered, showing the same woman as if she'd been drawn by a police sketch artist. 'And here's what Picasso would have made of her.' Another click, another monitor, this time, the cubist rendering.

'Lichtenstein,' said Dearborn, with a click. Another monitor showed her as a comic book illustration.

'Serat.' A pointillist portrait.

'Manet.' Impressionist.

'In the movie *Tron*.' A 3-D graphic.

'A character on *The Simpsons*.' Google-eyed.

Dearborn continued on until all the monitors were glowing. 'This is how I like to see a woman,' he said. 'From twelve different perspectives.'

Each and every one looked exactly like Emma.

If she'd wanted a still image of her face to self-serve into William's head, now she had a dozen to choose from. But she wouldn't need them. As he said, they were stuck in his mind already.

She whispered to Vic, 'Thank *God* I'm wearing a beard.'

He said, 'That must have been some kiss.'

On stage, William waited for a reaction. For all his confidence, he seemed a little worried.

But then the awe broke open and the audience erupted. People started leaping onto the stage to congratulate him. Someone handed William a bottle of champagne and he sprayed the crowd with it. The techno music began throbbing again, ear-bleedingly loud. And through all this mayhem, Emma could feel a pinprick in the center of her forehead, as if someone were jabbing at her. Rubbing the spot, she scanned the crowd. Up on stage, a pair of hazel eyes bored a hole into Emma's brow.

Victor noticed too. 'I take it Daphne is not aware that you and William have met.'

Emma said, 'She's on a need-to-know basis.'

'I think she knows,' he said, gesturing to the portraits before them. 'Whether she needs to or not.'

Emma couldn't help staring at the portraits, especially the original, in Dearborn's own style. Emma always had to brace herself when confronting her likeness – the wild hair, the odd eyes, how much she resembled her mother. Studying the portraits, though, she felt a strange, homey happiness. In them, Emma saw herself as art – sublime and beautiful. Which was, apparently, how Dearborn saw her.

But, she reminded herself, the image wasn't *really* Emma. It was idealized, a fantasy. The cold reality: William had remembered her face, but he hadn't captured her soul on screen. He'd painted his invention of it. She was as plastic a model to him as Marcie was to Daphne. Just a surface, nothing underneath. Despite the intensity of the kiss, and both of their apparent lingering fascination with it, she and William were complete strangers to each other. Worse than that, she thought. He was a target. 'It's just a job,' she said aloud.

Victor said, 'If you're going to hit Dearborn, you'd better hurry up. He's being eaten alive.'

'Let's get a bite,' she said.

They pushed toward the stage, penetrating the buffer zone around William three layers deep. The inner circle proved impossible to crack, even for Marcie Skimmer, coming up alongside Emma (Emeril), elbowing her (him) in the jaw to press her way forward, nearly dislodging the beard (which would have been disastrous). With one hand on her facial piece, Emma plowed forward in Marcie's wake and managed to get almost within arm's reach of William.

Luckily, Dearborn had removed his jacket and rolled up his shirtsleeves, revealing two forearms' worth of exposed skin. He was flanked by Daphne and Tweedy, the gatekeeper. Marcie fought her way to the front and kissed Dearborn on the lips. Cameras flashed. Emma took another elbow in the face from a guy in a khaki suit.

'Mr Dearborn? Over here, sir,' said the guy, shoving and pushing. 'Mr Dearborn. I'm a big fan. One minute of your time. Sir! Sir!' And then the khaki suitor was pushed back. Emma got a right shock when she saw his face before he disappeared into the throng.

Hoffman Centry, as she lived and breathed through a tuft of synthetic hair.

Tweedy shouted to Dearborn, 'Dave Kushner from the *Times* business section on your left.'

Marcie shouted, 'Liam! Kiss me again for the paparazzi!'

Dearborn ignored the model and started talking to the reporter. Marcie pouted. Daphne had spotted Emma and was imploring her, mouthing, 'Go!' Locked in a current of people, Emma found herself pushed behind Dearborn, still two layers of people away. If she could stick her arm through a gap and just graze her fingertips against his arm . . . she pushed . . . inches away, closer, closer . . .

A surge backward. She saw Daphne to the right looking anxious. She also spotted Victor nearby but then lost sight of him. If only she had Daphne or Marcie's height. She could reach over the bodies. But if Emma was lacking in stature, she made up for it with perseverance.

Despite the noise, Emma could hear Dearborn's conversation. 'Who's the girl?' the *Times* man asked the artist.

'What girl? You mean her?' Dearborn gestured at Marcie.

'The girl in the portraits,' said the reporter. 'If I'm going to reprint some of the images in the paper, I'll need a release.'

'No need,' said Dearborn. 'She doesn't exist. She's made up, a fantasy. Like a fairy or a mermaid. Or a witch.'

Emma gasped when he said 'witch'. She couldn't help it. The reporter's eyes turned toward the sound. He made eye contact with her before turning back to Dearborn. He said, 'A witch, you say? Her face appeared like magic?'

'Gads, don't write that,' said Dearborn. 'She's totally imaginary. Have you ever seen eyes that color in your life?'

Emma was right behind William now. One touch was all she needed. Two seconds to implant Daphne in his mind. She lifted her hand, an inch away from his elbow.

The reporter said, 'Actually, I have seen eyes like that before. Right behind you. That short guy with the beard.'

'Where?' demanded Dearborn. The reporter pointed at Emma just as she touched Dearborn's elbow. But he moved, spinning around and ensnaring her wrist. Instantly, on contact with his skin, her own ignited under his hand, and a sudden heat rolled upward from her wrist to her shoulder and into her chest. Her cheeks under the fake beard felt hot, sticky, and itchy.

'William? Are you okay? You're sweating,' asked Tweedy, studying his face.

Beads of sweat were forming on his forehead, his eyes fixed on Emma, his mouth open to take quick breaths.

Daphne moved into Emma's line of sight. She mouthed, 'Do it! Do it!'

But Emma couldn't concentrate. She didn't dare close her eyes. She felt trapped and anxious, vulnerable, exposed. She had to get out of there. A flash of panic and adrenaline took over. She tugged free and spun backwards, letting herself be swallowed by the crowd.

Her size was an advantage now. She scurried like a mouse through holes in the crunch of bodies, and all she could think was 'Get out!'

She heard Dearborn yell, 'Stop that man!'

Victor's voice rang out: 'He went that way!'

Her friend was, no doubt, pointing in the opposite direction of where she actually was. Emma tried to calm herself. She slowed down. Running would only draw more attention. She walked at a rapid but normal pace at the periphery of the crowd. She was almost safe. Only a few more yards. She prayed no one saw her, or noticed that she was in costume.

As she passed the sushi table, the human platter stared

at her and said, 'Hey! Wait just one minute. The message is for you.'

The Good Witch said, 'Excuse me?'

The girl said, 'The writing on the wall.'

Emma glanced up at the characters. 'What does it say?'

'It says, "From my perspective, I see that you're either a eunuch or a transvestite." '

'It says all that in four characters – one of which I'm pretty sure means house?' asked Emma.

Sushi Girl said a pithy, 'Yes.'

Emma reached into her jacket pocket and found her wallet. She removed a fifty (Mr Cannery would so *not* approve), and held it against the flat fly of her trousers. 'You didn't see me. You didn't talk to me,' she said. 'I am invisible.'

Sushi Girl said, 'Slide the bill under my shoulder and keep walking.'

11

William Dearborn sat on Emma's white couch, fluffy pillows on either side of him. He was shirtless, in jeans and bare feet. His hair was damp, just out of the shower, and marvelously sloppy. Placing a hand on his belly, he closed his eyes. His hand rubbed his hard ab muscles, dipping into the waistband of his jeans.

And then he opened his eyes and looked right at Emma. He said, 'Are you just going to stand there gawking? Come over here. Have a seat. You're not going to make me wait all night, are you?'

Emma's eyes snapped open. She'd been in bed, lazing on a Sunday morning, ignoring the phone that had been ringing since 8:00 a.m., replaying her favorite daydream about Dearborn. But this time he'd broken form – and talked. That was not in her script. And, frankly, she didn't appreciate the improv. Everything was wrong. She couldn't even fantasize right.

Pulling the covers over her head, Emma wanted to hide in her bed forever. What would she say to Daphne (who, she assumed, was the person calling every half hour)? How to justify her colossal failure at Haiku last night? Her pathetic attempt to hit Dearborn. And then the mad panic and wild dash. And the portraits! Daphne would surely want an explanation about those. Emma threw the covers off and reached for her phone to turn the ringer off. She didn't work on Sundays. It was in the contract.

But the phone rang in her hand. Instinctively – as in, before she remembered not to – she hit the on button and said, 'Hello?'

'I'm in love,' said Victor. 'I'm also on my way up with coffee and cupcakes.'

Emma said, 'I'm in my pajamas.'

'Me too,' he said.

He let himself in two minutes later. As promised, he wore a pair of drawstring flannel pants, a gray sweat-shirt, and unlaced hiking boots with no socks. He handed her a large cup of coffee and said, 'Have you ever noticed, when you're in love, that senses are heightened? The sun seems brighter. The air smells fresher. The coffee tastes better?'

Emma placed both hands around the cup and drank greedily, burning her tongue just a little. The coffee was delicious. She peeked under the window shade. The sun was bright today. Cracking a window, she inhaled the city air, which was remarkably fresh. Did this mean she, too, was in love? Shaking her head, she reminded herself that her senses were always heightened.

'Who's the lucky girl?' she asked.

'The woman with the clipboard,' he said. 'She wouldn't let us into Haiku last night.'

'Tweedy?'

'She wore a tweed skirt, if that's what you mean. Her name is Ann Jingo. She's William Dearborn's right-hand woman.'

'And what exactly, as William Dearborn's right hand, does Ann Jingo do for him?' asked Emma, sounding oddly jealous.

'Her job requirements vary. For instance, last night, she spent half of the party searching for a short bearded man in a wool suit. I helped her. But we never found the guy. We spoke to nearly everyone at the party. Including the sushi girl, who pretended not to speak English.'

'So I'm safe?' she asked.

'Not quite,' said Victor. 'Ann remembered that we were together at the door. She remembered that you claimed to be Emma Hutch, but no one admitted to putting a woman of that name on the guest list. Daphne, FYI, is an excellent liar. I had to swear I'd never seen you before last night.' He took a sip of coffee. 'I asked Ann out. She's thinking about it and will get back to me.'

'You'll hear from her today,' said Emma. 'I've got a *feeling*.'

'You don't get *feelings*,' he reminded her. 'I hope you're right anyway.'

'Why is Dearborn so bent on finding me?'

'You know why. He's a Bewitched Brit,' said Victor. 'A moment for self-congratulations: my costume was flawless. Dearborn thinks that the bearded man is related to his mystery woman – a brother or a cousin.'

Emma was flooded with relief. If William had recognized her through the beard, she might as well resign from the case, lose the cash cow client, walk to the bank, and turn over her keys today. On the other hand, if she weren't working for Daphne, she could reveal herself to Dearborn and maybe kiss him again, an idea that was as terrifying as it was tantalizing.

'I'll have to get him when he's alone and unprotected,' said Emma. 'I can't concentrate at parties. The noise, the lights. It's too much for me. I'm a deeply, achingly sensitive person.'

'So you say.'

'When Dearborn grabbed my wrist, I felt a million eyes on me. I wanted to jump out of my skin.'

'It was weird to watch. Like you two were in a bubble together,' said Victor. 'Maybe something about him is jamming your signal.'

'Whenever we touch, I get hot,' she said.

'I told you he shouldn't be underestimated,' said Victor. 'You should fuck him and burn off all that heat. Then you'd be able to work on him for Daphne.'

'I'm sure the client would object.'

'You're right,' he said, smiling wryly. 'What was I thinking?'

He'd been thinking the same thing she'd been thinking. For two days already. Nearly non-stop.

Buzzer. Emma pushed the talk button and said, 'Hello?'

'Good morning. My name is Ann Jingo,' squawked the speaker. 'I'm looking for Emma Hutch.'

'It's her!' Victor mouthed excitedly.

'Emma moved. She couldn't pay her mortgage and fled to escape debtors' prison.'

The speaker squawked, 'Does Emma Hutch have any relatives in the area? In particular, a diminutive man with a full beard, dark brown hair . . .'

'Emma doesn't have family,' she said. That was true, at least.

The intercom kept squawking. 'I'd appreciate five minutes of your time. I have a sketch of the man. If Ms Hutch could take a quick look at it . . .'

'I told you: she's not here,' said Emma, sadness turning to anger.

'Is there a way I can get in touch with her?'

Emma said, 'No, goodbye,' and clicked the speaker's off button.

'Doesn't she have the sweetest, cutest, coolest voice?' said Victor. 'I think she's from Chicago.'

'Michigan,' said Emma, whose ear for accents was sharp.

'There's no such thing as debtors' prison.'

Phone. Emma checked caller ID. Daphne Wittfield. She took a deep breath and answered. Before her client had a chance to berate, Emma started in with, 'I'm very angry with you, Daphne.'

'You're angry with *me*?' asked the client.

'You put me in a terrible position last night. I won't stand for that kind of treatment. If you do that to me again, I'll cut you as a client – keeping your initial payment for the time I've already spent on your case, which is in the contract.'

Daphne said, 'I agree that the event wasn't the best setting for our purposes. I'm faxing you William's schedule for this week. Try to get him coming or going from his appointments.'

'You do realize that he has a girlfriend?' asked Emma.

'You mean Marcie Skimmer? You use the term "girlfriend" lightly,' said Daphne. The fax machine on Emma's desk started humming.

'Do you always work on Sunday?' asked Emma.

'By choice.'

Emma caught the fax sheet hot off the printer. She scanned it for an optimal stakeout. 'William has a one o'clock lunch at the Four Seasons tomorrow.'

'It's a standing reservation,' said Daphne. 'But he hardly ever misses it.'

'I'll be there from noon on,' said Emma. 'I'll hit him coming *and* going.'

'Good,' said Daphne. 'One more thing. The portrait William used to demonstrate ArtSpeak last night. Did it remind you of anyone? Anyone you know?'

'You bet it did,' said Emma. 'It looked a lot like you, Daphne. The colors were slightly off, but feature by feature it was you all over.'

'I thought it looked like someone else.'

'I can't image who,' said Emma. 'I immediately thought of you.'

'My other line,' said the client. She hung up.

Victor said, 'Did she buy it?'

'I'm not sure,' said Emma. 'People believe what they want to believe.'

'Which could be the summation of organized religion,' said Victor. 'And love. Here's the thing: I don't want to lie to Ann about you. But I will, for as long as I possibly can.'

'And how long is that?'

'Until she gives me a start-to-finish blow job,' he said. 'My allegiances will shift at that point.'

'I understand completely,' said Emma. 'Can you hold off for two weeks?'

'That depends on Ann,' he said.

Victor's cell phone rang. He took the call in the kitchen. When he returned, Emma said, 'That was her?'

He beamed. 'I'm seeing her tomorrow night. She invited me to an exhibit at the Brooklyn Museum of Art.'

Emma looked at William's schedule. 'I'll see you there,' she said. 'But you won't see me. Now get out. I've got one day to organize two brilliant disguises.'

'Need help?'

She pushed him toward the door. 'I can handle it.'

A limo pulled up at the East 57th Street entrance to the Four Seasons Hotel. The driver opened the rear door for three men in Armani. The men strode toward the hotel. Poised to receive them, two people held the handles of the double doors, one on each side, like bookends. The taller one, an older man, swung the heavy door open, bowing. He wore a black tunic, black slacks with gray piping, black patent shoes, a black cap with a shiny bill, and white gloves. His co-doorperson – a woman, shorter, curvier, her bronze hair in a tight bun – had on the identical uniform, minus the gloves. She also wore opaque black Ray-Bans.

Hanging high above their heads, flags from four nations flapped in the October breeze, calling attention to the I.M. Pei designed building, as if it needed the help. The Four Seasons was one of New York's most famous hotels. The Pool Room was the ultimate power lunch spot for the media and advertising elite. Being a doorman at such a luminous location was a privilege.

'Not just a privilege,' said the older man, name of Mr Reade. 'It's an honor to stand under this canopy and open the door for these fine citizens.'

'Yes, sir!' said his female colleague.

'I'm old but I'm not deaf,' he said. 'I hear your sass. Trainees get worse every month. Where did you say you worked before?'

'I didn't,' Emma responded. She'd been trying to deflect conversation since she showed up an hour ago, but Mr Reade insisted on chatting away the excruciatingly uneventful minutes. She was impressed, though, at how the hotel guests and luncheoneers completely ignored her, as if she were a handle-happy robot, programmed to swing and shut but not to speak.

'Nearly one o'clock,' said Mr Reade. 'Go on your break.'

'I can't,' said Emma, expecting Dearborn any minute. 'You go first.'

'No, I like one o'clock. This is when the famous people come.'

'I want to see famous people, too,' said Emma. She was primed for it. For one famous person anyway. Emma had been visualizing the transfer all morning. She'd forced herself to study the 'sun out of ass' photo of Daphne so that it'd rocket out of her head and into Dearborn's with the slightest touch. She planned to pull open the hotel door for him, brushing his hand with hers. It would seem like an accident. He'd never notice, as long as she didn't heat up. But she wouldn't. She'd be cool. Emma made a pledge to herself that she'd think of Dearborn as a target only. That said, she was butterflies-in-gut excited to see him.

Another limo. Another flutter on the wings of

anticipation. Another group of men in suits chewing on unlit cigars. No change in the clientele since the last time Emma staked out the Four Seasons. She'd trailed men here before (which was why she had the uniform). The influx of guests got heavy for a spell and time moved more quickly. When the foot traffic slowed, Emma asked Mr Reade for the time.

'One thirty. Take your break now or never,' he said.

'Bullocks,' she said. Dearborn was either late, or he wasn't coming. He could have slipped inside via another entrance, but why would he do that? He didn't know he was being staked out. This was beyond frustrating. She'd never had so much trouble getting close to a target before.

'Okay,' she said. 'I'll go on my break now.' Emma decided to roam the lobby. If she'd somehow missed him, maybe she could find him inside.

But then a taxi pulled up to the entrance. A handsome man hopped out and snapped his fingers at the door people.

Mr Reade jumped (creakily) to serve. Emma took her time walking over to lug three heavy suitcases to the entrance.

'Bring these inside and take them to the bell station,' said the man Emma had recognized immediately.

Her chin down, Emma asked, 'Under what name, sir?'

'Roger,' he said. 'Mr Roger.'

'Yes, sir,' she said, doffing her cap. 'Will you be staying long, sir?'

'Long enough,' he said, paying the cab driver. 'Let's go. Come on! Jesus Christ, do you want a tip or not?'

Emma remembered what a lame tipper he was. She said, 'Roger. I mean, yes, sir!'

He stopped. 'Are you trying to be funny?' he asked.

Mr Reade said, 'She's a trainee, sir.'

'Just bring in the bags,' said Mr Roger, otherwise known as Jeff Bragg. Emma marveled at the vehemence of his condescension. She was the size of a bug to him. A mite on the bug. A speck on the mite. If Susan could only see how he treated the servant class, she'd be ashamed of herself for fucking him. Emma felt a pang of said shame. She owed Susan a phone call, even if she had nothing to report.

Emma dragged Jeff's bags inside to the bellhop stand and filled out the tags. Jeff strode up to the concierge desk. She lowered her chin practically to her chest to get past him and then wandered into the lobby proper. She made a tour of the bar and the restaurant and couldn't find Dearborn. Shit and double shit! thought Emma. Where was that slippery Brit?

Back in the front lobby, Jeff Bragg was just now getting a room key card. He went straight for the elevators. A family of six entered after him trapping him way in the back. Not sure why (frustration? curiosity? commitment to her client?), Emma rushed into the elevator, too, just before the doors closed.

When the car got to the ninth floor, Jeff pushed through the family and out of the elevator. Just as the doors were closing, Emma ducked out. She skulked down the hallway, keeping a distance of thirty feet between her and Bragg. She felt like a private eye, a sleuth, a shamus. She smiled crookedly, liking her accelerated pulse, the actual thrill as opposed to the vicarious kind she was used to. But what did she hope to achieve, following him? Maybe she was taking the risk for the sake of it. Putting herself out on a limb. That would show Susan Knight and her theories. If nothing more, Emma would know where to find him, not that she'd send Susan anywhere within fifteen blocks of him.

Jeff turned a corner. Emma double-timed. She was wary of rushing, but she didn't want to round the corner and find an empty hallway.

Which was exactly what happened. She walked slowly down the corridor, her ears pricking, her skin prickling. She looked left, then right, searching for sound and motion. As she tiptoed past the ice machine closet, an arm reached out and grabbed her by the uniform sleeve, pulling her into the closet.

Jeff slammed her against a Coke machine, hard.

A can of diet Dr Pepper clunked into the tray on the bottom.

They both looked at it.

'My favorite,' said Emma.

'Who are you?' demanded Jeff, gripping her shoulders. Emma felt the cold penetrating her uniform tunic, slowly seeping into her flesh. William turned her into a flame; Jeff turned her into a block of ice.

'I'm just the doorperson,' she said. 'I wanted to apologize for my impertinence. I'm only a trainee, sir, and I'm still struggling to act as lowly as I should.'

'How did you find me?' he demanded.

'I wasn't looking for . . .'

'You're lying, Connie Quivers, or whatever your name is.'

Emma said, 'Okay, okay. You've got good eyes, Mr *Roger*. You're right. I am spying on you. My people want to know where you are, at all times, and if you try to sneak off again, you'll wake up in a pool of your own blood, dead.'

'I'll wake up dead?'

'You'll wake up nearly dead, and then you'll die. And it'll look just like this,' she said and then put her bare fingers on his neck.

Emma tried to conjure up a scary scene from a horror movie. Any bloodbath would do. She closed her eyes and transmitted the first image that came up.

Jeff released her and lunged backwards across the closet and crashed against the opposite wall. He said, 'A crazy picture just popped into my head.'

'That's what I'm going to do to you,' said Emma, menacingly.

'You're going to turn me into a naked blond with a klieg light up my ass?'

'Don't think I won't!' she screamed. Emma grabbed the diet Dr Pepper and ran down the corridor into a conveniently waiting elevator. She rode down to the lobby and ran out the front door, which Mr Reade held wide open.

'Break over?' he asked. And then, 'Slow down. Watch out!'

Emma hit someone, hard, and fell on her ass on the sidewalk, soda, cap, and shades flying.

'Trainees,' said Mr Reade. 'All sass. No class.'

'Hello, Emma,' said the man she'd careened into. He wore a tan suit and offered his hand.

'Hello, Hoffman.' Emma accepted his help, and he yanked her to her feet. She bent down to pick up her accessories and the bottle. 'What a coincidence,' she said. 'Running into you here.'

'I've been waiting all day for someone, but he never showed,' he said. 'I ate alone.'

'What'd you have?'

'Lamb chops,' he said. 'What are you doing here? And why are you dressed like a doorman?'

'You were waiting for William Dearborn?' asked Emma, deflecting his question. From Hoff's bashful look, she knew she was right. 'I saw you try to talk to him Saturday night at Haiku.'

'You were there?' he asked.

'Well?' asked Emma.

'Well . . . done?' asked Hoff.

'Did you feel a spark? Did you get excited in Dearborn's presence? Did the sight of him send high voltage to the groin?'

'The only groin jolt I felt all night was when I saw your face on the computer screen. Times twelve,' said Hoff. 'None of this makes any sense. And just now, seeing you sprawled on the ground, your legs splayed, hair a mess' – he whispered the next part – 'it gave me a hard-on. I've still got it. When I saw Dearborn the other night, nothing. But I wanted to see if, in a different setting . . . I thought I'd ask him if he'd ever considered working on a book project.'

Emma wanted to end Hoff's sexual-identity crisis. No reason he should be tormented with longing for William Dearborn. Especially since she was tormented enough for both of them. 'Hoff, I need to confess something to you,' she said.

'What?' he asked.

She hesitated. Guilt. Fear he'd be angry. She should have been upfront from the start. Her mouth felt dry. She unscrewed the cap of the diet Dr Pepper. Promptly, explosively, the agitated soda erupted like Mount Vesuvius. Brown liquid doused her eyeballs, flew up her nostrils and between her parted lips causing her to blink, sneeze, and cough at the same time. Her tunic and hair were soaked.

Mr Reade and Hoff started pounding on Emma's back, forcing her head between her knees and then attempting to get her to drink the few drops of Dr Pepper that remained in the bottle.

'Stop,' she insisted, pushing the bottle away.

The two men backed off. Hoff looked her up and down, and said, 'This is the second time in a row I've seen you in a soaking wet top.' He paused. 'Not that I'm complaining.'

Mr Reade said, 'The boss isn't going to like this. Employees have to represent the proper image of the hotel. And this' – he waved at her clinging tunic – 'isn't the kind of image the Four Seasons wants to present.'

Emma said, 'Tell the boss I can't continue to work under these dictatorial conditions.' She turned to Hoff. 'You can stop staring at my chest now.'

He said, 'I don't think I can.'

'Me either,' said Mr Reade.

Emma shook her head with disgust. 'This is just the kind of thing that happens when you go above 14th Street,' she said, taking her cap, empty bottle, glasses, and wounded pride west on 57th Street.

12

Susan Knight was frantic. 'Jeff's home phone has been cut off,' she ranted, pacing in Emma's living room.

The Good Witch had found Susan on the bench in her lobby when she returned home. Her friend looked distraught, her hair in a disheveled pony, the drawstring of her track pants (on a workday!) untied, her shirt misbuttoned.

Emma brought the sad rabbit upstairs to her place, made her a cup of soothing chamomile tea, and told her to drink it while she rinsed off the diet Dr Pepper. Emma cleaned up and, dressed in a bathrobe, returned to her guest on the living room couch.

'Why aren't you at work?' Emma asked.

'How can I work when the man I love is missing?' asked Susan, no calmer, despite the tea. 'I think something terrible has happened to him.'

Emma said, 'I know where he is. But I'm not going

to tell you. He's out of his mind, Susan. Completely paranoid. Possibly delusional. He thinks I'm spying on him.'

'You are spying on him,' she said. 'And why haven't you called me?'

'I've been busy with that other case,' said Emma. 'Let me ask you something, and then we'll get right back to wasting our breath on Jeff Bragg.' Susan nodded. 'When you picture a scene in your imagination of, say, people in a room, are you in the room, too?'

'I don't understand the question,' said Susan, who preferred reality to fantasy.

'I observe the scene, like I'm the audience,' said Emma. 'But lately, in my daydreams, this one person seems to see me. He looks at me, talks to me.'

'Honestly, I have no idea what you're talking about.'

'It's like a movie, when a character looks into the camera, talks into it. It's called breaking the fourth wall.'

'So?' asked Susan, impatiently.

I am that wall, thought Emma. She certainly felt broken into. Dearborn had somehow come to life in her fantasies. 'I'm wondering if I'm having a psychotic break,' she said. 'Or an emotional breakthrough.'

'You're not having a psychotic break,' said Susan. 'But emotional breakthroughs are few and far between. You certainly need one, so we'll go with that.'

Emma liked her logic. 'Jeff Bragg is staying in a hotel – I'm not telling you which one. He must have moved out of his apartment with a few days left before leaving on his permanent vacation.' Emma felt a chill remembering

Friday night at Bull when Jeff literally made her blood run cold. 'He's moving to an island. To stay.'

Susan couldn't believe it. 'He'd never do that. It's childish! It's irresponsible!'

'From what I've seen, that fits.'

'You don't know Jeff at all,' said Susan.

'How well did you know him?' she asked, having a sketchy idea of their relationship.

'Intimately,' she challenged.

'How many times did you go to his apartment?'

'He never invited me to his place, but he had good reasons. He traveled a lot. Or his apartment was too messy. Or he had no food in the fridge. Or he was out of toilet paper.'

Emma asked, 'What about his friends? Colleagues? Did you meet any of them?'

'We didn't socialize,' she admitted. 'It seemed like a waste of time when what we really wanted to do was hole up at my place, order in Thai, and make love for hours.'

'Not all night long?' pushed Emma.

'Jeff was particular about sleeping in his own bed.'

'Did he ever leave stuff at your place? A shirt? A toothbrush?'

'You're missing the point.'

Emma waved her off. 'You never saw his place, met his friends – if he had any – or spent a whole night together. You don't find that odd?'

'No.'

'Did he bother taking off his shoes when you had sex?'

Susan said, 'Most of the time.'

The Good Witch could hardly believe her exceptionally sensitive ears. 'You call this love?' she asked.

'I don't expect you to understand,' said Susan. 'You've never had phenomenal sex. You can't appreciate how hard it is to lose it.'

Emma's frustration with Susan rose to the boiling point. 'I'm putting myself out for you,' she snarled. 'In return, you remind me how empty my life is.'

Susan sighed. 'I'm sorry. I'm acting reprehensibly. It's the break up.'

Not good enough, thought Emma. 'This is exactly why I don't want to deal with the endings. I only get involved with the beginnings. The fun part. The joy, the bliss. I'm not supposed to be in the picture when it all comes tumbling down. I make a point of avoiding that part. I don't want to see it, and I don't have to. It's in the fucking contract.'

Susan's eyes got round. Emma glared into them. 'I'm going to get dressed,' she said. 'Give me five minutes, and we'll sort this out.'

Susan nodded numbly. The Good Witch went into her bedroom and crashed around in her closet to find a long-sleeved T-shirt and velour track pants. She crashed around in her bathroom to brush her hair. When Emma returned to the living room, Susan was gone and she'd left a piece of paper on the couch. It read:

Emma,

You have obvious objections to working on my case. Consider it closed. Please write up a detailed report

*of your encounters with Jeff Bragg so that I might
continue the investigation on my own. Send your
material to my office.*

That is all,
Susan

Along with the note, Susan left a check for one
thousand dollars.

Emma picked up the phone and called Susan's home
number. She left this message: 'I just read your pink slip.
Forget about a detailed report. You might be determined to
bury yourself with this loser, but I'm not going to hand you
the shovel. The next sound you hear is me ripping up your
check.'

Emma hung up, put the pieces of the check in the
trash, went into her bedroom, and assumed the fetal
position on her soft white coverlet.

Sex had the power to turn otherwise coherent women
into desperate maniacs. Susan behaved as if Jeff Bragg's
touch was food, water, and air. That she'd starve and
suffocate without it. Emma hugged her knees, afraid for
her friend's sanity (and safety). She felt tired suddenly,
weary. She closed her eyes.

And there was William Dearborn again, on the white
couch, shirtless, shoeless, bangs grazing his long lashes. He
was unfastening the buttons of his jeans, plunking them
open one by one, revealing more of his flat belly, an inch at
a time. Then he looked up – right at her – and shouted,
'What the hell are you waiting for?'

The entrance plaza to the Brooklyn Museum of Art had recently been redesigned to resemble the Louvre's in Paris, although the glass and steel structure looked more like a hovering UFO than the French pyramid.

The renovation – millions of dollars and years in the making – was impressive, if bizarre, and Emma oohed and aahed as she walked underneath it. She moved slowly, with the aid of a wooden cane. She pulled the mesh veil on her pillbox hat low to cover her rose-colored specs and to obscure the penciled-on crow's feet and forehead creases. She gripped her cane and shuffled in orthopedic shoes to the revolving doors at the entryway.

Two cops stopped her. One held out a hand and said, 'The museum is closed to the public tonight, ma'am.'

'Isn't there an exhibition?' she asked in her old lady voice.

'I need to see an invitation or check your name off the

list,' said the black cop. He was short but wide with a mustache – and a clipboard.

Not again. Could one go nowhere in New York City unless one's name was on a list? Emma formed an orange lipstick smile. She fished into her needlepoint purse for her wallet, extracting a laminated rectangle and waving it in their faces.

'This is my museum membership card,' she said. 'I used a social security check to pay for a lifetime membership, and I want to see the Delado exhibit.'

The other cop, doughy and white, also mustachioed, said, 'Not tonight, ma'am. The exhibit is open to the public tomorrow.'

Emma adjusted her velvet opera coat and said, 'Lifetime membership! Says so on the card. And considering that my lifetime isn't going to last much longer, I need to see this exhibit now.' She paused, laying on the schmaltz. 'Would you treat your own mother this way?'

The black cop pursed his lips tight. Clearly, he would not treat his mother this way. 'What's the harm?' he asked his partner. To Emma he said, 'Promise you'll be in and out in an hour. Or we'll come and get you.'

'You are a dear!' said Emma, shuffling toward the revolving door. 'Your mother would be proud.' She turned to the other cop. 'Yours, too.'

'My mom was a drunk,' he said. 'She beat me with a belt.'

Emma pretended not to hear that and shuffled into the museum as quickly as she dared.

Safely inside, Emma headed toward the atrium gallery. A sign on a silver pole directed them to the Delado exhibit opening night party, and through a small corridor to the event. Unlike the claustrophobic, crowded party at Haiku, this gathering was spacious and sparse. Half a dozen sculptures were lined up in the center of the cathedral-sized room. About forty people milled around the artworks, a dozen more stood at the table in the front of the gallery, picking at the platters of yellow and orange cheese cubes, crackers, and green grapes. No naked women as food platters in sight, which was both a disappointment and a relief.

Emma avoided the samplings. She was focused. Nothing, not even cheese, would distract her from her mission – transmitting Daphne's portrait into Dearborn's mind. She would not imagine him undressing himself. She would not turn into a human fireball when she touched him. Most of all, she would remind herself that she was doing a job for payment which she direly needed. November first was less than a week away. Time to get serious.

Harnessing her powers of concentration, Emma scanned the thin crowd for her prey. Dearborn wasn't at the refreshment table. She looked down the length of the gallery. The room was too long (even for her) to see everyone. She'd have to stroll among the sculptures, blend in.

As she neared the first sculpture on display, Emma smiled at a man with golden dreadlocks in an army jacket. He wore ink-blue jeans, worn Nikes, and a bright red T-shirt. 'Hello. I'm Alfie Delado,' he said. 'Thank you for coming. I couldn't possibly express the full extent of my gratitude.'

The artist. Emma inhaled. He smelled like good coffee and better marijuana. She liked him instantly. 'Congratulations on your show,' she said, still scanning the room for Dearborn.

Delado said, 'Thank you, thank you. The exhibit is a dream come true.' He got a bit choked up. Emma was afraid he might cry. Were all artists insatiable beggars for the approval of strangers? What a living hell that had to be, thought Emma.

'I've heard some wonderful things about your work,' she said, taking pity, trying to extricate herself and find her target.

'You have?' said Delado, incredulous. 'Please, let me show you my favorite piece.'

A hand on her back, Delado steered the gimpy, cane clattering Emma toward his first sculpture. He said, 'I call it *Penis Christ*.'

The piece of art, at first glance, was a Christian cross. On closer inspection, Emma saw that the two intersecting parts were shaped like penises. On the top of the vertical shaft, and on either end of the horizontal, Delado had fashioned the glans to resemble little fists. The base appeared to be a squat scrotal sac.

Delado said, 'The penis shape with a fist represents the masculine brutality of Christianity.'

'And this?' asked Emma. She'd shuffled toward the next sculpture. It was a gold-plated Star of David. The three arms of the two interlocking triangles had the same fisticock motif. 'Does this represent the masculine brutality of Judaism?' she pondered.

He grabbed Emma by the shoulders and shouted,

'YES! Exactly! Finally, someone understands what I'm trying to say.' Then he hugged Emma tight.

'Get off me,' she demanded, sensing other people's attention, the opposite of what she wanted.

A glance up the gallery confirmed her worst fears. William Dearborn, of fucking course, was bearing down on them. He was followed by Ann Jingo in tweed again, and Victor Armour in his chocolate brown Hugo Boss – the suit he wore only on special occasions (when he thought he might be laid).

Alongside William, taller than him in moon-high heels, Marcie Skimmer clung to his arm like a life preserver. She was breathtaking in pink sequins.

Panicking for release, Emma cracked Alfie Delado on the skull with her cane. He let her go and rubbed his dreadlocked noggin. Emma screwed up her face (trying to form genuine wrinkles) and said, 'Keep your hands to yourself!' She shuffled away as fast as her orthopedic shoes could carry her.

As expected, Dearborn and his posse stopped to gather around the artist, ignoring the little old lady who (1) couldn't further their careers, and (2) wasn't a potential sexual partner.

Except for Victor. He continued on, toward the curmudgeon with the cane. He caught up to her by the sculpture of an Islamic crescent.

He asked, 'Excuse me, ma'am. Are you all right?'

'I'm fine, young man,' she said.

'You sure showed that guy,' he said.

'I sure did,' she agreed.

'You could show me, too,' he said.

'Pardon?' she asked.

'Show me what you've got under that opera coat,' he said. 'I can tell you've got quite a rack. I'd love to see it. And your granny panties. I bet they're baggy. And graying, with big holes. Just how I like 'em.'

'Victor, you sick perv,' said Emma.

'I knew it was you as soon as you walked in,' he said, chuckling. 'But that's just me. No one else will recognize you.'

Now she wasn't so sure.

'Who's your friend?' asked Ann Jingo, appearing at Victor's side. She slid her arm around him like a serpent. Emma suspected that Victor's allegiances would soon shift.

He said, 'I was making sure this woman was all right. She came to appreciate the art, not be mauled by the artist.'

'Do you find Alfie's work titillating?' asked Ann.

'There's nothing tit about it,' said Emma in her best crotchety voice.

Ann's laugh was genuine – a light sound, a chime in a ball. Emma smiled back, couldn't help it, and she felt her makeup crack. 'Are you young people friends of the artist?' she asked.

'I am. I've known him for years. Alfie, Liam, and I were best friends in college,' said Ann.

'Liam?' asked Emma Crone.

'That tall man in the brown suit,' pointed out Ann.

'The one who needs a haircut?' asked Emma. 'Why are all those people fawning all over him? Shouldn't the artist be the star at his own exhibit?'

Ann said, 'Alfie doesn't care about being a star. He just

wants to show his work. Liam made this exhibit possible.'

Victor said, 'Dearborn is that big a fan?'

Ann said, 'Liam will do anything for a friend.'

Emma and Victor watched William and Alfie, the two old pals, standing side by side at the cheese and wine table. William whacked Alfie on his back. Alfie punched Liam on the upper arm. William slapped Alfie on the cheek. Alfie slapped him back.

'You see how they are?' asked Ann, smiling affectionately.

Emma saw only one thing: her target. Dearborn might as well have had a red bull's eye painted on his face.

Ann waved over Emma's shoulder, 'Victor, there's someone I want to say hello to. Nice meeting you!' she sang and led Victor away. He shrugged at Emma with a helpless puppy face. Ann had him on a short leash. Would all night, apparently.

More people trickled in. The room was getting slightly crowded, but Emma had only minor party panic. The music was classical and low. The lighting was white and soft. She was focused on the job and never lost sight of Dearborn. At the moment, he was touring the room with Marcie. The model girlfriend was strikingly pale, as if someone had stuck a tap in her side and drained out the color. Her hair was platinum, skin white as powder, lashes spider black, dress shimmering, waist cinched like a sack. How had this woman ever been fat? marveled Emma. Marcie seemed chiseled out of an ivory column. She was an organic sculpture, crafted by stylists and makeup artists.

Emma spotted Daphne at the cheese table. She was also keeping one eye on William and Marcie. Dressed for business tonight in a bland blue suit, her hair in a French twist, Daphne looked like a frustrated librarian. Emma checked her watch. She'd been waiting for a chance to get next to Dearborn for nearly an hour already. She hoped the cops out front had forgotten about her.

Watching from under her veil, Emma spied William and Marcie sneak out an emergency exit in the back of the gallery and into the dark autumnal night. Quick as she dared, Emma followed.

The Brooklyn Museum of Art sat on the northwest corner of the Brooklyn Botanical Garden, an oasis of photo-synthetic splendor in a borough better known for wiseguys than wisteria. Keeping at a safe distance, Emma tailed the couple deep into the garden. Fallen leaves made the ground soft and squishy. Her orthos were adequate for the terrain.

Emma kept her eyes trained on Marcie's luminous platinum high hair and shimmering dress. The model was as loud as she was reflective, rambling incessantly. Her stream of nonsense was painful to listen to from a distance, and the Good Witch could only imagine the agony Dearborn was in walking next to her.

Marcie cooed, 'Look, Liam. It's a rose garden.'

Hand in hand, the lovers entered the park's famous rose garden, boasting hundreds of varieties of the flowering bush. A white lattice fence surrounded the garden. Emma found a particularly dark spot outside the fence. She lay low and watched the couple inside.

'It's pretty here,' said Dearborn. 'Better in June than October.'

'We should come back together,' said Marcie. 'In June.'

William said nothing.

'Roses can be *our* flower,' suggested the mannequin.

'Like San Pellegrino is *our* water,' said Dearborn. 'And Wednesday is *our* day of the week.'

'Don't make fun of me,' said Marcie flirtatiously. They were standing at the center of the garden, under a trellis coiled with dormant vines.

This would have been the perfect moment for William to sweep her up in his arms and pepper her sweet cheeks with kisses.

Didn't happen. William said, 'We should be getting back.'

Marcie laced her fingers behind William's neck and pulled him into a kiss. Emma closed her eyes, gave them privacy. But she couldn't shut off the sound of smooching and increasingly theatrical female moans.

Dearborn said, 'Could you please shut up?'

Emma nearly guffawed. Marcie's moans were as phony as the platinum hair. The model pouted and said, 'We've been together for almost a month, Liam.'

Through the slats in the fence, Emma watched him turn away. He'd been expecting this talk. And dreading it.

Marcie continued, 'It's time we went public. A discreet leak, through publicists.'

'We are public,' he said. 'We're seen together.'

'We go out in large groups to dives like Ciao Roma,' she said. 'Take me to the Four Seasons for your Monday lunch.' He shook his head. She said, 'I want the world to know how much I love you.'

'Marcie, please,' he scoffed. 'Your feelings are inflated.'

From the fence, Emma saw Marcie's fists take shape. 'Don't say "inflated" to me!'

'You have a *bloated* idea of what this relationship is,' he said.

'Don't say "bloated"!' she said.

'You've grossly *overweighed* my feelings for you,' said William with real bite.

Ann Jingo had portrayed Dearborn as the bestest buddy in the whole wide world. But here was a jerk who needled an insecure woman in her most vulnerable spot. Emma felt her mind drifting, wondering where, between the two extremes, was the real William Dearborn. And how far was he from the man who'd kissed her, painted her portrait, and spoke to her from the inside out.

In the moment of ponderous distraction, Emma slipped and snapped a twig under her ortho.

Two heads turned in her direction. Emma shrank into a small ball, her dark clothes blending into the backdrop of night.

'What was that?' asked Marcie, primping as if on cue, fixing her hair for what she assumed was a paparazzi photographer.

'I think we should break up,' said Dearborn.

'You want to see other people?' she asked.

'I mean we shouldn't see each other.'

'But . . . but . . . but I'm thin.'

'It doesn't matter,' he said.

'How can my weight not matter?' she asked. Emma felt a pang of sympathy for the model. Talk about myopia. Marcie's number on the scale carried the weight of her world.

But Dearborn didn't give her an ounce. 'Look, Marcie. This isn't love. It's never going to be love – for either one of us. If you want to keep having sex, though, I suppose I could agree to that. But you have to promise not to speak at all.'

Marcie did not take him up on his kind offer. Instead, she slapped him hard, resoundingly, the crack rolling across the great lawn. Marcie followed that with a hysterical 'Fuck you!' and stormed out of the rose garden, her heels sinking into the earth, each step a slurp.

He waited until she was gone and then said loudly, 'You can come out now.'

Who was he talking to? wondered Emma.

'You, by the fence,' he said. 'Are you just going to gawk at me? Come over here. Have a seat. You're not going to make me wait all night, are you?'

Emma froze. He'd given the same speech to her before. But it was all in her head that time. She stood up, creakily, and shuffled into the rose garden. She tried to sound ancient and pitiful when she said, 'I was at the museum, but I must have gone out the wrong exit.'

'The museum is two blocks that way.'

'Hell of a wrong turn,' she said, pulling her veil down and her coat close. 'Chilly tonight.'

'October,' he said. 'Please, sit.' He sat down on a stone bench at the head of the rose garden. He patted the spot next to him.

Okay, this was weird. Dearborn was asking her to hang? Some lost little old lady?

'I know you heard my conversation with that woman,' he said. 'I'm not accusing you of spying.'

She was spying. He glanced furtively at Emma and then looked away. She got it: he felt guilty about what he said to Marcie. He wanted absolution from an impartial bystander.

She shuffled slowly toward him and sat down, making sure she didn't make physical contact – yet. 'You treated that woman atrociously,' she said.

'She was using me,' he said. 'And she lied. When someone lies to me, I go berserk.'

'You were rude,' said Emma. 'Regardless of what she did.'

He looked at Emma more closely – too closely. She pulled her veil down. 'You remind me of someone,' he said.

Her heart thundered. Did he recognize her? 'Your mother?' she asked.

'My grandmother,' he said. 'My mother died way before she got old.'

'I'm sorry to hear that.' Emma immediately thought of her own mother.

'I don't want to talk about it,' he said.

'I'm pretty sure the exit is that way,' said Emma, pointing, her hand shaking genuinely with cold. She wanted to do her job and go. Sitting with him, talking. It was wrong. He was an invention in her head, just as she was on his computer screen. Talking, sitting, they were in danger of getting to know each other. More accurately, she'd get to know *him*. He was talking to an old lady who didn't exist. She was lying to him too.

'I like this,' he said. 'Talking to a stranger in the dark. I feel like I can trust you.'

How wrong he was. Emma frowned, felt guilty. But then she pinched herself. Stay focused, she thought. Don't look at his lips. Or his eyes. Her hands itched to touch his hair, only inches away.

She said, 'I like your accent.'

'It's pretty faint by now. I'm half English. My dad is an American. My English mother was paralyzed in a car accident when she was thirty-five. In London. She died of a lung infection a year later, and that's when my dad and I moved to New York. I think I've held on to the accent for her. I can still hear her voice.'

Emma could still hear her mother's voice, too. And smell the cinnamon that seemed to rise from her skin. Whenever Emma got a vicious headache, she imagined her mom's fear in those last minutes of her life.

'Did you hold on to your mother's language, too?' asked Emma.

'Her language?'

'English words like chuffed and barmy and kip.'

He shook his head. 'I use American slang, not British. Sometimes I use her phrase "a cracking headache." I like that one.'

A cracking headache? Had he really said that? She felt a chill, not just the air.

He laughed to himself. 'That woman, the blond. I dated her for a month and never told her about my mother. I tell you in three minutes.'

Emma said, 'You sensed something. See, I also . . .' She stopped herself. He'd almost sucked her into a genuine conversation. 'I also pour out my heart to little old ladies. We're irresistible.'

'If only I could find an irresistible woman my own age,' he said.

An opening. 'What about other women in your life? Someone you might have overlooked. Perhaps a colleague?'

He said, 'I did meet a woman a few days ago. Sort of met her. I can't stop thinking about her. This is going to sound very odd, but she talks to me in my head.'

As did he, in hers. 'What does she say?' asked Emma, almost whispering.

'She says, "Come and get me." She screams it, actually. But I can't find her. She's disappeared – like magic.'

Like magic. The Good Witch dared to sneak a peek at his face. He was looking at her and their eyes (hers behind glasses) connected. A surge of energy rocketed through her. She was shaking – from cold, fear, or desire, she wasn't sure. 'I'm absolutely freezing,' she said.

Taking the hint, he stood up. 'I'll walk you out.'

She would send a telegraphopathic transfer to him now, no matter what he'd said or how she felt about him. The sooner this case was concluded, the better. She could get back to her life as it was, secure and happy, in the bubble.

Emma held out her bare hand, closed her eyes, and concentrated. But he lifted her, two handed, by her upper arm.

'Your arms are pretty muscular for an old lady,' he said.

Accidentally, he brushed his knuckles against her breast. Her breath caught. 'Let go,' she snapped.

He dropped her arm instantly. Embarrassed, he said, 'Sorry. I wasn't trying to grope you or anything.'

Emma's throat got tight. She wanted him to grope her, brush her breast with his knuckles – and much more –

every day, for the rest of her life. But what she wanted didn't matter. Emma and sex didn't mix.

She must have looked mightily upset. He said, 'I'm sorry! Honestly, I didn't mean to offend.'

Emma said, 'I was just thinking.'

'What?' he asked.

'I was thinking that roses could be *our* flower.'

He laughed, hard and loud. 'If only I'd met you forty years ago.'

'When you were in diapers?'

'I would have liked you, even then,' he said, his eyes twinkling.

Emma took a deep breath. She said, 'Young man, it's obvious to me that you could have your pick of girlfriends and probably always will. But you squander yourself on women like that blond. You have no respect for your power. If you did, you'd choose a woman who had power of her own.'

'What, like super powers? A woman who can lift huge restaurant bills with one finger?'

Emma laughed, catching herself in time, made it sound old. She said, 'Choose a woman who is your equal. Someone who's successful, confident. A woman who doesn't want to use you or change you. A woman with vision.'

'Artistic vision?' he asked.

'Someone who has plans, someone who can see into her own future,' she said. 'Now, close your eyes and try to imagine a woman – someone you might already know – who is powerful, attractive, and successful in her own right.'

He closed those beautiful green eyes. Emma closed

hers, too, concentrating. Her fingers icy from cold, she put them gently on his cheek. The portrait images of Daphne appeared in her mind, all three of them, clicking one after the other behind her eyelids. Emma breathed rhythmically and sent the pictures into William Dearborn's mind. Daphne's white pose with the backlight; the red pose, a human flame; the blue one, electrified. She managed three rotations, and then Emma's fingertips got hot.

She pulled her hand away. The entire transfer had taken several seconds.

He said, 'I just had the most peculiar experience.'

'Were you thinking about a woman?' asked Emma. 'Someone who's your equal?'

'My cheek feels hot,' he said. 'Right where you touched me.'

Emma rubbed her forehead. The brain fuzz was coming on strong, proof that she'd done a successful transfer on Dearborn.

'I've really got to go,' she said. 'Sudden headache.'

'Is it cracking?' he asked.

A flashlight beam flitted across her face. A loud voice said, 'That's her. Oh, my God! She's with Dearborn!'

The two cops – those who'd granted her an hour some two hours ago – started running toward Emma and William. If they caught her, her cover would be blown.

Emma looked around and saw her only way out. She dropped her cane, hiked up her skirt, and galloped in her orthos to the fence surrounding the park. Adrenaline speeding in her blood, she scaled the fence like a monkey and heaved herself over the barbed wire on top – scratching her thigh, losing a patch of velvet on her opera coat, but otherwise uncut – and landed solidly on her thick rubber soles. And, bonus, the exercise cleared her headache before it got bad.

The cops, meanwhile, had reached William. The three men stared at Emma from the other side of the fence, speechless. They weren't going to pursue her, she realized, so she waved goodbye and walked away.

Before she got too far, she pricked up her super ears, and heard one cop say, 'Ever seen a geriatric scale a fence like that before?'

'Hardly seems possible,' said William. 'It's almost as if she were a young woman dressed up like an old lady.'

Silence. Then the two cops in unison: 'Nah.'

The wrinkle lines didn't want to come off. Emma scrubbed and scrubbed until the skin underneath was red and raw.

She'd go at them again in the morning.

It was midnight when Emma got home to the Village from Brooklyn. The cab ride cost twenty dollars. Victor had left two messages via cell from the museum. Emma half listened while shedding her granny gear. There'd been, as Victor reported, some scuttlebutt when Dearborn and Marcie went MIA. When Marcie returned alone and upset, she began stuffing cheese chunks down her gullet with frightening speed. Daphne dragged her weight-loss spokesmodel out of the museum before Marcie started eating the table. 'Not the food on the table, Emma,' Victor noted in this message. 'But the table itself.'

Daphne left Emma a message from her Town Car. She said, 'I'm taking a friend home from the party, and I'll have to stay with her for a little while. But my cell phone is on.

Call me the second you get in. It's VERY IMPORTANT.'
Before Daphne clicked off, Emma could hear Marcie
shouting at the driver to pull into a McDonald's drive-thru.

That conversation could wait, she decided. Emma took
two Tylenol PM tablets. She wanted sleep to come fast.
And it did. She had dreams of William at ten, a mop-haired
English schoolboy in a blazer, short pants, knee socks, and
a cap.

THE FIVE QUESTIONS EMMA IS ASKED
MOST OFTEN ABOUT HER SKILL

1. Are your parents gifted too? When in a bitchy mood, Emma told people, 'My mother was Nancy Reagan's personal psychic – don't believe those Joan Quigley lies. My father has bent spoons with his mind all over Europe. He's currently in India, studying with the Maharishi.'

The truth: Anise, Emma's mom, could guess – accurately, within a few days – the last time someone had sex. She could also guess – accurately, within a few pounds and months – someone's weight and age. Anise had long credited her keen intuitive powers to 'a soft spot in her brain', a prescient description that haunted Emma daily. Her father Harry was a muggle.

Both her parents were gifted with patience and tolerance, necessary attributes for raising a loner child who seemed to see and hear everything she shouldn't. Emma's peculiar eye and hair color only exacerbated her chronic friendlessness. Anise and Harry tried to help her fit in, moved to the Village from suburban New Jersey when Emma was twelve, assuming city kids would be more inclusive. And they were, to a point. Emma was an oddball's oddball, even in a private school full of 'gifted' children. She put herself in a protective bubble and stayed there. Emma called it self-imposed isolation with a dash of self-pity. Anise called it adolescence.

2. Have you always had your power? Clients loved this answer: 'My skill awakened when I lost my virginity.'

The truth: She'd always had it. Anise claimed that, while breastfeeding Emma, she had beautiful kaleidoscope visions. Anise hadn't been afraid of the visions; she claimed to dig them, telling Emma years later that the colors and patterns were like 'being on mushrooms – the magic kind,' said Anise. 'In fact, I was high on mushrooms when you were conceived, so it made sense.'

3. Wouldn't you like to see what's in other people's heads, instead of just putting images into them? Emma's rap: 'I have a giving nature, and ask for nothing in return.'

The truth: She'd love to receive messages, thoughts, ideas, anything and everything, from someone worth taking from. Try as she might, she couldn't do it. Simply put, Emma was a pitcher, not a catcher.

4. Where does the power come from? The usual response: 'God only knows.'

The truth: God only knew. At Berkeley, the researchers told Emma that brain waves could be amplified via heightened senses of hearing, smell, touch, taste, and sight

– and Emma scored off the charts in those areas. Her talent could be genetic. Her mom *was* intuitive. And, as a matter of fact, Anise did have a soft spot in her brain, which resulted in a deadly aneurism. Since Anise's fatal burst, Emma had undergone numerous CAT scans to see if the soft spot was inherited or if there was anything unusual about her brain. Did she have an enlarged cerebral cortex? A nerve-dense oblongata? Scan after scan showed the same thing: normal. No weak vessels, no peculiar areas, no uncharted nerves. The annual confirmation (which Emma paid for out of pocket to the tune of two thousand dollars per scan) didn't erase the fear that someday, something would spontaneously pop in her brain. And it wouldn't be a sexy picture of a man in his skivvies.

5. If you could, would you give up your power to lead a normal life? The rap: 'I've been given a gift. Helping others find happiness makes up for any personal sacrifices I've had to make.' She'd said as much to Daphne when they first met. And Daphne had laughed at her.

The truth: Would she like a passionate sex life? A regular job? One that didn't land her in the sticky wicket of helping another woman seduce the man Emma wanted for herself?

Of course she wanted a normal life! But since Emma had been an isolationist for so long, she didn't think it possible to work in an office, fit in with ordinary people. She'd started The Good Witch, Inc. because it addressed all of her needs to: (1) use her unique skill, (2) maintain a safe emotional distance from the people she worked with, and (3) acquire a steady supply of vicarious romantic thrills.

The job both suited and doomed her, by her own design.

Although, since Dearborn came into the picture (as it were), Emma wore the doom more than the suit.

'Hit me,' said Deirdre, Emma's favorite waitress at her favorite breakfast spot.

Emma took Deirdre's outstretched hand and pictured a pair of eggs on a slab of ham and an English muffin smothered in Hollandaise sauce.

The waitress said, 'Benedict?'

'Eggcellent,' said Emma, grinning.

Deirdre groaned. 'Do you have to do that every time?'

'If I don't, Victor will,' said Emma. 'No sign of him yet?'

'Means only one thing,' said Deirdre. 'Juice?'

'Grapefruit. Thanks.'

Emma sat in a booth at Oeuf, a tiny restaurant only half a block from her building. As one might hazard to guess, Oeuf served egg dishes eggsclusively. Omelets, frittatas, quiches, soufflés. Emma and Victor had breakfast there a few times a week. From her seat in the window, Emma kept one eye on the front door of Victor's building and the other on the Village's multi-ethnic parade of cool jerks, leatherettes, tourists, students, yuppies, and the ubiquitous artistic types. She could always spot the freelance writers, starving painters, and struggling actors at a glance. She felt a bond with them, feverishly flinging thoughts into the world, hoping that something good – love, success, money – would be flung back in return.

Emma checked her watch. She dialed Victor's number on her cell. He picked up.

She said, 'Are you coming to Oeuf?'

'Nope,' he said.

'Why not?'

'I'm already here,' he said.

On cue, Victor pushed through the door of the restaurant, snapping his cell phone closed.

Ann Jingo was right behind him.

Before Emma had a chance to react (or run), Victor said, 'Don't move! I'd like to introduce you to Ann. Ann, this is Emma Hutch.' Even thought they'd met twice – as Emeril and the Crone – Ann was looking at Emma as if for the first time.

Apparently, the sight made her angry. To Victor, Ann said, 'Emma Hutch? This is the friend you wanted me to meet? You swore you didn't know Emma Hutch. I've asked you ten times. She's clearly the woman in Liam's portraits.'

Victor held up his hands. 'I lied. You're right,' he said.

Emma said, 'This is an ambush.'

'Just calm down,' he said. 'Both of you.'

Ann sat, as did he. Victor dramatically removed a pack of Big Red from his jacket pocket and dropped it on the table. He said, 'The great Raymond Chandler once wrote that if you don't know what to do next, have someone walk into a room carrying a gum.' The two women stared at him, not amused. 'Just trying to break the tension.'

Emma turned to Ann. 'Friendly warning: if you don't like puns, you should not be involved with Victor.'

'As it just so happens,' said Ann, 'I'm a bit of a punster myself.'

Deirdre came over and placed Emma's breakfast on the table. 'Are you eating, Victor? How about you?' She pointed her pencil at Ann.

Victor explained the Oeuf menu concept to Ann. He ordered number two. Ann selected the number four.

Deirdre said, 'Okay, that's the usual for Victor and two scrambled with hash and home fries for you.'

'Eggsactly,' said Ann, grinning.

Victor, Emma, and Deirdre blinked. Ann asked, 'Is something wrong?'

Victor smiled and kissed her cheek.

'And then there were three,' said Deirdre before heading back to the kitchen.

Emma inhaled the smell of breakfast. Still hot, her eggs Benedict was a dripping island of heart-stopping cholesterol on a plate. She dug in.

Victor said, 'It's been a long, long time since I felt this way about a woman.' He squeezed Ann's hand. 'And keeping you two apart seemed like a waste of potentially stimulating conversation. Emma is my best friend and we work together sometimes. We've never been more than friends. Just so you know.'

'Are you a photographer, too?' asked Ann to Emma.

So Victor hadn't told her about The Good Witch, Inc. That was a relief, thought Emma. Down the road, though, if Ann stuck around, she'd have to hear about it. For one thing, Ann would want to know why Victor took photographs of women in leather chaps and peekaboo bras.

'I'm a consultant,' Emma said. 'Sometimes, I outsource to Victor.' That was nebulous enough.

Ann said, 'That was you on the intercom yesterday, wasn't it?'

'I'm a very private person,' explained Emma. 'And sensitive, too.'

'Deeply,' added Victor.

Ann asked. 'So why not just tell me that? Why lie?' To Victor: 'Repeatedly.'

Victor said, 'It might help to put my explanation in a historical context. Back in 1987, when I was twelve . . .'

'Oh dear God,' said Emma.

'*When I was twelve,*' repeated Victor, 'and my parents were divorcing, they both confided in me without realizing what the other was doing. It was a horrible time – destroyed my childhood. Looking back, as I have, often, I wonder if I should have told Mom what Dad was saying, and vice versa. If their marriage could have been saved. I'll never know. I kept their secrets, as I was trained to do. But I learned a valuable life lesson.'

'Was it, "Don't discuss your painful childhood too early in a new relationship"?' asked Emma. 'Because you could use a refresher on that.'

'I should use my own judgment about which secrets to keep,' said Victor. 'That was the lesson. I did keep Emma from you, Ann. But only for a day, until I came to my senses.'

Ann patted Victor's hand and said, 'Thank you, dear.' To Emma, she said, 'I'd like to schedule a meeting for you with William Dearborn. As soon as possible.'

'No can do,' said Emma.

'You're refusing to meet him?' asked Ann, as if Emma had declined an audience with the pope.

'I've already met him,' said Emma.

'Yes, I know,' said Ann, testily. 'And since you two "met", he's had me scouring the city to find his mystery woman. That was you in drag at the ArtSpeak event, wasn't it?'

'No,' said Emma.

'Yes,' said Victor. Then, 'OUCH! Don't kick me, you witch.'

'You mean *bitch*,' said Ann. 'You called her a witch.'

'Yes, BITCH,' said Victor. 'With a b, as in, why do I fucking *bother*?'

Ann said, 'You sneak into Haiku to get close to Liam, but now that I'm offering to set up a meeting, you refuse. I don't get it.'

Emma shook her head. Clearly, she couldn't explain Daphne's case or her dire need for the cash it would provide. Or how her own attraction to William terrified her and made her want to sit in the corner with her back to the room. She said, 'I'm sorry, Ann. I have my reasons.'

'He wants to use the portraits of you to market ArtSpeak. You could get rich,' said Ann. 'And famous.'

Deirdre appeared, dropping more plates on the table. Emma watched them eat, the words 'you could get rich' rolling around in her head. But the 'and famous' part ruined it. Emma prized her anonymity, for work and peace of mind. She was horrified at the idea of millions of strangers looking at her face, judging her.

Emma asked, 'Dearborn produces his own ads?'

Ann said, 'He partners with an advertising company. He hasn't decided which one to choose yet, though. He's auditioning three different agencies now. He's supposed to make a final decision soon.'

'When?' asked Emma sharply.

Ann said, 'About a week and a half.'

Victor squinted at Emma. He mouthed, 'Are you thinking what I'm thinking?'

She nodded. Daphne wasn't after William's love. She wanted his business. She must have thought that seducing him would lead to a job.

Emma asked, 'What do the ad agencies think of using my face?'

'They love whatever William suggests.' Ann laughed to herself. 'The creative director at Crusher Advertising – Daphne Wittfield – is wild about the portraits. For some reason, she thinks they look just like her! Liam lets her believe it. He's a little intimidated by this woman. Rumor has it – no, I shouldn't say anything.' She paused. 'Then again, it's not like you two have any personal or professional ties to this woman. According to the grist mill, she once killed a man.'

'Murder?' asked Emma.

'Self-defense,' said Ann. 'This was about five years ago. She met a guy at a party. Brought him home. He got rough with her, and she pushed him into the corner of a glass coffee table. Face first.'

'If I still had an appetite,' said Emma, who'd cleaned her plate, 'I'd have just lost it.'

'How do you think I feel?' said Ann. 'I have to work with her.'

Victor, who'd worked with Daphne in the nude, said, 'Can't imagine what that's like.'

On one hand, Emma could feel free, ethically speaking, to dump Daphne as a client. She'd deceived Emma about her intentions. On the other hand, Mr Cannery at Citibank was not going to say, 'Ethical standards are far more important than mortgage payments. Take all the time you need.'

Ann said, 'One meeting with Liam. Ten minutes.' Emma shook her head. 'You have to tell him "no" yourself. Just to get him off my back. Please.'

Victor said, 'Do it for me, Emma. For the greatest good.'

The greatest good? Was Victor saying he was in love with Ann? After one night? 'Am I to assume your allegiances have shifted?' asked Emma.

Victor blushed.

The passionate beginning. Emma's favorite part of the show. She smiled at her best friend, wishing him well. Wanting to be involved – up to a point. And then she'd have to turn away.

Ann asked, 'What's this now? The greatest good? Shifting allegiances?'

Emma distracted her with good news. 'I'll do a ten minute phoner with William Dearborn,' she said. 'But that is it.'

'Today,' said Ann. 'Where can he call you?'

They arranged the details – he'd call Emma's landline at three p.m. Ann sent the message to Dearborn via Blackberry before Emma could change her mind.

15

Emma left Oeuf as soon as possible. Ann and Victor stayed to moon at each other over their dirty plates. She was happy for him, of course, but the sight was enough to make a single witch sick. She decided to take a walk around Washington Square Park. The snap of cold air made her pull her coat closer. Halloween was fast approaching, as was November first, her deadline. Regardless of what happened between now and then, Emma vowed to hold herself together. William was calling soon. That would certainly test her emotional fortitude.

Her cell vibrated in her pocket. She clicked on. Before she could say, 'Hello,' the caller screamed, 'Where the hell have you been?'

'Daphne,' she said coolly. 'I'm glad you called.'

'Listen carefully, Emma,' said her tentative client. 'You have to get to Liam today. He called early this morning and asked me to his studio tonight. He wants to paint me! I don't know if it's an official first date. But if you hit him beforehand, I'll write you a check for five thousand dollars tomorrow morning.'

The Good Witch gulped. She'd been all ready to dump the client. And now she was stymied. William had asked to paint Daphne? If that wasn't a come on, what was? Had one transfer turned his head to Daphne so easily? What about the mystery woman? Some loyalty he showed her (that they'd never 'officially' met didn't matter at that moment of irrationality). Emma said, 'Okay. I'll do it.'

'Good,' said Daphne. 'You're getting quite a deal, considering how little work you've done on my case.'

Emma said, 'I nearly killed myself getting him good last night.'

'When?' asked Daphne. 'At the museum?'

'Remember a little old lady at the exhibit? Velvet opera coat? Pillbox hat? Gray wig?'

'No,' said Daphne.

'Well, I saw you,' said Emma.

'I didn't stay long. I spent most of the night cramming food down Marcie Skimmer's garbage disposal.'

'I guess SlimBurn pills don't prevent emotional eating.'

'Like I care?' said Daphne. 'We're selling bottles by the millions. Go to Dearborn's office. He'll be there until five.'

Daphne hung up.

Emma put the cell in her pocket. It was one o'clock. She was supposed to do a phoner with William at three. If she had any guts at all, she'd tell William everything and come clean. Or she could do one last hit and clean up.

The choice was clear. Emma headed home to plan a

costume for the afternoon hit. Janitor? Mousy secretary? Gender-ambiguous Xerox repairperson?

The cell phone again. Had to be Daphne with more demands. Emma clicked on and said, 'Hello?'

A man's voice said, 'I'm trying to reach Emma Hutch. My name is Armand Chicora. I'm an orderly at St Vincent's Hospital.'

'This is Emma.'

'I'm afraid I have some bad news. Hoffman Centry has been mugged.'

'Is he okay?' she asked.

'It's not serious. He walked himself into the emergency room. But he has a broken rib.'

'Oh, no.'

'And a gash on his cheek.'

'Poor Hoff!'

'He's got a black eye too.'

'Is that it?' she asked, horrified.

'Like I said, nothing serious. He's in the ER. I'm calling you from his cell phone. The mugger didn't take it. Or his wallet, or his keys.'

'Some mugger,' said Emma.

'Mr Centry has been asking for you.'

Emma was surprised to hear it. 'Really?' she asked.

'He's been moaning your name since he came in.'

'I'm coming now,' she said, aiming her black boots uptown.

'They won't let you in unless you're listed as his emergency contact, and according to the insurance information, you're not. Are you family?'

'No, a friend,' said Emma.

'Then you won't get by security,' he said.

Yet another New York hotspot she'd have to sneak her way into. 'Are you saying what I think you're saying?' she asked.

'Mr Centry has been asking for you,' said the orderly. 'I'd do whatever I could for a friend.'

He hung up.

Emma stared at her phone. Was this a ruse of some kind? A joke? She checked her caller history and redialed. On the other end an operator said, 'St Vincent's.'

In three minutes, Emma was back in her apartment rummaging through her costume closet. It took some digging, but she managed to locate the white polyester uniform, white stockings, white orthopedics (same ones she wore last night), and the nameplate for 'Nurse Ratched'. She tucked her bronze waves into a black-plaited wig and put on rose-shaded glasses. She grabbed a white cardigan and bolted.

St Vincent's Hospital was on the corner of 11th Street and Seventh Avenue, about ten minutes by foot from Waverly Place. Emma jogged uptown and got there in six. Hot, she took off the cardigan and put it over her arm. Emma marched purposefully through the emergency room waiting area. At that hour it was relatively vacant. Only a dozen seats were claimed.

For some unknown reason, every eye in the room landed, and stuck, on Emma. Painfully self-conscious, she rushed for the set of double doors to the triage area. She pressed the wall plate; the doors opened automatically. She went inside.

Emma rounded a tight hallway corner, following signs

with arrows to the triage area. To penetrate that layer of security she needed a prop. On an unattended checkpoint dais, Emma spotted an empty manila folder. She snagged it and studied it with great absorption as she churned her orthopedic shoes past the next security desk. No one stopped her, but she felt eyes boring into her back.

A narrow hallway opened cavern-like into the ER staging area. The room was sectioned off with curtains into several dozen stations. Each station had a number, a bed, and a chair. Some of them also had patients. Pretending to study the folder as if it contained the knowledge of good and evil, Emma did a lap around the ER, having to walk past the nurses' island in the middle. Five nurses sat in and around the island – all black or Hispanic women in boxy monochrome checked or striped pastel-hued tops.

None of them were dressed anything like Emma with the white poly dress and triangular cap.

So hospital uniform codes had relaxed since Emma bought her get-up. She'd purchased it at a novelty store years ago, along with her French maid costume. So what if she was a bit retro? Nothing wrong with old school. Emma smiled nervously at the nurses. They stared at her, their mouths round with what appeared to be astonishment. A couple of them put on their glasses to get a better look.

Emma hurried along. Station Six: an old man snoring loudly. Station Ten: an old woman snoring loudly. Station Fifteen: a young woman, ripped panty-hosed feet peeking from under her blanket. Station Three: a man with twenty wires attached to his chest. When he spotted Emma peering around the curtain, he shouted, 'I need a doctor!' Emma jumped back.

Station Twenty: a young man, his face a map of bruises and cuts. He was grimacing and clutching his ribs.

'Oh, Hoff!' she said at the terrible sight, tears pooling in her amber eyes. The glasses got foggy.

'What the . . .' he said, one eye widening at the sight of her. 'Is this some kind of twisted *joke*? I'm not in the mood.'

'It's me, Emma.' She removed her glasses.

Hoff gaped at her, then started to laugh. Then stopped laughing and started moaning.

'Hurts when you laugh?' she asked.

'Hurts when I breathe,' he said. 'Did you, by any chance, look at yourself in the mirror before you went out in that get-up?'

In her rush to get to his side in his hour of need, she hadn't paused in the mirror, no. She said, 'I realized the uniform is a bit dated . . .'

'It's a bit diaphanous,' he said. 'More than a bit.'

Emma looked down. 'You mean you can see . . .'

'Everything,' said Hoff, his smile spreading, despite the gash on his cheek. 'Black bra with a tiny ribbon on the front. The black bikini panties, ribbons on the sides. Do you always wear black underwear? You were wearing a black lace bra under that red dress the other night. Oh, no.'

Hoff pitched a tent with the hospital bed sheet. He moaned.

'Hurts when you get a hard-on?' she asked, sympathetically.

'Since puberty,' he said.

She remembered the cardigan on her arm. Slipping it on, she asked, 'Who did this to you?'

Hoff shook his head, wincing at the movement. 'I did

most of it to myself, unfortunately. I was downtown for a lunch meeting at Union Square Café. A man I'd never seen before called my name. I turned around. He came up to me, smiling. I was trying to place him, and he pointed a gun at me. He directed me into a deserted loading dock and then started asking questions. When had I last heard from "the man whose name won't be mentioned"? Was I working with Connie Quivers? I insisted I didn't know any Connie Quivers. But the mugger said the doorman at the Four Seasons saw me talking to her. That's when I realized: he meant you. I didn't tell him anything, though. Don't worry.'

'He tried to beat it out of you?' she asked.

'Not quite. During a lull, I screamed, "Look! A rat!" and then I ran, tripping over a forklift on the way out, falling on my face.' He touched his eyes and lip. 'Then I scrambled to my feet, ran into a garbage can, and fell on top of it.' He touched his ribs. 'I suppose you could say I mugged myself.'

'How did this guy know where to find you?'

'I've been thinking about that. I gave the Four Seasons doorman my business card. To give to William Dearborn, should he ever show up. The doorman must have given it to the mugger. The card has my name and office address. The Ransom House website has my photo.'

'I'm so sorry this happened,' Emma said, leaning over the bed to kiss his non-bruised cheek.

'Ouch!'

'Your cheek hurts, too?'

'It's the hard-on again,' said Hoff. 'Listen, Emma, I knocked some sense into myself today. Whatever popped into my head that night at your place, it wasn't real. It couldn't have been. When that bastard pointed the gun at me, I thought of you. Not Dearborn. You're the one I want. Take off that wig. Let me see you.'

He reached for her wig, and she grabbed his wrist.

If she couldn't be honest with the man she wanted, she'd at least tell the truth to the man who wanted her. It was a start anyway.

'Close your eyes,' she said. 'Do you see the man who mugged you?'

She pulled an image of Jeff Bragg out of her memory: his angry face when he'd pinned her against the soda machine. She concentrated on the details. Jeff's flat eyes. His straight nose. The tiny cleft on his chin.

Hoff said, 'Interesting.' He opened his eyes. 'The mugger's face popped into my mind. But without the Yankees cap he was wearing. Why would I conjure a memory of him that I don't have?'

'You wouldn't,' she said. 'I put that image in your head.'

He squinted. 'How could you do that?'

'And I put the image of William Dearborn in your head too.'

'That doesn't make any . . .'

'I have this skill. My brain waves are like radio signals. But, as I've recently learned, thanks to you, I slip sometimes, sending images by accident. When you saw Dearborn in your head that night, it was because I had him in my head too. He's still there, Hoff. If it's any comfort, I'm haunted by that night too.'

'I don't believe this,' he said.

She took his hand, closed her eyes, and pumped a slide

show into his head. 'Yorkshire terrier,' she said. 'Golden retriever. Schnauzer. French poodle. Llasa Apso. Great Dane.'

Hoff said, 'Enough.' He took his hand back. 'Why didn't you tell me about this before?'

'I tried to tell you,' she insisted.

'Most women withhold the truth about their adolescent acne, college weight gain, and string of regretful one-night stands.'

'I withheld those, too.'

Hoff sighed. 'I'll have to get used to this if we're going to be together.'

'We're not going to be together,' she said softly.

Hoff looked into her eyes. She sent him a message the old fashioned way without tricks and cheats. He said, 'I see.'

They sat uncomfortably for a moment. 'Are you going to be admitted to a room?' she asked.

'No need. They've done all they can. I'm waiting for a prescription for Vicodin, and then I'm free to go. I've already spoken to a police officer when I first came in. I've got his card somewhere.' He had her search in his wallet. She found the card for a Detective Marsh. 'You should call him and tell him what you know about the man who attacked me.'

'His name is Jeff Bragg,' she said. 'I followed him for a client. We had two conversations. He thinks I'm spying on him. He seemed kind of nuts, but I'm surprised he followed you and pulled a gun. You're sure it was real?'

'Not at all,' he said.

'Even if the gun was fake, he's not the average,

everyday loopy paranoiac I took him for.' Emma thought of Jeff's puzzling secrecy around Susan. How he'd never let her see his place or introduce her to his friends. 'I'll call the cops as soon as I leave,' she said, slipping the card into her bra. She'd have to call Susan, too. 'Do you think Bragg knows where you live?' she asked.

'I'm listed,' said Hoff. 'It's possible.'

Emma stood up. 'You can't go home until he's caught. Where are your apartment keys?'

Hoff said, 'In my jacket pocket.'

'When are you getting out of here?' she asked, fishing for the keys.

'I'm just waiting for paper. I'm sure it'll arrive sometime this month,' said Hoff.

Emma looked at the wall clock. It was after three. She'd missed the call from Dearborn and had only two hours to get home, dress, get to his office, and hit him before his dinner with Daphne.

'I have to leave,' she said. 'But I'll make arrangements for someone to take you straight to the Tribeca Grand Hotel from here. I'll go to your place, get some clothes, and meet you at the hotel later.' Bragg had only seen Emma in costume. If he were staking out Hoff's building, would he recognize her as herself? It was a risk, but she'd take it.

She kissed him on the forehead. 'I'll see you soon,' she promised and left.

As she was walking by the nurses' island, a fat nurse with a pink smock chewed her gum in Emma's direction. 'What are you supposed to be?'

'I'm a nurse,' she said. 'From the psych ward.'

'Nurse Ratched,' read Ms Pink. 'From psych.' The other nurses burst into riotous laughter.

'That's right. And I want to know what the hold-up is on releasing the man in bed twenty.'

'Oh, that was good. Very forceful. Authoritative. I was almost convinced for a second.' Ms Pink looked Emma in the shades and said, 'Do it again.' Her colleagues hooted.

Emma said, 'I'm serious.'

'I'm sure you are,' said Ms Pink. 'That's a very serious *uniform* you're wearing.'

'Where is orderly Armand Chicora?' demanded Emma.

'On break.'

'When is he coming back?'

Ms Pink said, 'I'm not his mother.'

Another nurse in an orange smock said, 'He's over there.'

Emma turned. A lumbering caramel-skinned man in a white smock and green pants entered the ER. He had long hair, tied back in a pony, and a hard bone structure. Part Native American, part Latino, she guessed. Emma walked over to him. He must have liked what he saw. He didn't smile or do anything overtly friendly. But he stopped and gave her his full (and intense) attention.

Emma said, 'Armand Chicora?'

He nodded.

'Follow me, please.' Emma led him out of the cuckoo's nest, through triage and waiting room, and outside the hospital. He followed behind her obediently and didn't ask questions.

Once outside, Emma removed the hundred dollar bill she'd tucked into her ortho. She handed it to Armand and

said, 'I'm Emma Hutch. You called me about Hoffman
Centry? I'm giving you this money for two reasons: first, to
thank you. Second, to pay you for a job.'

Tucking the bill into his pocket, he waited for her to
speak. So she did. 'Keep an eye on Mr Centry until he's
discharged. Then take him by cab to the Tribeca Grand
Hotel. Help him check in and get settled in the room. Then
call me with the room number. I'm going to his apartment
to pack him a suitcase.'

Armand said, 'Two hundred.'

'One fifty.'

'I'll miss dinner,' said the orderly.

Emma sighed. 'Okay, two hundred. But cab fare comes
out of it. And be careful with him,' she said.

He put his mitt-sized hand on her shoulder. The heft
made her slump. 'Don't worry,' he said. 'I'm sensitive to the
fragility of the human body. I'm orderly. Especially for an
orderly.'

She looked into his intense eyes and believed him.
Then Emma hoofed south, quite sure without checking
that Armand watched her go.

At home, Emma dared to look in the full-length mirror at
her disguise. *I'm a Naughty Nurse, just like it said on the
box*, she thought. *I look like I've just stepped off the set of
Horny Hospital IV.* Cheeks flaming with post-traumatic
embarrassment, Emma shed her dress, tights, and orthos.
She checked the time. Four o'clock. That gave her only one
hour to change into a disguise, get to midtown, locate
Dearborn, and hit him. She'd never make it. Not unless she
had a flying broomstick. Fuck it, she thought. So she

wouldn't get paid tomorrow. She'd tell Daphne what happened, although Emma doubted 'I was visiting my friend in the hospital' would fly with the blond crusher.

Emma put on jeans, a black crew-neck cashmere sweater and her boots. She fluffed her hair, cleaned her blue-tinted shades on her sweater, and dropped Hoff's keys into her bag. Without checking her answering machine, she left the building. On the street, Emma didn't need super vision to spot the long, black limousine idling out front.

Before she could lift her arm to hail a cab, the limo's rear door opened. From inside, a man said, 'Can I give you a lift?'

Emma slouched to look inside. William Dearborn was perched on the edge of the bench seat, one hand on the door handle, the other beckoning Emma to come over, have a seat right next to him, don't make him wait all night.

She blinked rapidly; the surprise of seeing him made her eyes water. She stood there, uncertain what to do. He seemed amused by her indecision and said, 'What are you waiting for?'

Another echo from her daydreams. She said, 'Take me to Gramercy Park?'

'Yes, Gramercy Park. Tower of London. Mount Rushmore. Just get in here. Make yourself comfortable.'

Emma slid in, pulled the door closed, and settled into the bench seat. She gave William Hoff's 20th Street address. He repeated it for the driver.

The limo pulled into early rush-hour traffic. Emma's stomach lurched. She was finally alone with him – without a costume to protect her. Nervously, she checked her cell phone, fiddled with her hair. She turned toward William and he was beaming at her.

He opened the bar cabinet and said, 'Thirsty?' She shook her head. He opened the mini-fridge and asked, 'Hungry?'

'Sorry I missed your call,' she said. 'You didn't have to come downtown. We could have rescheduled.'

'I'd rather do this in person,' he said. 'I wanted to come and get you.'

He'd found out where she lived and he'd come to get her, just as she asked him to in his daydreams. In reality, Emma felt flattered, but also stalked. She'd stalked dozens of men, not thinking the least about their feelings. *Maybe I should have*, she thought now.

'It was so dark at Ciao Roma,' said Emma. 'And I didn't stick around long after the lights came on. I'm surprised you could remember my face so well.'

He tapped his temple. 'Photographic memory.'

'I thought you might feed me a line about my indelible beauty.'

'I'm an artist, not a poet,' he said. 'But that was an indelible kiss.'

Emma said, 'Ann Jingo said you want to use my portrait in your marketing for ArtSpeak. I'm going to have to say no.'

'I can make you famous,' he said.

'My preference leans in the other direction,' she said. 'And, not to tell you your business, but it's a bad idea. I'm not that gorgeous.'

'You're autumn leaves,' he said. 'Warm cider, pumpkin pie. Orange and black, a sleek little cat. You're Halloween,

the treat and trick. Come over here and sit on my dick.'
He waggled his eyebrows at her.

Emma laughed. 'I though you weren't a poet.'

He said, 'Emma Hutch – nice to know your name by
the way – you have an extraordinary face. You should show
the world. And ArtSpeak is revolutionary. You should be
proud to represent it.'

Emma thought of Marcie Skimmer, who'd shown her
extraordinary face to the world representing diet pills. She
certainly didn't seem proud of it, or anything.

'I'm sure it's a good product,' she started to say.

'It's a *great* product,' said William, not humble about
his work. 'The smallest child has the instinct to fist a crayon
and draw on the wall. The human brain is hardwired to
create. If we can't, we die. My mother was a painter. She
lost her ability to paint and it was the end of her life.
ArtSpeak is for everyone who can't hold a paintbrush. And
it's for everyone who can but doesn't know what to do with
it. People *need* to create. Like they need to eat.'

'I'm sorry about your mother,' she said sincerely.

He nodded, changed the subject. 'You're a visual artist,
right?' he asked.

'I'm not . . . actually, I am,' she said.

'Paint? Clay? Watercolors?'

Brain waves. She said, 'I'm more of a performance
artist.'

'What's your message?' he asked.

'The greatest good,' she said.

He started to say something but stopped. Then he said,
'The truth is, Emma Hutch, although I do want to use
those portraits, I needed an excuse to talk to you. About

our kiss at Ciao Roma. You were like a human flame in my arms. I saw visions. Fire, smoke, a burning mountain. The whole experience was distracting, to say the least. And it's stuck in my head, like a tune. Piano music in the wind. Almost eerie.'

'Haunting?' she said.

'Yes!' he agreed.

'That's how I've described it,' she admitted.

'I think about you constantly. Your face pops into my head all day long. I know this sounds crazy, since we don't know each other at all, but I think I might be in love with you.'

He'd as much as dictated The Good Witch, Inc.'s operating principle. But she was popping into his head without the aid of telegraphopathy. One might describe his reaction to her as organic love. Since he'd set up camp in her head, logic (and magic) would have it that she was in love with him too.

Without warning, William lifted Emma by the waist and deposited her sidesaddle onto his lap. He kissed her before she could object. As soon as their lips touched, she felt her pulse quicken, a heat wave on her skin. Lightning struck again, in the same exact spot. She closed her eyes and saw a spark, like a match spontaneously igniting. As she always explained to clients, it was up to them to fan that spark into a flame.

Or not. It was a choice – the woman's choice – to go forward with a relationship or to back away from it. If Emma moved forward with William, how would it end? With him running away from her bed, carrying his clothes in a bundle under his arm? Would he announce one day that he was quitting the relationship to move to an island forever? Would the pounding flow of blood and heat of sex burst a blood vessel in her brain, rupturing the soft spot she just knew was there, no matter what the doctors had to say? Anise was dead at forty-seven. Only thirteen years older than Emma was right now.

She felt cold suddenly. Scrambling off William's lap, she looked out the limo window. 'I'm going through a transitional period right now,' she said by way of an explanation.

'Emma, my lips are on fire,' he said.

'Drink your seltzer,' she said.

'Why are you rejecting me?' he asked, his English lilt growing limp. 'I know you're attracted.'

'I just can't do it,' she said. For days, she'd been resisting because of professional ethics. Now Emma knew her fear of getting close to William ran much deeper. If Susan were in the limo, Emma would tell her, 'Emotional breakthroughs might not be as few and far between as previously thought.'

William reached over to stroke her hair. She turned to look at him. She loved his face. His bangs, the soulful green eyes. 'Okay. I'm going to tell you the truth, Liam,' she said. He smiled, eager for it. 'The truth is, I'm anorgasmic.'

Emma waited for him to say, 'You're *what*?'

But he said, 'Bullshit. You have earthquake orgasms with lightning speed, and since our kiss in the dark, I've been the cause of every one. I know. I've seen them.' She must have looked shocked. He tapped his forehead. 'In here.'

Just as she'd seen his orgasms in her head.

Emma said, 'I have to get out of here. Pull over.'

'You're afraid of me,' he said. 'Of my reputation with women.'

'That too,' she agreed.

'What else? Just tell me what the problem is,' he pleaded.

'You don't know a thing about me,' she said.

'So tell me,' he pleaded.

She was tempted, certainly, to unload. But she'd learned from age nine that people reacted predictably when she told the truth about herself. At first, everyone – including Victor – recoiled with distrust.

Emma said, 'Don't you have somewhere to go?'

16

If Hoff's doorman recognized Emma from the one time she'd been there before, he didn't acknowledge it. He merely smiled and flipped a page in his magazine as she hurried to the elevator bank. She rode to floor seventeen, found Hoff's two-bedroom exactly where he'd left it. The key worked too.

Flicking on the lights, Emma was struck again by Hoff's color scheme. Slate, pewter, navy, charcoal. Dark and darker. It'd been puzzling for Emma, having thought of Hoff as a lighthearted, happy fellow, to enter his blue and gray space. Emma accused him of falling for an interior decorator's line about a 'masculine palette'. But Hoff insisted he'd picked his own colors, finding them calming and comforting after a long day of fluorescent oppression at work.

Emma searched his closet for a suitcase. Finding an L.L. Bean duffle, she chucked a week's worth of clothes into it. His closet and dresser drawers were organized, but not pathologically. On top of his dresser, a framed photo of preppy ten-year-old Hoff with his family caught Emma's eye. His mom was blond and plump, a generous face and relaxed manner. His dad grinned down at his wife, Hoff, and his younger gap-toothed sister. They were sitting on a boulder, a lake in the background, a station wagon with Connecticut plates in the foreground. A summer trip? Their country house?

She plopped down on Hoff's blue bed and missed her own parents suddenly. After Emma's mom died, Harry, her dad, moved out of New York. He was still young – forty-nine at the time – and he wanted to see America. He didn't stop moving for five years, keeping in touch with Emma via postcard and cell phone. He met his new wife, Claire, a woman Emma still had never met, in Santa Fe, where they lived and worked, running a bed and breakfast out of their house.

Emma closed her eyes and tried to conjure a snapshot of her family sitting on a boulder by a lake. An impossible task. Emma's family trip memories were of museums in foreign cities, meals at five-spoon restaurants. An only – not to mention lonely – child, Emma's parents treated her like a mini adult. And she behaved accordingly, which explained, in part, her awkwardness with other kids.

The cell phone rang, mercifully dragging Emma back to the present.

'Armand?' she asked.

He said, 'Yes. We're here. Room 512.'

'Great. I'll be there in twenty minutes,' she said.

'With the money,' he reminded her.

Emma hurried to finish packing, riffling through Hoff's top dresser drawer for underwear. She found two dozen pairs of the Banana Republic boxers she'd seen on him, in a variety of colors, along with ball after ball of cashmere socks. Underneath those, she found a roll of cash. Next to the roll, the bundled pages of a manuscript.

The cover sheet was a letter from a copy editor, with a page-by-page breakdown of errors and typos. Emma flipped a few sheets in and saw the title page. *Smoke and Mirrors: How Greedy Underlings Made Millions Disappear and Blamed Me for Their Crime*, by Seymour Lankey.

The book was slight, less than two hundred pages. She knew this was Hoff's top-secret project. She weighed packing the manuscript in the duffle but decided against it. Emma peeled four fifties off the money roll (reimbursement and another hundred for Armand) and put them in her pocket. She threw the rest of the cash into the duffle. The doorman didn't look up from his magazine when she left.

In the cab downtown, Emma called Susan Knight. 'Are you still not speaking to me?'

Susan asked, 'You have news?'

'Meet me at the Tribeca Grand. Room 512. If you walk fast, you can be there in twenty minutes.'

Susan should hear what Jeff Bragg had done to Hoff from his own lips. Emma would enjoy the redemption, and she wanted an apology from Susan. Emma also wanted some emotional service – handholding, shoulder leaning. She needed a friend. A female friend to make her feel better. Emma had pitched long enough; tonight, she wanted to catch.

'I can't leave the office right now,' protested the petite lawyer.

'Just be there,' said Emma and then she hung up.

The Tribeca Grand was Emma's favorite hotel in New York, mainly for the understated lobby design. She liked the autumnal hues of the interior, the reds, browns, and oranges that made up her body's color wheel. The piped-in music was consistently pleasing, ranging from Josh Redman to Steve Earle. Unlike the opulent palaces uptown, the Tribeca Grand didn't overwhelm its guests with Honda-sized crystal chandeliers, obsequious epaulette-bearing valets, five-story floral arrangements, and tarted-up gilt tables and chairs. The Tribeca Grand was warm and cool, simply elegant. Emma inhaled deeply when she hit the lobby. Apples and allspice with undertones of new carpet.

Emma took the elevator to five. By the time she stepped out of the cushioned box, her mood was better. Change of setting couldn't be overestimated to lighten one's emotional load. She'd forgotten her simpering dip into childhood. Her errands for Hoff forced William from her mind. Emma felt relieved and glad to be alive in New York City with a rising moon, cash in her pocket, and one-touch room service.

She knocked on the door of 512. Armand let her in. Nothing too fancy about the room, except the pinkish-purplish recessed lighting that cast strategic spotlights, including a glow over the bed where Hoff lay propped up with pillows.

He was in bad shape. Armand had tended to him,

covering him with a comforter, putting a pitcher of water, a vial of Vicodin, and a few ice packs on the night table.

Emma turned to the orderly orderly. 'Do you work on Wednesdays?' she asked.

Armand said, 'Unless I call in sick.'

'Calling in sick to the hospital,' said Emma. 'It seems so wrong. That said, how about doing it tomorrow and coming here instead?'

Armand didn't have to think too hard. 'Fifty an hour?'

Emma hoped Hoff was good for it. She said, 'Around nine?'

He nodded. But he didn't leave.

'Oh, right, the hundred.' Emma reached into her pants pocket for the bills, having to tug because the jeans were tight, flashing a bit of tummy by accident. She slapped the cash into Armand's hand. He slapped his hand over hers, trapping it. He didn't let go.

Emma closed her eyes.

Two seconds later, Armand squeaked, released her hand, and fled the room. She called down the hall, 'See you tomorrow,' shut the door, and then sat on the edge of the bed.

Hoff was awake. He said, 'You put a picture in his head?'

'A fat nun, with chin hairs.'

'Why would that scare him?'

'She was naked. Except for the wimple.'

Hoff laughed, then groaned, clutching his ribs.

Emma asked, 'How are you feeling?'

'Waiting for the Vicodin to kick in,' he said. 'See what all the hubbub is about.'

Emma said, 'I invited a friend to come over.'

He said, 'I'm in no shape to entertain.'

'On the contrary. We have a mini-bar. Room service. Prescription opiates. The makings of a swell party.' He looked horrified. 'Kidding,' said Emma. 'She's not going to steal your drugs. That's what I'm here for.'

He reached for her hand, squeezed. He said, 'You may not know this about me, but I've led a pretty sheltered life. I grew up in Greenwich. Went to boarding school. Exeter. Not a very tough crowd there. Until this morning, I've never felt the threat of physical violence. Granted, I beat myself up. But the experience was rich, and it'll make me a better person for having had it.'

'Only you could put a positive spin on a mugging,' she marveled. 'You're a keeper, Hoff.'

'Thanks,' he said. 'For arranging this room. For being honest with me about your . . . what do you call it?'

'Telegraphopathy,' she said.

He approved. 'Very Latinate.'

'I came up with it myself.'

Hoff grinned as much as his bruising would allow. 'I also want to thank you for being my friend,' he said. 'If you're sure we can't be more than friends.'

Emma said, 'I promise not to rattle your sexual identity or put a maniac on your trail again.'

'In that case,' he said, 'you may take *one* Vicodin.'

Knock on the door. Emma let Susan in.

Susan melted as soon as she saw Emma. Clearly, the strain of being angry was too much for her. 'I'm sorry I fired you!' she said. 'I was upset and hurt, and confused . . .'

'Shut up and meet my friend Hoffman Centry.' Emma

steered Susan into the room and toward the bed.

Hoff sat as upright as possible. He said, 'I apologize for my appearance. I wasn't expecting company.'

Susan said, 'My God, what happened to you?'

He said, 'I was mugged.'

'By Jeff Bragg,' said Emma.

'That's not possible,' said Susan. 'Jeff wouldn't hurt anyone.'

'Technically, he didn't hurt me,' said Hoff. 'But he did pull a gun on me.'

'And he threatened me – twice,' said Emma. 'The fact is, Jeff Bragg is paranoiac and weirdly secretive. His peculiar habits. His anti-social behavior. Think about how well you really know him. Turns out, not so well.'

Susan asked, 'You're sure it was Jeff ?'

'Emma helped me identify him with her *telegraph-opathy*.' He smiled, liked saying it. Or maybe the Vicodin was taking effect.

Susan said, 'I swear, when Jeff and I first met, he was a mild-mannered – albeit insanely handsome – guy. Just another accountant among a hundred others at a corporate lunch.'

'I agree with the insane part,' said Emma.

Hoff said, 'Hold on. Do you mean to tell me that the savage who stuck a gun in my face is an *accountant*?'

Susan looked at Hoff, at his bruised skin and missing tooth. She sat down on the edge of the bed and said, 'He was my boyfriend, on and off, for a year. It's off now. I'm sorry I got Emma involved with him.'

'Unfortunately, my involvement dragged in Hoff,' said Emma.

Susan sighed. 'I wish I'd never met Jeff.'

Hoff said, 'And I wish you'd never met him, too.'

Emma wanted to ask more questions, but she'd lost her audience. Susan was busy arranging Hoff's ice packs. The butterfly grace of her dainty wrists was hypnotic. Hoff stared at her, was at her tender mercy.

Emma said, 'Susan is a vice president at the Verity Foundation. She's in charge of the class action suit against Riptron.'

'I'm impressed,' said Hoff.

'Hoff is a vice president at Ransom House. He edited the Seymour Lankey book that's coming out later this week.'

'We have Riptron in common,' said Susan.

'And we're both vice presidents,' said Hoff.

Susan asked, 'How do you two know each other?'

Emma fielded that one. 'We met in my neighborhood. At a liquor store.'

Hoff said, 'I was buying a bottle of wine for a dinner party, and Emma was buying a bottle of Bailey's.'

'For personal use,' said Emma. 'We got to talking. Hoff asked me out.'

'You two date?' asked Susan, surprise and disappointment in her voice.

'We went out a few times,' said Emma.

'Six,' corrected Hoff. 'Which was enough for us to realize we're better as friends. And how do you two know each other?'

'Emma is one of the plaintiffs in the class action suit against Riptron,' said Susan. 'I interviewed her, and the conversation turned to our personal lives. We decided to meet for drinks and got to be friends.'

The three smiled at each other. 'I'm glad to be here,' said Emma. 'Among friends.'

The lonely child inside would always doubt. But Emma did have friends. They were all she had, in fact. And, if she nudged gently, her friends seemed primed to have each other.

Hoff said genially, 'Well, friends. I have a mini-bar. Room service. Vicodin. How may I entertain you?'

'I feel restless,' said Emma. 'I'm going to take off.'

'You can't leave Hoff alone,' said Susan.

'You stay,' said Emma.

'Good morning!'

The greeting was so loud and proud it hurt Emma's ears. She said, 'It is?'

'Welcome to Crusher Advertising. My name is Natasha. How can I help you?'

Natasha at the front desk was about twenty-two years old with huge black-lined eyes, a closely shorn head, dangling gold earrings, latte-colored skin. Her outfit was an exact knockoff of the gray suit Daphne wore at Emma's apartment.

It was eight o'clock in the fucking morning. This Natasha had no right to be so put together at the ungodly hour. She smelled good, too, like black tea and mint. Emma said, 'Daphne Wittfield wanted to see me.'

'Your name?'

'Emma Hutch.'

Natasha paused. 'The mutant?'

Emma sighed. 'Yes.'

'You were expected an hour ago.'

'I'm not used to impromptu seven o'clock meetings,' growled the Good Witch in a bad mood. Daphne had called her at six.

'Ms Wittfield demands total commitment from her employees.'

Emma squinted. Was Natasha being snarky about Ms Wittfield and her 'demands', or was she a faithful member of Daphne's flock? 'I'm not her employee,' said Emma.

'I thought you were,' said Natasha. 'Follow me, please.'

Emma did, warily. She knew she was about to be fired. What else would explain the six o'clock summons? Emma wanted to get it over with, go home, and crawl back under the covers where she belonged.

The Crusher Advertising office building was located on Madison Avenue at 38th Street. Not a glamorous block. The building itself was limestone with ornate cornices. Otherwise, the high-rise was uninspiring and utilitarian. Crusher Advertising occupied the top four floors. Daphne's office was at the tippy-top.

As she was escorted to her execution, Emma checked out the framed print ads that hung on the hallway walls. Crusher had some huge accounts, including a pharmaceutical company that revolutionized anti-depressants, a food company that invented low-carb cookies, and a beverage company that promised good health and long life in five fruity flavors. Emma slowed to examine the series of ads for SlimBurn diet pills.

Emma stopped and said, 'I haven't seen this one before.'

'It's not out yet. We're debuting the "after" part of

the ad on a Times Square billboard on Friday.'

The top text line of the ad read, 'Fat to Fabulous.' Underneath the copy, there were two photos. In the 'before' shot, a rotund Marcie, wearing a tent-cum-evening gown, was seated in front of a lavish spread of food on a well-set table. She was laughing, a Henry VIII turkey leg in her fist, grease on her lips. The photo was staged, but it was supposed to look like a candid paparazzi shot.

The 'after' photo was also a staged candid that must have been photo-shopped down to the last pixel. The picture was a full-frontal shot of Marcie on a beach in a bikini. She was laughing, her jaw tilted back to showcase her sinewy throat. Slim fingers flitted on her jutting collarbone. Her bikini was brief, showing a flat tummy and slim hips. The text underneath the two photos: 'It's Time.'

'Marcie is an inspiration to us all,' said Natasha. 'A beautiful woman and a great humanitarian.'

'Okay, that time I'm positive you were being snarky.'

Expression blank, Natasha said, 'Here we are.' She knocked on the four-paneled door and walked away, quickly.

From inside, Daphne called, 'Come in.'

Emma entered the spacious corner office. As she'd suspected, Daphne's window blinds were closed, blocking out natural light and the view. The furniture was cushy and expensive looking, including a leather couch and desk chair, a titanium-legged desk, and a computer stand to match. Emma's olfactory nerve endings detected the faint scent of oiled machinery.

'Close the door,' said Daphne. She was well turned out at that ridiculous hour, too, in a suede jacket, black skirt, and knee-high boots.

Emma closed the door. She stood by it, since she would be leaving soon anyway.

Daphne said, 'What did you do to Liam Dearborn yesterday?'

'I can explain. A friend of mine was mugged . . .'

'That's too bad,' interrupted Daphne. 'Now, tell me about your encounter with Liam. Precise details.'

'I wish I could,' said Emma. 'My head is a bit fuzzy at this hour.' No way was Emma going to describe the heartache she'd felt in the limo with William, wanting him, but knowing that, for at least three good reasons, she'd never have him. One of those reasons was sitting behind her titanium desk, glaring.

Emma said, 'I take it that my work here is done.'

Daphne snorted. 'You got that right.'

The Good Witch nodded. She'd been teetering on the edge of disaster for months. With this firing, she'd officially fallen off. Somehow, Emma was relieved. Dreading a disaster might be worse than living it, she realized. She'd had a ten-year run as the Good Witch of Greenwich Village. She still had time to sell her apartment before the bank took possession. She'd make a profit, start over somewhere else. Do something else and be brave about it. Grace, a flower rising from the mud, blossomed with acceptance and resignation.

I am that flower, thought Emma.

Daphne opened the top drawer of her desk and reached inside. She pulled out a black ledger. She opened it and clicked a pen. 'I'm writing the check to cash,' said the blond.

'The check?' said Emma.

'I'll make it for ten thousand. Five for completion and a five thousand dollar bonus for getting the job done in less than a week.'

Her eyes fixed on the swirling pen, Emma asked, 'Completion?' And then, *'Ten thousand dollars?'*

Daphne ripped the check out of her book and waved it in the air. Emma inched close enough to the desk to snatch it.

Ten thousand. To cash. Emma said, 'I don't understand.'

Daphne grinned arrogantly. 'I had a lovely evening with Liam last night.'

Did he sleep with Daphne? Impossible! Emma said, 'In what sense?'

'We had a delicious dinner at the Broome Street Grille. And then he brought me to his studio on Greene Street and sketched my portrait for an hour. Emma, it was the red pose I'd done for Victor.'

'The human flame.' The words William had used to describe Emma in his arms.

Daphne nodded. 'After I saw the rough sketch, I knew you'd done your job and done it well. William and I shared a bottle of wine, talked business. Came to some agreements there. And then he kissed me goodbye.'

'Was this a deep, passionate kiss with open lips and tongue?' asked Emma.

'That's none of your business,' said Daphne shortly.

'That's exactly my business,' corrected Emma.

'It satisfied my definition of a first-date kiss,' said Daphne. 'Liam wants me.' She laughed suddenly, as if remembering a private, intimate moment between them. 'Yes, he most definitely wants me,' she repeated.

Emma smelled something bad – sudden and overwhelming. On top of that, her ears started ringing and her eyes stung from a glare that wasn't there. Her senses were reacting aggressively to this news, or Daphne's presence. Emma had to leave immediately. She said, 'If you're happy, I'm happy. I'll let you get back to work.'

Daphne said, 'I wrote that check on the condition of total confidentiality. You can't tell anyone about our transaction. Is that understood?'

'It's in the contract,' said Emma. The Good Witch reached for the knob. But she stopped and said, 'I'm curious about something.'

'Yes?' asked Daphne, not hiding her impatience.

'Marcie is your friend,' said Emma. 'You said so at Victor's. But you went behind her back, hiring me to steal her boyfriend.'

'And?'

'And I was curious why you'd do that to a friend.'

Daphne said, 'I knew they wouldn't last.'

'And your seduction had nothing to do with getting William to hire you for the ArtSpeak campaign? You gave me two weeks to lure him to you, and he'd given you two weeks to audition for the job.'

'You do have big ears,' said Daphne. 'Where'd you hear that?'

'Little bird.'

'You should be ashamed, Emma,' said Daphne. 'You call yourself a matchmaker and you can't recognize a woman in love when she's sitting right in front of you.'

Reason to be cheerful: she was suddenly rich.

Reason to be miserable: William wanted Daphne.

Emma was not in a reasonable mood, either way. She'd achieved her goal, secured her future, but now the future seemed bleak and gray. Sunshine free. As soon as she left Daphne's midtown office building, Emma headed straight to Victor's. She sought succor. And Victor had always been a super succor. Granted, his comfort would be cold (i.e., platonic). But she'd take what she could get.

She had a set of keys for his place, so she let herself in the front doors. Emma rode the grindingly slow elevator to Victor's third-floor studio. As the box ascended, she heard music, the rhythmic techno Victor used for fashion shoots. Fine. She'd watch him work. She'd be happy to watch him clean out his freezer. Just as long as she didn't have to be alone.

The pulsing beat got louder. Victor's apartment

gradually came into view as the platform rose (he'd forgotten to close the loft-side elevator door again). As the room came into full view, Emma blinked in confusion at what she saw. In the middle of the loft, Victor was dancing in a frenzy, a belt with silk scarves tucked into it around his waist and a feather boa around his neck. On the floor, draped in a gold and sequined cloak, a bejeweled crown atop her head, Ann Jingo lounged on the beanbag chair, yelling, 'Faster, faster,' over the music.

Before Emma could punch the buttons to take her down, Victor did an impressive twirl and saw her standing inside the steel cage. He froze. Ann turned toward Emma and then buried herself in the beanbag. Victor unfroze and turned off the music.

Emma said, 'Why do I suddenly feel like John the Baptist?'

Victor opened the elevator cage door. He put his hand on Emma's shoulder. Gently, lovingly, as only a best friend could, he pushed her further back in the box, and stepped in with her. He rammed the gate closed and pushed the down button.

As they descended, awkward with each other for the first time in years, Victor said, 'You caught me between the fourth and fifth veils. Another few minutes and this might have been embarrassing.'

'Because it's nowhere near embarrassing now,' she said.

'Ann was Salome last night,' he said. 'We're taking turns. She's a better dancer than I am.'

'It's nine o'clock in the morning,' said Emma.

'We never went to bed,' he said. 'I mean, to sleep.'

'You'll be a wreck all day.'

'I cancelled my appointments,' he said. 'Ann's taking a personal day. We couldn't stand the idea of being apart.'

'I'm happy for you, Victor.'

He said, 'If you hadn't taken me to Haiku that night, I never would have met Ann.'

They reached the lobby. Emma said, 'You should close the inside elevator door when you go back up.'

He nodded and smoothed his veils. 'How do I look?' he asked.

'Ridiculous,' said Emma. 'But hot.'

'Exactly what I was going for,' he said.

Victor opened the cage for her to go out and then slammed it shut. He pushed the up button. 'Did you need me for something?' he asked as it inched upward.

She shook her head. 'I was in the neighborhood.'

'You're always in the neighborhood.'

'I got a fat check from Daphne. I thought we could celebrate.' Or commiserate. Whichever.

'Great! We definitely will,' he said, stooping to see her as the elevator lifted him back to his girlfriend, back to bliss. 'I'll call you in a couple of hours.'

'Don't you dare,' she said. 'You and Ann should be alone. I'll find someone else.'

Once outside, Emma called the Tribeca Grand. The operator connected her to Hoff's room.

'Hello?' asked Hoff.

'It's me.'

'Emma!'

'You sound better.'

'I feel like a new man.'

'How many Vicodin have you had today?' asked Emma.

'Just one,' he said. Then he put a hand over the mouthpiece. The voices were muffled, but she heard every word, clear as teardrops. 'Should we tell her?' he asked. 'Now? Not in person?'

'Tell me what.'

'Susan's here,' he said.

'She came over first thing?' asked Emma.

'Actually, she never left,' said Hoff. Muffled giggles. Hoff put his hand over the mouthpiece again.

'She must need to leave for work,' said Emma. 'Is Armand there yet? Should I come over?'

'I completely forgot about Armand,' said Hoff. 'Susan already called in sick. Don't bother coming over. You should take a day for yourself. Get some alone time,' he said.

That was the last thing she wanted. 'If you're sure,' she said.

Hoff changed the subject. 'Susan and I are getting married!'

Emma blurted, *Married?*

'If she can love me the way I look now, imagine how she'll feel after I've had cosmetic dentistry!'

'She's got good taste,' said Emma. 'I'm thrilled for you both.'

'We had a fantastic time last night. I think I broke another rib. But it was worth it.'

Muffled giggles. Emma said, 'Oops, my cell battery's dying. I'll check in later.'

'Susan wants to talk,' he said.

'Half a bar! I'm losing you.'

'We want to thank . . .'

She pushed end.

This had to be an all-time record for Emma. She'd engineered two new couples in a single week. (Three, if she could take credit for Daphne and William.) Her friends' happiness and joy, though, wasn't having the usual effect on Emma. Not that she wished them ill. It was just that she wouldn't mind a little happiness for herself.

Seeing only one kind of joy on the horizon, Emma walked across the street and into the Citibank on Sixth Avenue.

Mr Cannery was surprised to see her. 'Ms Hutch. Back so soon?' He wore a red bow tie today. 'I've got good news for you.'

'Really?' she asked.

'Yes. According to my screen, November first is on a Sunday. That means you have until Monday, November second to pay the mortgage. You get another day!'

'Don't need it,' she said. Emma sat down in front of his desk and slid the check across the blotter. The banker picked up the piece of paper and made a yummy sound when he read the amount. He held the check close to his nose, sniffed it, caressed it, folded it, unfolded it. Made love to it.

Emma said, 'You should buy the check dinner first.'

He said, 'I assume you'd like a deposit slip.'

'And a withdrawal slip, too.'

'I advise you not to make a withdrawal until the check clears.'

'It's good,' said Emma dismissively. 'Make it five hundred in cash. Twenties and fifties.'

Mr Cannery nearly moaned at the thought of all that green. He consulted his screen, printed out some slips, gave her receipts, and counted out the cash into Emma's palm with his languid, shaking, lingering fingers.

'Thank you, Mr Cannery,' said Emma. 'And may I congratulate you for choosing exactly the right job for your passion and skills.'

'You're welcome,' he said. 'I wish the same for you.'

She exited the bank. He wished the same for her? Emma had always thought she *was* in a job that matched her passion and skills. Her skills, anyway. And her passion? Problem there. If today was any indicator, she'd lost her ability to derive vicarious thrills from other people's romantic happiness. She felt a sudden gnawing in her stomach.

'Why so glum?' asked someone on the street.

Emma looked up. It was the Jew for Jesus who'd refused to sell her his T-shirt the other day. 'I'm not glum,' she said. 'I'm hungry.'

He said, 'You look like you need someone to talk to.'

Emma said, 'You just want to convert me.'

'That is the mission,' he said. 'But I can restrain myself.'

'I don't want to talk,' she said. 'But I'll just stand here, if that's okay. And, if you talk, I'd rather hear from your Jewish side.'

'My name is Martin,' he said, offering a hairy-knuckled hand.

'I'm Emma,' she said. 'Can I buy a shirt yet?'

'I'm still waiting for the bulk delivery.'

'Give me a stack of those pamphlets,' she said. 'I'll help you disseminate.'

Martin raised his bushy eyebrows. 'Are you sure you want to do that?'

'We'll be the Two Pamphleteers,' she said.

'Don't be discouraged,' he said, 'if most people C&D the brochures. That's crumple and dump.'

I am those brochures, thought Emma.

'I have to ask,' she said. 'Why?'

'You mean, why turn my back on one religion and embrace another?' he asked. 'The 2004 election was a real wake-up call for me. I figured, if you can't beat them, join them.'

'That's a bit defeatist,' said Emma.

'We were defeated,' said Martin.

Together, the two pamphleteers stood on the corner of Sixth and Waverly, passing paper. In five minutes, at least a hundred people zipped by. Emma handed out a dozen pamphlets. All of them were C&Ded. She was called 'freak show', 'wacko', 'sicko', and a few other slurs that didn't end in 'o'.

'Whenever you're ready,' Martin prompted. 'You obviously have something to get off your chest.'

'I'm not a religious person,' she said. 'My parents were atheists. I've never walked with Jesus. Never been carried by Jesus. Definitely not at this weight. I'm at the high end of my range. I doubt he could lift me.'

Martin offered a pamphlet to a hurried man in a cashmere overcoat who said, 'Go to hell.'

'Have a nice day!' Martin called after him. To Emma, he said, 'Hungry, lonely, and pagan is no way to go through life.'

'*Pagan?*' She guffawed. 'Not sure about that. I am

definitely hungry. I might be alone, but I have friends, and I'm good to them. Just last night I set up two friends and now they're engaged.'

'That's impressive,' he said. 'Matchmaking is your gift?'

'Among others,' she said.

'Having a special gift can take over your life,' said Martin. 'That's pretty standard. From Moses to Jesus to Spider-Man.'

He fanned a few pamphlets at a pack of moms pushing strollers. The kid in the lead stroller said, 'You're fat and hairy.'

Martin beamed and said, 'Children are a blessing!'

'How can you stand this?' Emma asked. 'These people are so rude. They're not buying what you're selling. They think you're a nutcase who creates litter and hogs the sidewalk.'

Martin agreed completely. 'They loathe me. I fill them with contempt. I could stand on this corner for ten years and I won't convert a single one of them. It's fruitless.'

'So why bother?' she asked.

'I'm on a quest. And unlike ninety-nine percent of the people who spit at me, throw pamphlets back in my face, kick my shins, disown me, divorce me, keep me from seeing my children, get restraining orders against me – unlike those lost souls, *I have conviction*.'

He waved a brochure at an elderly woman with a plastic shopping bag. She said, 'Fuck off, Christ killer.'

'Jesus loves you!' he shouted after her. To Emma, he said, 'What about you, Emma? Do you think I'm a raving lunatic?'

'Not raving,' she said.

He laughed. 'You know the second standard catch about having a special gift?'

'I'm afraid to ask.'

'You can never give it to yourself,' he said. 'But that shouldn't deter you on your quest.'

'My quest.'

'We're all on a quest,' he said. 'Whatever yours is, however fruitless it seems, if you've got conviction, you've got to keep trying. When you stop trying, you might as well be dead.'

'I'll take that under advisement,' she said.

'Should all else fail, there's always God,' said Martin.

A memory rose from the cauldron of Emma's mind. She was nine or ten, in her room in New Jersey, her black cat Cloudy on her lap. Emma was hypnotized by Cloudy's twitching whiskers, her lush fur, the round eyes. Emma believed that, if there was a God and if she looked hard and long enough, she would see Him (or Her) in Cloudy's golden eyes.

Emma said, 'Shake?' She held out her hand to Martin. He shook it, and gave her a little squeeze. The Good Witch sent the image of Cloudy's feline face into Martin's consciousness. She held it a few seconds and then dropped his hand.

'I put that picture in your head,' she said. 'Don't ask how. My gift to you.'

'What is it about pagans and cats?' asked Martin.

E mma made a quick stop and then headed across the street, back home to her white sanctuary.

A man was loitering outside her building. He was prematurely balding in an expensive suit, around her age, around her height, and had the tiny feet (in loafers) of a ballet dancer.

'Are you Emma Hutch?' he asked. 'Otherwise known as "The Good Witch"? Nice flowers, by the way. Roses are your favorite?'

'They remind me of someone,' said Emma, shifting the just-bought red dozen from one arm to the other and lifting her key to unlock the front door.

'You are Emma Hutch?'

'The one and lonely,' she said.

'The . . . I'm sorry, did you mean, "The one and *only*"? Because you said, "The one and *lonely*."'

'I'm a very busy woman,' she said, walking into her lobby.

He followed. 'I represent a certain person who has heard about your success in a certain area. This person would like to hire you on a limited yet exclusive basis, for an inflated fee, if you are available immediately.'

Emma walked toward the elevators. She said, 'In my limited yet exclusive experience with certain people, fee inflation tends to match ego inflation. Just how much hot air are we talking about?'

The man said, 'I speak of the fee, not the ego.'

'Of course.'

'Are you familiar with the Good Year blimp?'

'That bad?' She jabbed the elevator button. 'Tell your certain person I'm not interested.' She wasn't. With Daphne's cash, she was okay for a month or two. She decided she was burnt out and needed to take some time off, to get away from women and men and the pursuit of love.

The man wedged himself between Emma and the opening elevator door. He said, 'This is an emergency.'

She kicked him in the knee. He went down. Stepping over him and into the elevator, she said, 'A matchmaking emergency. I like that. Dial 911-match.'

The doors began to close. The man blocked them with his arm. Emma kicked at his hand. While fending off blows, he shouted, 'Twenty thousand dollars!'

She stopped kicking. Emma stepped over him and back into the lobby.

'Twenty thousand dollars?' Her keenly sensitive hearing had to be mistaken. For that amount, she felt suddenly refreshed and ready to work.

'You stomped my pinkie,' said the short man, standing,

rubbing his finger. 'And, yes, I said twenty grand.'

'That figure is quite the blimp,' she said. 'Who's the client?'

He stood up, dusted himself off, and said, 'I didn't go to Harvard Law School for this.' He handed her a business card.

She read, 'Sherman Hollow, Esq. of Park Avenue.'

'I do entertainment and contract law,' he said. 'Currently, I'm acting as personal manager for one of my clients.'

'The client with the matchmaking emergency,' said Emma.

'She's waiting for you around the corner. In her limo,' he said. 'When you speak to her, don't tell her that I referred to the Good Year blimp in our conversation. In fact, don't use the word "blimp" at all. Or "inflated".'

Emma followed Sherman Hollow, Esq. back outside. They walked down Waverly Place and onto Gay Street. A six-door white limousine with blacked-out windows idled at the curb. As they approached, one of the rear doors opened. Emma peeked inside.

Marcie Skimmer squealed, 'Roses? For *me*?'

The blond bombshell swiped the roses out of Emma's hand, buried her bobbed nose in the bouquet, inhaled deeply, and then tossed the bunch at Sherman Hollow. He obediently – one could say, slavishly – received them and placed the flowers in the front seat next to the driver. Then he joined the ladies in the back.

Sherman said, 'Marcie, this is Emma.'

They shook hands. Marcie said, 'Have we met?'

Emma was still adjusting to the model up close. At

eleven on a Wednesday morning, Marcie looked like Saturday night. Platinum hair piled atop her head, strands artfully flowing downward with haphazard perfection. Her makeup, especially the black vamp eyeliner, was penciled on with the precision of a diamond cutter. Her lips were glossy and frosty, her skin spritzed with peony perfume, dazzling Emma's eyes and nose.

The Good Witch said, 'We haven't met. I'd remember.' But they had. Twice. At Ciao Roma (but Emma looked a lot different that night, with straight hair, no shades, and full makeup), and with Victor at Haiku, when she'd been disguised as Emeril. Also, like hundreds of others, Marcie had seen her face in William's portraits.

The model almost connected the dots. She said, 'You seem so familiar.'

'I must have one of those faces.'

Frowning, the model said, 'No, your face is unusual. That low forehead and pinched chin and too-wide cheekbones, those kooky blue glasses.'

Sherman Hollow, Esq. interjected. 'Marcie, why don't you get to the point?'

'I hear that you are a witch and you cast spells and boil potions, then invade the minds of men and haunt their dreams and make them fall in love with whoever you tell them to.'

Emma laughed. 'Your sources are a bit off. I'm a telegraphopathic matchmaker. I can't boil an egg, much less concoct a magic potion. And I don't haunt men's dreams or make them fall in love.' Except for William, or so he claimed. But then again, he'd given up on her after only one polite rejection. That couldn't be love.

Marcie said, 'So what do you do?'

Emma said, 'I guarantee a first date. Although I find it impossible to believe that you can't get first dates on your own.' It occurred to Emma that Marcie might've come to her to lure William back.

'You've been working with Daphne Wittfield,' said Marcie.

'I can't say,' said Emma.

Marcie pouted. 'Just between us girls.'

Emma said, 'What's it to you?'

'Daphne and I are old friends,' said Marcie.

'And colleagues,' added Emma. 'The diet pill ads. You as a cow. A parade float. A whale.'

Sherman winced. Red dots surfaced on Marcie's otherwise flawless cheeks. Her voice jumping an octave, Marcie said, 'I lost fifty pounds. And it was brave of me to do it. Very brave and very hard.'

Only in America was dieting considered an act of heroism, thought Emma.

'You should be proud,' said Sherman.

'I am proud,' said Marcie to Sherman. To Emma: 'Tell me about Daphne. Who she's fucking, for how long, and how it got started. I have a right to know.' Like a spoiled child, Marcie was used to getting what she wanted.

Sherman whispered, 'Twenty thousand dollars.'

'I can see that you have a real concern for Daphne's well being,' said Emma. 'That your interest in her romantic life comes from a giving, loving place.'

Marcie said, 'That's exactly right. I love her and want to make sure she's chosen a deserving, trustworthy man.'

'Such devotion,' said Emma, marveling. 'How long have you and Daphne known each other?'

'We were college roommates,' said Marcie. 'Which didn't always work out for Daphne romantically. What could I do? Hide in my bedroom? Ignore her guests? How could I remember to close the shower door *every time*?'

Emma nodded sympathetically. 'You can't help being beautiful,' she said.

'Daphne blamed me when she got dumped,' she said. 'For years, I've been trying to get her to see the truth: it was her own fault for making poor choices in men.'

'I get it now,' said Emma. 'You want to test her new boyfriend? Prove his mettle?'

Marcie trilled, 'That's it!'

'You have a plus-sized heart in a size four body,' said Emma.

Sherman said, 'All Marcie wants is a name.'

'I give you a name and you give me twenty thousand dollars?'

'Marcie is an extremely wealthy woman,' he said, reaching into his pocket and removing a checkbook. 'Shall I make it out to you or cash?'

'I don't want your money,' said Emma.

Marcie said, 'You have to take it! Sherman, make her take the check!'

'Settle down,' said Emma. 'It would be wrong for me to take your money to further assist the needs of a client – although I won't confirm whether she is or not.'

'But you'll give me a name?' asked Marcie.

Emma would send Marcie to William exactly one day after Hell froze over. Then again, maybe she should point

Marcie in his direction. Daphne had had no compunction about stealing William from Marcie. It would serve Daphne right to put Marcie back on the trail. Perhaps William and Daphne and Marcie deserved to be locked in a lovers' triangle together. Emma could stay on the outside, and watch. Except the thought of William kissing either of the ruthless blonds was too horrible to imagine.

But then she got a better idea.

'As I said, it'd be wrong for me to violate my oath of confidentiality,' said Emma. 'I can't talk about it. But I will do something to help. And I'll do it for free.'

Sherman said, 'Free is good.'

Emma said to Marcie, 'Give me your hand.'

Marcie handed herself over. Emma held on, and closed her eyes.

'Oh!' said Marcie, as if she'd been goosed. 'Oh! Oh, my!'

'What is it, Marcie? Are you hurt?' asked the solicitor.

Emma let go and said, 'Did the image of a man pop into your head?'

Marcie said, 'Yes!'

'Do you recognize him?'

'Absolutely!'

'Then go get him,' said Emma, brain fuzz coming on.

Sherman said, 'Are you sure you won't take a check?'

'I couldn't possibly.'

'Thank you so very much,' said Marcie.

Emma climbed out of the limo. The door shutting behind her, Emma heard Marcie yelling, 'Luis! Luis, to Brooklyn. NOW!' The driver peeled out. Marcie sped off to find her man and throw herself at his feet like Cleopatra to Caesar.

Alfie Delado, penis artist, was in for the surprise of his life.

Emma watched Marcie's taillights zoom downtown. Brain fuzz approaching, she did some jumping jacks to clear her head. She was puzzled by the ringing in her ears – that wasn't a usual symptom. The sound of a weakening vessel? But then she realized: cell phone.

'Hello?'

'It's Susan,' said her newly engaged friend. 'I'm in the lobby at the Tribeca Grand, hiding behind a column and watching Jeff Bragg eat an early lunch. At this very moment, he's chewing.'

Alarmed, Emma said, 'Stay away from him. He's dangerous. I'm hanging up and calling the police,' she said, fumbling in her purse for the card Hoff had given her.

'Don't you dare,' warned Susan. 'That man took advantage of me, threatened you, and pulled a gun on my future husband. I want five minutes with him.' She drew breath. 'I'm going in.'

'No!' said Emma. 'Wait. I'm on my way. Don't do anything. Just keep an eye on him. Okay? You'll wait?'

Long pause. Too long. 'Okay,' said Susan reluctantly.

She started down Sixth Avenue and asked, 'By the way, what's he eating?'

'Burger. With mayonnaise. The sick bastard.'

'I'll be there in ten minutes,' said Emma, hanging up.

Eleven minutes later (Emma spent the extra sixty seconds buying a pom-pom tam on Canal Street to hide her hair), the Good Witch walked into the lobby of the hotel, head down, hat on, glasses on, protective shield that transmitted 'don't talk to me, don't look at me, stay six hundred feet back' engaged.

As she unobtrusively walked through, she glanced at the lobby café. Jeff Bragg sat alone, reading the business section of the *Times*, his plate and cell phone on the table in front of him. With her super vision, Emma could make out the headline: 'Dearborn's ArtSpeak: Record Sales Projected.'

A tiny hand grabbed Emma's wrist and dragged her behind one of the lobby's load-bearing columns. Emma smelled vanilla.

'I might need this,' said Emma to Susan, detaching the vice-like grip on her arm. 'Engagement becomes you.' The petite brunette's cheeks were glowing pink, her lips bruised and swollen from kissing, and her brown eyes, which Emma had previously admired for their intelligence, crackling with excitement.

'Thanks,' said Susan. 'You look good, except for that horrible hat.'

'What do you expect for five bucks?' Emma gave her a hug. 'Congrats, by the way.'

Susan said, 'Last night was revelatory, being with a great guy who treated me like a queen. I fell in love with him when he gave me the most incredible back rub.'

Emma remembered his back rubbing talent fondly. 'He could do it with a broken rib?'

'Vicodin,' said Susan. 'Believe the hype.'

The two women crouched behind the column, taking turns poking their heads out to watch. Jeff put down the paper and looked out the window, showing his profile.

Susan said, 'So Jeff might be certifiably paranoid, but you can't deny he's a damned handsome man.'

Emma said, 'He does nothing for me. All right angles. Perpendicular. Emphasis on *dick*.'

'Perpendicular is bad?' asked Susan.

'In angles and men, I prefer acute. Emphasis on *cute*.'

'Like William Dearborn, for instance? He's acute.'

'Hoff told you about me and Dearborn?' asked Emma, surprised.

'He hasn't told me anything,' said Susan. 'Wait, *you know William Dearborn?* Can you introduce me?'

Emma shook her head. 'I would, but since I'll never see him again, I won't get the chance.'

'You can see him right now,' said Susan, aiming her finger at the front door. 'He just walked in the lobby.'

Emma's pom-pommed head swung to the left. Everyone in the lobby's head swung to the left. William Dearborn was magnetism itself. Only Susan stayed focused. She said, 'Jeff's leaving.'

Sure enough, Jeff Bragg was pocketing his cell, signing his bill, and standing up to leave. He walked out of the restaurant and toward the hotel elevator bank. Was he staying here now? In his paranoia, he must have checked out of the Four Seasons immediately after his confrontation with her.

Meanwhile, William was headed in the same direction. People had started to approach him, fawn over him.

Susan said, 'What now?'

Emma didn't want to be seen by either Jeff or William. 'Why do you want five minutes with Jeff?' she asked.

'I'd like to know the truth,' said Susan. 'Why he left me. What he's hiding. Just get answers. Ideally, some closure, or satisfaction. And then I can forget him.'

Emma would love to forget William too. But she was sure that five minutes with him would not get her closure – or satisfaction. Looking at him from fifty feet or five inches, Emma felt an instant physical reaction, a gravitational yank toward him. She imagined reaching all the way across the lobby to touch his lovely neck.

William's head suddenly turned in their direction. Emma quickly ducked behind the column.

Susan said, 'The elevator door is opening.'

'Go,' said Emma. 'Get in there. Act surprised to see him, and tell him you're visiting a friend at the hotel. Ask him to meet you for drinks tonight.'

Susan asked, 'Then what?'

'Don't get off the elevator before he does, but pay attention to which floor he's on.'

A quick nod and Susan was off. Emma watched as her gutsy friend greeted her ex with convincing astonishment. William, meanwhile, was occupied with some fans.

The elevator doors closed on Susan, Jeff, and William. Emma crept over to watch the numbers rise. The car stopped on the sixth floor. Then it went up to the tenth and top floor. Emma jabbed the call button and waited forever for an elevator to come back down.

Assuming she'd find Susan back in Hoff's room, Emma went straight to 512. Armand let her in.

'You're here,' said Emma. It was after noon.

'Sorry I was late,' he said. 'I had to go to church.'

'On a Wednesday?' she asked.

'I've had unclean thoughts.'

Of a naked nun? wondered Emma. 'You smell spiritually clean now.' He did. Like Pine-Sol.

Hoff was napping. No Susan. Emma wondered if her friend was ballsy enough to go to Jeff's room and get her five minutes with him, unchaperoned.

Emma sighed heavily. To Armand, she said, 'I'll be back.'

Armand said, 'Mind if I watch TV?'

Emma could not have cared less. She helped the orderly find the remote, decipher the channel guide. She took the stairs to the sixth floor, intending to search methodically, pressing her ear against each door to listen for Susan's voice. She'd only done two doors when Emma's cell phone rang.

'Emma!' said Susan.

'Where are you?' whispered the Good Witch. 'Are you okay?' In the background, she heard music, laughter. She went back into the stairway to talk in private.

'I'm in the penthouse suite!' said Susan. 'This place is incredible. It's a triplex with an enormous roof deck. The furniture looks like giant rubber noodles. Someone told me – hello? – Emma, you there? This guy told me the suite goes for three thousand dollars a night. You have got to come up here.' A muffle. Susan said, 'Parker Posey just asked me where the bathroom was.'

One act of daring-do and Susan had both met *and turned into* a Party Girl. Emma said, 'You crashed?'

'William Dearborn brought me in.'

'William is at the party?'

'Yes, he's standing right here. He asked me to call you.'

Emma blurted, 'He's right there? How did he . . .'

'He saw us together in the lobby.'

Another muffle. Perhaps Jude Law was asking for a cigarette.

'Hello, Emma,' said the voice on the phone.

'Susan, that is a pathetic British accent.'

'Funny,' said William. 'Are you coming up? It's just a little impromptu get together. The host signed his divorce papers two hours ago and decided to throw a party. Isn't this a lucky coincidence, the two of us in the same place at the same time.'

Usually, they were at the same place in each other's mind.

Emma said, 'I'm not good at parties.'

'Do you like very small crab cakes?'

'I love crab cakes,' said Emma wistfully.

'Get them while they're hot,' said William.

'White Russian? Gin and tonic? Madras? Screwdriver? Whiskey Sour?' asked the bartender.

'The party theme is 1983,' said Susan at Emma's side. 'The year the host married his ex-wife.'

The Good Witch got a White Russian. Only four thousand calories per glass. 'What happened with Jeff?'

Susan said, 'He was shocked – shocked! – to see me. He agreed to meet me for drinks tonight at seven at Nancy's Whisky Bar across the street.'

Emma knew Nancy's well. It was, bar none, the sleaziest hole in lower Manhattan. 'Perfect,' said Emma. 'You'll get your five minutes. I'll go in costume to make sure you're safe. Then we call the cops and have him taken away. Jon Stewart and Amy Sedaris at three o'clock.' Stargazing was good sport – and this party was like shooting stars in a barrel. She'd already spotted a dozen semi- and full-blown celebs. In the corner, an ex-junkie swimsuit model was canoodling with an up-and-coming singer-songwriter whose big hit was a ballad to his wife (not the ex-junkie). A rap impresario rolled joints for a cinema-verité movie director. To the right, the most downloaded Internet pin-up girl shared a cigarette with the *other* darling/muse of independent films. By the stairs, a lad magazine editor turned novelist talked to a famous aging alcoholic satirist. On the couch, the daughter of a pair of politicians sat on the lap of an ex-Yankee slugger with a steroid addiction.

Susan said, 'I may be the only not-for-profit person here.'

'I don't know where to gawk first,' said Emma.

'Start here,' said William Dearborn, materializing at her side. 'And please take off that horrible hat.'

Emma couldn't help smiling at him. In a room full of eye catchers, he was a standout. Despite her aversion to parties, in this unreal setting, with familiar faces all around, one drink in her already, Emma felt okay. She sipped her drink and drank in William, tipsy from both.

He asked them, 'Do you want to meet anyone?'

Like peace on earth, Susan was all for it. 'Will you introduce me to John Mayer?' she asked, grinning lustily.

'Come along, Susan,' he said, taking her hand. 'John Mayer waits for no woman.'

Emma watched as Dearborn deposited her lawyer friend on a velour-covered couch between a famous female downtown designer and the Grammy award-winning guitar player. Then he returned to Emma, snagging a tray of crab cakes from a server along the way. She loved to watch him walk, the long strides, his sleek, slim body in the usual brown suit, his eyes trained on her, only her, with far more beautiful women to the right and left. Any thoughts about William's date with Daphne evaporated from Emma's mind.

William offered her the tray. She nibbled delicately, girlishly, letting herself soak up the flavor of his attention.

'You're cute when you eat,' he said, grinning.

Due to the alcohol, the surreal setting, Emma's guard was way down. 'This party is like watching TV, but live and in person.'

'Does it make you uncomfortable?' he asked, as if he hated the idea that anything on earth would bother her.

'I'm usually ready to leave a party after five minutes. But not now, weirdly.'

'This party is okay for me too,' he said.

'Don't tell me,' she said. 'You're not a Party Boy?' Nearly every time she'd seen him, he'd been at a party, the center of attention.

'As a matter of fact, Emma Hutch, I treasure my

privacy. I wish I could have more of it.' He seemed testy. 'I do not like it when people make assumptions.'

She did not like his tone. 'You want privacy, you can have it.' Emma took a step.

'Don't go,' he said quickly. 'I've been meaning to talk to you about something philosophical.'

First Martin and his Quest Theory. Now William. 'Okay, I'm comparison shopping,' she said. 'Lay it on me.'

'I have one abiding philosophy of life. Based on my accumulated experiences.'

'Which is?'

'I won't cheat myself.' She waited for elaboration. He said, 'It's one thing if you're bamboozled in business. Or hoodwinked by circumstances beyond your control. Or cheated out of time with someone you cared about because of illness or death. That's bad luck, bad business, fate, what have you. But denying yourself something you really want? That's a self-inflicted wound. Cheating yourself out of love is suicidal.'

'That's fascinating, William,' she said.

'You could learn a lot from me, Emma.'

'About philosophy,' she said.

He squinted at her, baffled. 'Philosophy?' he asked. 'For God's sake, woman. I was talking about sex.'

Emma laughed. 'I'm not determined to cheat myself,' she said. 'I'm practicing self-preservation.'

She ate another crab cake. Wiped her lips. Across the room, Susan was talking to Heidi Klum while Seal listened. Susan was half Heidi's height.

'Is there another man?' asked William. 'That has to be it.'

'Aren't you the least bit curious who I am?' she asked. 'Where I come from? What I do for a living?'

He said, 'Emma Hutch, born in June, 1974, in Livingston, New Jersey. Mother: Anise Janis, homemaker. Father: Harry Hutch, architect. You grew up in Short Hills, New Jersey and moved to Manhattan at age twelve. You went to the Big Blue middle and upper school on Greenwich Street, graduated from NYU, class of 1995. You currently live on Waverly Place. You are a self-employed personal shopper, hired by private clients on a freelance basis.'

Emma blinked. 'Private investigator?'

'Google.'

'I'm sure you have better things to do,' she said. That bit about being a personal shopper – she'd given that line to the NYU alumni office.

'Your high school yearbook photo,' he said, grimacing.

The photo was Cousin It-like, her wavy hair covering her face. Only a sliver of her nose showed. She was hiding then – from the photographer, from her classmates. The picture was illustrative of Emma's defining contradiction: she could see everything, but she was terrified of being seen.

Emma looked up at William, from under her hat, behind her glasses. He'd seen her, even when she tried to hide from him. He'd seen her when she wasn't even there. Emma now knew that she couldn't hide from him or avoid what they both wanted. If she had a fatal burst in his arms, at least she got to be held first. If he ran away screaming, at least she didn't cheat herself out of trying. The simple fact: Emma wanted to be seen. Not by the wide world (she was a million years away from that level of emotional evolution). But she longed for an audience of one.

She said, 'Can we go somewhere more private? To be alone. Together. If you get my meaning.'

Not missing a beat, William said, 'Right this way.' He put his hand to the small of her back and steered her out the door. 'My company keeps a room in the hotel. Down one flight.'

'Not right this very second!' said Emma, hesitating. 'We need to talk more first.'

'As if talking is the way you get to know someone,' he said.

He led her into the room Dearborn International kept on the ninth floor. The space was comfy despite the modern furniture and graphic art; it was twice the size of Hoff's room several floors below.

The bed itself was the size of Emma's entire apartment. Or maybe it just loomed large. The black cover appeared to be sateen, which seemed sort of cheap. Emma ran her hand over the material. No, not sateen, she realized. Satin. The real thing. Yards and yards of it. A circus tent's worth.

Emma sat down on the edge of the bed. William stood in front of her and unbuttoned his pants.

'You, too,' he said.

'I'm not undressing in front of you!' she said, looking away. And then looking back.

'Then undress behind me,' he said, turning around, continuing to strip. In a flash, he was naked as the city, his ass within arm's reach. She'd imagined him nude many times. And her fantasy had been pretty close to reality. The dusting of dark hair on his long legs. The rounded butt, big rabbit feet on elegant ankles. His spine was a shallow gutter in the center of his back, snaking upward to his boxy shoulders and long neck. His arms were larger than Emma had expected, but by no means beefy.

Glancing over his shoulder: 'Emma! You're still dressed.'

He spun around. She gasped. Not all of William Dearborn was a slim bean.

'I can see why you're so popular with the ladies,' she said, her eyes big.

He smiled wickedly and said, 'That would be much funnier if I weren't the only one naked,' he said. 'Your turn, Emma.'

He came toward her, his hard-on bobbing as he walked. He lifted her to her feet. First, he pulled the pom-pom hat off her head and threw it across the room. Then he took off her shades, folding them carefully – and then threw them across the room. He pulled her black shirt over her head, her hair falling around her bare shoulders. He expertly unhooked her bra and slid the straps down her arms. As the bra hit the floor, William started to unbutton and unzip her jeans. He pushed them down her hips before gasping himself.

She said, 'I don't wear panties with low-rise jeans.'

'Is this a common practice?'

'You'd know better than I would.'

'Most of my dates wear complicated lingerie.'

'And you find it refreshing to undress a woman who wears nothing at all?' she said.

'Refreshing is one word for it,' he said and then lowered her by the shoulders onto the bed. He got on his knees and grabbed her ankles, unzipping her boots and pulling them off along with her pants in a fluid flourish.

She sat naked on the bed. William was kneeling nude in front of her. She closed her eyes and braced herself for his touch.

William said, 'You should see the expression on your face.'

Her eyes snapping open, she said, 'What?'

'Look at me. Right in the eyeball,' he said. 'Good. I want you to keep your eyes open and on me.'

She nodded. Still not touching her, he leaned forward and gave her a peck on the thigh. Emma's lids lowered.

'Don't close your eyes,' he repeated.

'It's hard to keep them open,' she said.

'Try again.'

He sat next to her and kissed her lightly on the lips. This time, Emma kept her eyes wide. His were partly closed. She stared at his eyelashes, the sprinkle of pale freckles on his cheeks (hadn't noticed those before), the few blond strands in his brown fringe. He smelled of marshmallow, graham cracker, and chocolate. And she wanted s'more. She put her arms around his neck and deepened the kiss.

But he pulled back. 'You smell like ginger snaps,' he said, sniffing along her nape. Emma, who took the aromatic measure of everyone she met, had never been fragrantly appraised before. She felt flattered, appreciated, expansive, like she was filling the room with her essence.

'Making me watch you,' she said. 'Is this about vanity?'

'You seem nervous,' he said. 'And if you keep your eyes

open, you'll stay focused on what's happening and forget whatever's putting you on edge.'

A simple but brilliant notion. It could have more profound benefits, given Emma's particular sex-related problems. She couldn't fantasize if she were in the moment (although, with William, this didn't seem to be a problem). With her eyes open, she was incapable of transmitting – even accidentally. Regarding her overheating, her extreme sense of touch seemed to be minimized in combination with her sense of sight.

William guided her farther back on the bed so they could lie next to each other, their heads on satin-covered pillows. He put his hand on her belly and kneaded it gently. She watched, relaxing into his hands. She flashed to the night with Hoff, how she'd flinched when he touched her stomach. Not so now. She wanted William to touch her wherever and however he wanted. She wished he had eight hands.

William said, 'I hope you don't mind if I just grope you for a while. Your skin is so white and soft. Have you *ever* been to the beach?'

She laughed. Emma had been to the Jersey shore once, but she got so sunburned, she threw up and vowed never again.

'Which is more important to you,' she asked. 'Art or sex?'

'Art and sex go together,' he said. 'They're my religion.'

'What's bigger than art and sex – and religion? And love?'

'Is this a riddle?' he asked. He was touching her breasts. She alternated between watching his hands and his face. His green eyes roamed her body. His fingertips were like fine-bristled brushes, painting her pink.

'Not a riddle,' she said. 'It's the key to my philosophy.'

'I'm stumped,' he said. 'What could be bigger than love, sex, art, and religion? Form a good answer and I'll give you two orgasms.'

She said, 'You're so sure there'll be one?'

'Would you like that now?' he asked.

Emma took a deep breath and nodded. He said, 'You'll have to keep your eyes open. No cheating. Yourself.'

She nodded. He slid one arm under her neck and pulled her tightly against his body. Their foreheads were touching, and when they blinked their eyelashes twined. He kissed her cheek and the corner of her mouth. She imagined the ginger snap scent filling his head, saturating his senses.

William's hand glided along on her ribs, over her belly. He seemed to need to touch every inch of her, to learn her skin. Running his hand over her bottom, William's breath changed. He moaned and pressed himself against her. She put her hands against his chest, her fingers exploring, moving around to his back. She kissed his chin, licked his lips.

His warm hand slid over her hip and between her legs. Emma let her eyelids flicker.

He whispered, 'Open up, Emma.'

She looked at him. His face was close and his clean breath tickled her ear. She focused on his lips, how red they were, parted slightly. She felt like she was in a waking trance. His fingers expertly busy, William's eyes were narrow and shiny and gloriously green. Emma felt every inch of him against her side.

An image popped into her head. An arrow, feathered quiver.

William said, 'You have the most beautiful eyes I've ever seen.'

And she came against his hand. He leaned in to kiss her mouth as soon as it started. She couldn't help closing her eyes with the quake, and a series of images crashed into her head. Stars and spinning planets, a slash of orange, red, and yellow across a black sky like the aurora borealis. Emma herself wearing a pointy hat, zooming on a broom across the moon, a trail of fire in her wake.

Eventually, she returned to earth. He stopped kissing her and said, 'I hope that felt as amazing as it looked.'

She said, 'How did it look?'

'Cosmic,' he said.

'That is exactly right.'

They lay hugging on the bed. He brushed hair off her forehead. 'Now tell me,' he said, 'what is bigger than sex, love, art, and religion?'

'Magic,' she said.

'As in, hocus pocus?'

'Mysticism, the unknown, what we feel but don't see, what we can't understand and don't question. The forces of the universe that have no reasonable explanation,' she said.

He continued toying with her waves, using a strand to stroke her cheek. 'Interesting. I will give that more thought,' he said. 'But not right now. I have an urgent concern' – which he proceeded to urge into her thigh – 'that has drained all the blood from my brain.'

She gripped him and he filled her hand like a bat. They both moaned. She couldn't help smiling at her own hunger for it. She thought she'd be hungry forever. Emma crawled on top of William. She rubbed him against her and then, slowly, eased him inside. He moaned again and his eyelids lowered. Emma almost asked him to open up, but then she figured, let him go. She'd watch him.

She rocked, squeezing him as she moved. Before too long, she closed her eyes, too. Instantly, her temperature went up five degrees. William turned to liquid beneath her and started making noises, a melt of alarm and abandon. She opened her eyes and concentrated on his face, his chest, glistening with sweat.

'Look at me,' she said.

He opened his eyes, grabbed her thighs, cried out, and came. Like an electrocution, he came, and Emma had to hold on or be thrown from the bed.

She lay flat on top of him, filled to the brim with relief and pride. She'd done it. She'd had sex. Hadn't burst a vessel. The man hadn't fled in terror. In fact, he seemed quite content, as she was. Sex was suddenly spread out before her like an all-you-can-eat buffet. She had years of starvation to make up for. She wanted seconds, and thirds. And fourths.

'That was the most fun you can have with your clothes off,' he said.

She would have laughed, but instead she wondered, had William said the same line before? To Marcie, perhaps? To any of the other women he'd been with? What about Daphne and her comment, 'William wants me.' Had he pressed his urgent concern against her thigh too?

And just like that, in a flash, Emma's bliss and joy were gone.

She felt herself spiraling downward – not the direction she wanted afterglow to go. The shift wasn't caused by jealousy alone. Even as she lay on top of William, his penis still inside her, Emma detected the odor of a swindle. She'd gotten a full dose of pleasure, true, but she felt cheated out of what she'd hoped sex would bring – love, a relationship, satisfaction of the soul. She'd faced her fears. That was good. She'd had a physical release. Also good. But she and William hadn't become intimate (as if sex was how you got to know a person). The sad truth was, nearly everything he thought he knew about her was a lie.

A tinny taste in her mouth, Emma rolled off William, climbed off the bed, and searched the floor for her clothes.

He sat up and said, 'You're getting dressed?'

Emma said, 'I had a wonderful time, William. Thank you.'

'That's it?'

'I've really got to go.' She put on her shades.

William said, 'After what just happened, you're going to disappear?'

She said, 'Like magic.'

And so Emma fled from William's bed – confused, rocked, and guilty – just like the dozens of men who'd fled from hers. She ran from the room, her clothes half-on, leaving William with all the sadness of all the times she'd been left.

S he rushed back to room 512. After Hoff admitted her,
she sank into an armchair and buzzed from the inside
out. Emma's thoughts were on a spinning wheel (relief,
pride, joy, anxiety, sadness, excitement, back to relief, etc.).
Her legs were shaking. Her hair tangled and wild. Her skin
flushed.

'You look different,' said Hoff.

'You do,' agreed Armand, looking up from baseball on
TV. 'Can I call room service? I'm hungry.'

'You haven't done anything but watch TV,' snarled Hoff.
'And I hate sports.'

'I only watch to divert my mind,' said Armand. 'Otherwise, I'll think about the fragility of human existence.
We're tissue paper. Our bodies are as flimsy as what we use
to wipe our . . .'

'The room service menu is next to the phone,' said Hoff.

Emma asked, 'Has Armand always been so morbid?'

'He says it comes from working at a hospital.'

'He's right, about the fragility of human existence,' she said. 'But courteous folk keep that to themselves.'

'Back to why your hair is such an unholy mess,' said Hoff.

'You say I look different?' Emma thought about adolescent claims that sex changed a woman's face. 'Different how? Glowing? Radiant?'

'I was going to say "upset" or "crazed". But radiant works,' said Hoff.

Armand said, 'Does anyone want a cheeseburger, too?'

'Wait a minute, Armand,' said Hoff. 'Now that Emma's here, I won't need you. I'm sure I can manage on my own anyway.'

'You never know,' said Armand. 'You could fall in the shower, crack your skull. I'm a trained professional. I know what to do in those situations.'

'What would you do?' asked Emma.

Armand said, 'I'd check for a pulse. Then dial 911.'

Hoff said, 'For this wisdom, I'm paying fifty dollars an hour? And, incidentally, I've taken two showers a day since I was twelve and I haven't slipped yet.'

'Two showers a day?' asked Emma. 'Every day?'

He said, 'None since the mugging, and it's making me nuts. I'm three showers behind.'

'One bit of advice,' said Emma. 'Save the news about your compulsive showering until after the wedding.'

'Where is Susan, anyway?' asked Hoff, wincing as he sat upright. 'God that smarts. I think it's time for a pill.'

'She's stretching her legs,' said Emma, watching Hoff sympathetically. He moved like a ninety-year-old. 'We'll have to keep Armand for the rest of the evening though. Susan and I have plans tonight.'

'Plans?' he asked with pretend casualness.

Emma wasn't sure it was a good idea to tell Hoff about the rendezvous with Jeff. He would object for sure. 'Don't worry,' she said placatingly. 'You have nothing to worry about. Susan is completely dependable, reliable, and upstanding.'

The door swung open, crashing against the wall. In the threshold, Susan Knight hiccuped and giggled, her arms around the neck of a tall man in a brown suit. She slurred, 'I'm in love with Seal! He's the sexiest man alive. He kissed me, on the lips. I got the Seal of approval!'

'Oh my God,' said Hoff, rushing toward the door with the sudden agility of an elf. He ignored Susan and offered a hand to her companion. 'Mr Dearborn, it's an honor. Hoffman Centry. I've been speaking with your staff all week. About a book project with Ransom House. I'm an editor there.'

'Vice president!' slurred Susan.

William gallantly deposited drunken Susan on a nearby chair and shook Hoff's hand. Emma tried to make herself invisible.

'Is that you, Emma?' asked William, her invisibility skills failing her.

'We can't seem to get away from each other,' she replied.

'Only one of us wants to,' said William. He sounded hurt. She couldn't believe it. Wasn't an afternoon of hotel sex with a near stranger what he did every Wednesday?

Hoff looked from William to Emma and back again.

He said, 'I'm a close friend of Emma's. Your doing a book with me was her idea, actually.'

'If Emma thinks I should write a book, I'll write a book,' said William. His cell chirped. 'Excuse me,' he said and answered it.

Emma whispered to Hoff, 'I suggested no such thing.'

'You slept with him!' declared Hoff. 'When?'

William hung up, frantic. 'Someone at the party upstairs is choking on a crab cake!'

THUD. Armand stood up so quickly, his chair fell to the floor. 'The threat of death, always lurking. Which way?' demanded Armand with confidence and authority.

'Upstairs,' said William.

Armand and William raced up the five flights, leaping three at a time. Emma ran behind them. They took the flights in about sixty seconds and burst into the penthouse suite. Armand steamrolled toward a woman on the couch, her lips a ghastly blue. He grabbed her around the middle and Heimliched her. A glob of pre-digested crab cake flew out of her mouth, but she didn't start breathing. Armand threw her on the floor and began CPR. It was both terrifying and exhilarating to watch. In about twenty seconds, she looked pinker. She began coughing aggressively. Armand helped her sit upright and patted her on the back.

When she stopped hacking, with her pallor normal and eyes no longer bugged, Emma recognized the woman instantly. William kneeled down beside her. He said, 'Chloe? Are you all right?'

'I'm fine,' said Ms Sevigny. 'I saw a tunnel of light. And then someone pulled me away from it, back to earth.' The princess of independent film looked into Armand's black eyes. 'It was you,' she said. 'You saved me. I owe you my life.'

'You might feel differently in a couple of hours,' he said, bashfully.

'I want to repay you. What can I do?'

Armand said, 'Donate blood every year to the hospital or blood bank of your choice.'

'I'll start tomorrow,' she promised. 'Will you help me get home?'

'Okay,' said Armand.

'Hey, what about Hoff?' asked Emma.

But Armand was lifting Chloe Sevigny into his arms and carrying her like a sack of laundry out of the penthouse suite and into the hallway. Chloe pushed the elevator button with the toe of her shoe.

She said, 'My apartment is only a few blocks from here. Should we get a cab?'

Armand shifted her to his other shoulder and said, 'I prefer to walk.'

After that scene, the party was done. What could follow? The beautiful and fabulous headed for the door. As they filed out, the newly divorced host accepted congratulations. Emma was pushed to the middle of the crowd. Somewhere behind her, William said, 'Emma? Are you still here? If you can hear me, please wait for me outside.'

She did no such thing. She rode a crowded elevator to the lobby. On a house phone, Emma called Hoff's room. 'All is well,' she told him. 'Choking victim's fragile human existence intact. Armand is no longer at your service. And please tell Susan I'll see her at seven.'

'Susan is passed out, face down, on the bed.' Hoff sounded kind of pissed off.

Emma said, 'At six, throw her in the shower and wake her up.'

'Like I can lift her with a broken rib? And what if she falls in the shower and cracks her skull?'

'Check her pulse and dial 911.'

'Yes, of course,' said Hoff. 'Someone's at the door. Got to go.'

Emma hung up, sighed with relief. Nothing like witnessing a near death to make a girl realize what life was really about: self-preservation. She'd flown high in bed with William. Couldn't deny that. But if sex with him was always going to end in a crushing crash landing, just the one encounter was enough. Victor had often theorized that successful sex would puncture Emma's protective bubble. How wrong he'd been. If anything, the bubble was thicker because of it.

With money in the bank and sex behind her, Emma could return to doing what she did best. Assisting other women in finding their bliss. Starting with Susan, tonight. She'd help her friend eradicate the last traces of Jeff Bragg from her consciousness.

This was one case Emma was looking forward to closing.

A couple of hours and three wigs later, Emma sat on a stool at Nancy's Whiskey Bar, a dive that held the stench of fifty years of cigars smoked inside its greasy walls. Emma checked herself out in the mirror behind the mahogany bar. She wore one of the scariest wigs in her collection: a mousey brown shoulder-length mullet, long in the back, short on the top and sides. The dishwater-gray aviator glasses and nude lipstick went perfectly with her ratty flannel shirt and black high-rise acid-washed jeans, a keychain hanging from the belt loop. On her feet, Timberland boots. Emma was going for a New Jersey bar dyke look, and she was pretty sure she'd nailed it.

No man would notice her. Or, if he did, he'd pretend he didn't. In keeping with her outer toughness, she ordered a whiskey on the rocks.

'What kind?' asked the bartender, an older man, shaved head, with deep wrinkles in his forehead, big shoulders, and knotty knuckles.

'What do you recommend?'

'For you, Black Bush.' The seedy drunk a few seats down snickered.

Emma grinned inwardly. Her disguise was a success. 'My favorite,' she trilled. 'And let me buy you one. Old Grand Dad?'

The drunk snickered again. The bartender poured their drinks and drained his glass before Emma lifted hers. She put a twenty on the bar and waited.

Ten minutes later, Susan walked in, freshly showered, hair in a pony but damp on the ends. She glanced around at the room and its three patrons – two drunks with few teeth and the New Jersey dyke – before sitting by herself at a stool two down from Emma's. As she walked past, Emma made a kissy sound at her. Susan's petite nose crinkled and she looked away, uncomfortably out of her element.

This pleased Emma. If Susan didn't recognize her, Jeff

Bragg couldn't possibly. She swiveled on her stool toward Susan intending to identify herself, but Jeff Bragg chose that moment to show up. Emma immediately swiveled back around and hugged the bar, keeping her mullet low.

Out of the corner of her eye, she watched Jeff, the wild card. He seemed cool and calm. Relaxed and confident. This was not the same man she'd seen at the Four Seasons. It was almost as if he had multiple personalities. A paranoid schizophrenic? Emma was ready to dial 911 at a moment's notice. She hoped Susan's five minutes wouldn't drag to ten. Emma looked, but she couldn't tell if Jeff was carrying the gun.

Jeff went straight for his ex, like a wolf to a sheep. She stood up to hug him. Emma was impressed with her bravery – and her acting. Jeff put his cell phone on the bar and said, 'I'm expecting an important call.' Then he looked Susan over and added, 'You showed up. I'm surprised. After the way I treated you, I thought you'd never want to see me again.' Emma eavesdropped easily; they were sitting only a few stools down.

Susan said, 'I'm a forgiving person, Jeff.'

He smiled. 'You look great, Susan. I like your hair that way.'

'I always wear my hair like this,' she said, touching her ponytail.

'I remember it differently.'

'How?' asked Susan.

'Splayed across a pillow,' he said and leered.

Emma wished she could punch him. How on earth had Susan ever responded to this amateur Lothario? Was this patter exciting to anyone? William, on the other hand, was a skilled seducer. He was sexual but not salacious, flirtatious but not crass. Emma peered into her Black Bush and saw William's face in an ice cube. She picked it out of her glass and sucked on it. The whiskey burned; the ice cooled. She thought of William shifting and moaning underneath her.

'We did spend a lot of time in bed,' said Susan, snapping Emma's attention back to where it should be.

'I've got a big bed in my hotel room,' he said. 'Wanna see it?'

'Why did you break up with me?'

Jeff didn't have a quick line to follow that. The bartender saved him from answering.

'Two martinis,' Jeff ordered.

Gin was the last thing Susan needed after her afternoon soak in it. But the bartender started mixing. Jeff checked his cell; Susan twisted her rings. That's when the Good Witch realized: Susan was worried. She must've thought Emma'd blown her off.

Emma wanted to give her friend some comfort. She tried to catch Susan's eye. The martinis arrived and Jeff immediately put lip to glass.

Susan said, 'Forget I asked that question before.'

Jeff said, 'What question?'

'Why you broke up with me,' she repeated. 'What I really want to know is why you asked me out in the first place.'

Yes, Emma thought. That was the heart of it. Unless one understood the beginning, there was no way to reconcile the sad ending. The beginning of Emma and William's story was mistaken identity in a dark room, mutual stalking, and a one-afternoon stand in a hotel room. This wasn't anything like the classic progression of increasingly intimate dates, leading to a relationship based on trust, attraction and respect. She and William had no chance of turning their twisted courtship into love. Already, so many lies had been told. Emma finished her whiskey. A sliver of ice remained in the glass, nearly invisible, clinging to the side, stuck.

I am that sliver, thought Emma. She sighed heavily.

Jeff turned to look at Emma. She smiled weakly at him. He said, 'What are you looking at?'

Emma said, 'Nothing much.'

Susan said, 'Jeff, I'm over here.'

He turned back toward his date and said, 'I asked you out because I thought you were hot. You're an incredibly sexy woman.'

The petite lawyer was cute. But hot? 'That's simply not true,' said Susan.

Emma couldn't help chuckling at her friend's honest self-appraisal.

Jeff sprang off his stool. 'What is your problem?' he demanded of Emma, putting his nose an inch from hers. She was reminded of his hot rubber stench. Staring into his malevolent eyes, Emma saw a hair-trigger temper. The guy was dangerous. She reached for the phone in her pocket to dial 911.

He said, 'I'm talking to you, Butch. You were spying on my private conversation.'

'I wasn't spying on you,' said Emma. 'You're paranoid.'

Susan had him by the arm. 'Sit down, Jeff.'

Not knowing (or caring about) his own strength, Jeff

shook Susan off with enough force to send the petite brunette tumbling onto the floor.

Emma rushed toward her friend, but Jeff shoved her back against the bar. She sputtered in reaction. It was an unfortunate accident that an errant bead of saliva flew out of her mouth and struck Jeff on the cheek. His eyes blazed. The Good Witch put up her dukes, optimistically and pathetically, and closed her eyes, waiting for the blow to strike.

But it never came. When she opened her eyes, Jeff was twisting like a hooked trout in the arms of Old Grand Dad.

Susan was back on her feet, pleading to the bartender, 'Don't hurt him.'

Emma said, 'Hurt him!'

The bartender said, 'I have a no-tolerance policy with this shit.'

'What about her?' cried Jeff, meaning Emma. 'She spit on me!'

'She didn't start it,' said the bartender. 'Besides, she reminds me of my daughter.' The bartender turned toward Emma. 'She drinks Black Bush, too.'

'A woman of taste,' said Emma.

'Jules, call the cops,' he said, saving Emma from doing it.

The snickering drunk hopped off the bar stool and ambled toward the door. He swung it open, whistled, and yelled, 'Yo!'

Old Grand Dad said, 'Police station's right next door.'

Out of the bar window, Emma saw two uniformed cops moseying up to the pub entrance. Jules waved them in.

Susan said to Emma, 'Incidentally, that wig does nothing for you.'

Emma laughed. 'Took you long enough to recognize me.'

Susan smiled. 'I knew it was you the whole time.'

The uniformed cops were talking to the bartender, trying to relieve him of belligerent Jeff who, in his flailing, kicked one of New York's finest in the ankle. Eventually, they slapped on the cuffs, and the two cops (one limping), dragged Jeff out of the bar, across the street, and up to the entrance of the Church Street police station.

The two women followed.

'We should call Hoff,' said Emma.

Susan nodded. She was unnervingly quiet, considering what had just happened.

Emma asked, 'Did you get what you came for?'

'No,' said Susan. 'I doubt five minutes of questioning – or five hours – would satisfy me. There are just too many things about our relationship that don't make sense. And it's bugging me.'

'Sorry I opened the can,' said Emma. 'Of bugs.'

Jeff, meanwhile, was screaming, 'I need my phone! Give me my fucking phone!'

Susan said, 'He was waiting for an important call.'

'He's going to miss it,' lamented Emma.

'We'll have to take a message,' said Susan, holding up a tiny black cell.

Thursday morning. Emma made a bright start to the day at the police station, where she'd spent much of the night before. She was at her first-ever bona fide police lineup. Six men stood on the other side of a two-way mirror. It was the ultimate invisibility. She could see them, but they couldn't see her. She loved it. She thought briefly of a career in law enforcement. Briefly.

'Turn to the right,' barked Detective March, the cop who'd interviewed Hoff in the hospital, to the men in the lineup. Detective Marsh had one lazy eye and one roving. The rover was focused on Emma's boobs.

'Remind me,' said the detective. 'Who are you again?'

'I'm the woman who was assaulted at Nancy's Whiskey Bar last night.'

'The description of that woman does not match you,' he said. 'Not by a long shot.'

'It was her,' said Susan. 'I was on the scene.'

'Witness?'

'And attorney,' she said. 'I'm representing both Ms Hutch and Mr Centry.'

The detective said into the intercom, 'Turn to your left.'

The six men did as they were told. Hoff took hold of Susan's hand and said, 'It's great having a lawyer in the family.'

'Recognize any of them?' asked Detective Marsh.

'Number three,' said Hoff, which Marsh repeated into the intercom. The cop in the lineup room nudged Jeff Bragg. He moved up a couple of steps.

Emma said, 'Can he say in a menacing voice, "Back off or I'll kill you, motherfucker."'

The detective switched on the intercom. 'Say, "Back off or I'll kill you, motherfucker."'

Jeff repeated lazily, 'Back. Off. Or. I'll. Kill. You. Mother. Fucker.'

'That wasn't very menacing,' said Emma.

'More menacingly,' said the detective.

Jeff sighed. 'I really need to make a phone call.'

'Say it,' barked the dick.

Jeff practically chewed his own cheeks off. Looking straight into the mirror, right where Emma stood, he said, 'I know you're there, Connie Quivers. Back off or I swear to God I'll kill you. Mother. Fucker.'

The detective asked, 'Who's Connie Quivers?'

'Sounds like a porn star name,' said Emma. 'Can he snarl like a dog now? Or snort like a bull?'

Marsh said, 'You're pushing it.'

Hoff said, 'I'm almost positive number three is the man

who mugged me. But I need him to recite what I've written on this piece of paper.'

'Menacingly?' asked Detective Marsh.

'Solemnly,' said Hoff.

The detective stared hard at Hoff. The battered book editor returned the look with the convincing Connecticut comportment that only old money could buy. Taking the paper out of Hoff's hand, the detective left the room and returned forthwith. The cop in the other room delivered the note to Jeff.

The prime suspect glanced down at it and said, 'This is bullshit. I'm not reading it.'

'How'd you like another hour in the rubber room?' asked the dick into the intercom. To Susan, he said, 'You didn't hear that.'

'After this, I get to make a phone call?' asked Jeff.

'Just read it,' said the dick into the microphone. 'With solemnity.'

Jeff cleared his throat. 'I'm sorry for the way I treated you, Susan. I took advantage of your kindness and your faith that all people are, at heart, good. But I'm not good. I'm a heartless thug, and I don't deserve your love. You should forgive yourself for caring about me, stop doubting your judgment, and get on with your life.' Jeff lowered the notepaper. 'I'm not reading it again.'

Hoff turned to Susan. 'Was that solemn enough?'

Susan said to him, 'You are the sweetest, most thoughtful man in the world.' She threw her arms around him.

'Watch the ribs!' he bellowed.

While they kissed, Emma and the detective smiled

awkwardly at each other and then gave thorough attention to the tops of their shoes.

Hoff said, 'Detective, that's him. He's the man who mugged me.'

The detective said into the intercom. 'Take them away.'

As the six men in the lineup were prodded out, the detective led Hoff, Susan, and Emma into another room at the station. Hoff had a ream of paperwork to do. Emma had to complete another pile (on top of the pile she'd filed the night before). An hour later, the trio left Church Street and walked the block back to the Tribeca Grand. Hoff wanted to pack up and go home. With Jeff detained, they agreed that it would be safe.

He packed and brought his duffle to the lobby to pay his bill. Hoff said, 'I feel bittersweet about leaving.' He took Susan's hand. 'Will you come to my place tonight after work?'

'I might be late,' she said. 'Should I bring dinner?'

While they sorted out the logistics, Emma watched them, appreciated them like a work of art. They were beautiful to behold. An advertisement for coupledom. The words 'love is the greatest good . . . love is all you need . . . if you stop trying . . . if you give up the quest . . . you might as well be dead' crawled across her mind like a news zipper on the side of a building. A bell rang in Emma's noggin. A bright, round sound, like a summons, a siren call, a wake-up call. So loud, so clear, Emma almost thought it was real.

'What's *that*?' asked Hoff.

'You can hear it, too?' asked Emma.

'The whole lobby can hear it,' said Susan, reaching into the pocket of her overcoat and producing a tiny black cell that was ringing at full volume and vibrating. 'It's Jeff's phone,' she said, handing it to Hoff. 'Answer it.'

Hoff said, 'Me?'

'You're a man,' said Susan. 'Let's find out who Jeff was so eager to talk to.'

Emma was curious, too. 'What's the harm?' she asked.

Hoff took the phone, opened it, and hit talk. He leaned down so Emma could listen too, and said, 'Yes?'

'What took you so long, shithead?' asked the voice, male, older. 'Never mind, write this down.'

Hoff grabbed a pen from the concierge desk. He cradled the phone against his shoulder and scribbled on a registry card.

'Got it,' Hoff said into the phone. He'd written GCNB 675688655. Under it, another number: 87988653.

The phone said, 'You need the password, asshole.'

'Ready,' said Hoff.

The man said, 'The password is the big day. You get it, moron?'

'Yes, thank you.'

'Fucking faggot,' said the voice and then he clicked off.

'I know this might sound crazy,' Hoff said, 'but I could swear I've heard that voice before.'

'In your nightmares?' asked Emma. 'GCNB. Maybe it stands for Grouchy Curmudgeon Needs Beeping.'

Hoff said, 'Let me check something.'

Emma watched as Hoff fiddled with the phone, finding the incoming call history. The phone had received only one call. And Hoff read the number aloud. It had a 203 area code. Connecticut.

'I know that number,' said Hoff.

'Who is it?' asked Susan.

'One second,' he said, hitting the button to dial the number.

Emma listened with Hoff. A message came on. 'You have reached an outgoing number at the Glatting Correctional Facility. Incoming calls will not be connected.'

Hoff turned off the phone. 'Just as I thought. It's Glatting. A low-security prison in rural Connecticut.'

Emma asked, 'You have friends in low-security places?'

'Just one,' said Hoff. 'You're not going to believe this. I can't quite believe it myself.'

'Who are you talking about?' demanded Emma for the last time.

'Seymour Lankey,' he said.

'Who?' asked Emma. Then, 'Oh.'

'Of Riptron?' asked Susan, her face darkening.

'My star author,' said Hoff.

'So there is a connection between Jeff Bragg and Riptron. What could it possibly be?' asked Emma.

Susan and Hoff said in unison, 'Money.'

'The reward for recovering the stolen pension fund is one percent,' said Susan several hours later. 'One percent of six hundred million is six million.'

Hoff, Susan, and Emma were sitting around Hoff's teak dining room table in his Gramercy Park apartment where they'd been all day long, theorizing, Googling, and eating Chinese takeout.

'Six million?' repeated Hoff. He had a wad of General Tso's chicken in his mouth and was having trouble swallowing the food – and the potential riches. 'Lankey insists in *Smoke and Mirrors* that he didn't hide the money,' he said. 'Dooey, Fleecum & Howe accounting books showed . . .'

'The Dooey, Fleecum team is just as guilty as Lankey,' said Susan. 'The Verity Foundation's come up with a six hundred million dollar shortfall. Most likely tucked away in an offshore bank – such as the Grand Cayman National Bank – hidden from the IRS, FBI, SEC, and reward hunters.'

'That would be us,' said Emma, licking her chops. A windfall of voluminous wealth gave her an enormous appetite, and she consumed a mountain of pork fried rice, pork fried dumplings, and moo-sho pork. 'Tonight, I am what I eat,' she announced. 'Is there any more greedy pig on this table?'

'Nothing left but us chickens,' said Hoff, holding up a chunk.

Since Emma's savings had been stolen by Lankey, the idea of stealing it back, from under the imprisoned CEO's nose, was the ultimate redemption. Then again, she thought having successful sex would be redeeming too, and, if anything, it had left her even more unsettled.

Emma said, 'If we stole the money back, would that be wrong?'

'Let's put morality aside,' said Susan.

'Good answer,' said Emma. 'So how do we steal the money?'

Susan shot her a look of contempt, irritation, and frustration. The lawyer had had a hard afternoon. In the timetable they'd constructed, Susan deduced that Jeff had initially approached her around the same time that the

Verity Foundation started investigating his accounting firm's liability in the Riptron case. Jeff had been a spy himself, for Dooey, Fleecum & Howe. Susan remembered that she had caught him going through her briefcase a few times and that he asked a lot of seemingly innocent questions about the investigation.

If nothing else, Susan now knew why Jeff had asked her out in the first place. Apparently, he'd graduated from stooge to a more lucrative position, working for Lankey.

Emma said, 'One thing I don't get. Why does Lankey need Jeff Bragg to be his money donkey?'

'Money *mule*,' corrected Hoff. 'Lankey must have recruited Bragg to help him set up the account either before he went to prison or after. Lankey can't access it himself. He can't place international calls from Glatting. He needs someone else to access the money for him.'

Susan said, 'Am I the only one eating the steamed vegetables?'

'You bet you are!' said Emma. 'What next?' she asked, her excitement mounting. 'I want that reward money. I deserve it. I've got this coming to me, fair and square. Six million, you say? Split three ways. Anyone?'

'You know it's two million,' said Susan. 'And I would give my share to the reparations fund. The Riptron employees and shareholders deserve it, not me.'

'As one of those shareholders, I'll keep my third,' said Emma. She'd pay off her mortgage. Or maybe she'd retire to an island somewhere – taking a page from Jeff Bragg's cooked book – and stay far away from any kind of threat, be it financial or sexual.

'We should tell our theory to the authorities,' said Hoff.

'Give them these bank account numbers.' He waved the scribbled on registry card from the hotel.

'No way,' said Emma. 'This is our discovery. I've been swindled out of that money once already. The feds will cheat us out of everything. Even with you watching, Susan.'

'It's all academic,' said Hoff. 'We don't know the password. The gentleman at the Grand Cayman bank said we needed the account number and the password.'

'Let's just tell them "the big day,"' said Emma.

'Three wrong guesses and they freeze the account,' said Hoff, finishing the chicken chow fun. 'Then no one can get the money.'

'So what is "the big day"? When Lankey gets released from prison ten years from now?' asked Emma. 'The book release date?'

'The book comes out November 1, 2006. 11-1-2006?' said Hoff. 'It might be worth a try. But I'd hate to waste a guess. I'm not sure Lankey cares too much about the book anyway. He only did it to pay his legal fees.'

Susan nibbled a broccoli floret. 'I want to check the Riptron figures again. Tomorrow, at the office.'

Emma drooled, 'Do you think the missing amount is *more* than six hundred million?'

The brunette nodded hesitantly. 'I just want to check.'

Emma pictured herself splashing nude in an ocean of hundred dollar bills. Her ivory breasts bobbing in waves of rolling green.

Hoff was watching her. 'I'd like to know what you're thinking.'

'Have a look,' said Emma. She touched his arm and sent him a picture that was worth a million dollars.

He blushed furiously.

Susan said, 'Stop that!'

Emma dropped her hand. The food was gone (except for the veggies). The conversation was concluded. She sat back in her chair, woozy with greed, MSG, and fatigue. Yesterday had been the longest day in the history of womankind. First the payoff from Daphne, the limo interrogation with Marcie, sex with William, the Nancy's near brawl with Jeff, the police station after that. And today, the lineup, the all-day Google fest at Hoff's. Emma was exhausted. She had to shut down, get unconscious. A good guest, she dumped the empty containers in a garbage bag and wiped the table. She doled out the hugs and kisses and left.

It wasn't too long a walk home from Gramercy to the Village. The brisk October air forced her to move quickly. She'd had a hell of a week. She saved her apartment. Had sex. Reclaiming her lost savings would be the ultimate redemption trifecta. Everything was looking up.

The street was crowded with people coming home from work on a weekday night. The ordinary sidewalk congestion produced a mechanical hum to her ears. But, on top of that, she detected the stutter of arrhythmic footsteps. Scampering, then stopping, then scampering again. As if she were being followed.

Her neck hairs stood at attention.

Emma turned slowly, scanning for a suspicious stranger. Finding no one, she faced west and walked faster. She had more than a dozen blocks to go before she reached Waverly Place.

The footsteps again. Closer this time.

Spinning around, Emma thought she saw the gray tail of an overcoat swing behind a bus shelter. She took one step toward it. Would have taken another, but a cab careened to the curb, only inches from where she stood. It disgorged a woman in a big hat and Emma immediately took her place.

'Waverly and Sixth,' she said. They rolled past the bus shelter. No one was there.

As soon as she got into her apartment, Emma double-bolted her door. She leaned against it and exhaled. 'You're paranoid,' she said.

She nearly jumped out of her skin when the phone rang.

'Hello?' she asked when she answered.

'Emma Hutch?'

'Yes?' she said.

'Detective Marsh. From the lineup this morning.'

'Hello, detective,' she said. Was he calling for a date? Of all the unprofessional, misguided . . .

'Jeff Bragg escaped from prison an hour ago,' he said.

For a ridiculous second, Emma was relieved he wasn't asking her out. 'Shit!' she said. 'I mean, fuck!'

'Bragg was out of control in lockdown, screaming about a missing cell phone. He refused to eat or talk to a lawyer. We sent in a public defender. Bragg attacked him, took the man's overcoat and hat, stole the case file, and got away.'

'What color was the overcoat?'

'Standard overcoat color.'

That helped. 'The stolen file included what, exactly?'

'The paperwork on the case,' said Detective Marsh. 'Your name and address were in there.'

She said, 'And Hoffman Centry's home address too.'

'Under the circumstances, I think I should come over to your place. For your protection,' he said.

She said, 'It's okay. I'll call someone.'

'A boyfriend?'

'A friend.'

'Do you have a boyfriend?'

'Detective,' she said, 'I'm anorgasmic.'

'Do you have a boyfriend or not?' he asked.

William's face popped into her mind. 'I'm not sure.'

Marsh took that in his stride. 'We're out in force looking for Bragg, and I'll keep you posted. I'm calling Mr Centry now.'

'Good. Thanks,' she said, hanging up.

Why had she refused his protection? Didn't she need it? Wasn't tolerating Marsh's roving eye a small price to pay for security? It wasn't that Emma was embarrassed to admit she was alone. She wasn't ashamed.

'I wish William were here,' she said to herself. 'Right now.'

A bang on the door at her back, so hard, Emma bounced. She ran from the sound and hid behind her white couch. The bang continued: thud, thud, thud.

Jeff had come for her. He'd sworn to God that he'd get her, and now he was going to keep his promise. Hands shaking, Emma reached for her phone, fumbled with the receiver. Before she could dial, a voice behind the door said, 'Emma? Are you there? Let me in.'

An English accent. Emma rushed toward the door,

flung it open, and sank into William Dearborn's arms like quicksand.

'You're here!' she said.

'You're glad to see me?' he asked.

'I wished for you and you appeared.'

'I appear like magic and you disappear,' he said, hugging her back. 'Do you realize that you send mixed signals?'

'Forget everything I've ever said before.' She dragged him into the living room and guided him to the couch. 'Come in! Sit! What can I get you? Something to eat? How about a drink?'

He squinted at her and then checked out her apartment. 'I take it you like white,' he observed.

'My own slice of heaven,' she said. 'You were expecting pink?'

'If anything, black,' he said. 'No trace of cat in the air.'

'I don't have a cat.'

'I thought you did.'

'You look gorgeous,' she said. 'The hour we spent together at the hotel was incredible, William. I loved every second of it.' The truth had been scared out of her.

'It was mind blowing,' he said. 'Mind exploding.'

Mind exploding. That phrase was like sandpaper on her already raw nerves. 'Oh, shit,' she said, but the hot spring of tears had already started flowing.

'What did I say?' asked William. 'Are you all right?' He had her sit down on the couch next to him. He put his arm around her and she felt comforted.

Emma said, 'Do me one favor.'

'Anything.'

'Don't use the phrase "mind blowing" or "mind exploding" around me.'

'Never again,' he said.

'My mother died of a brain aneurism,' she explained. 'Eight years ago. She and my dad – and a thousand other people – were on the number three train when it got stuck underground with the lights out for an hour. Mom had claustrophobia, and she freaked. Raving, clawing at the doors, screaming. And then the blood vessel popped. When she collapsed, the other people in the car applauded because she'd finally shut up. But when they realized she was dead, they all started screaming and clawing to get out. My dad said it was a living hell. He left the city as soon as he could. He's been a different person since then, lives a completely different life now. I lost him that night too.'

William listened, kept his arm tight around her. He said, 'I bet you don't take the subway much.'

She laughed – on the inside. 'Never. I walk or taxi. That's one reason I hate to leave the Village. I can't afford to pay for expensive cab rides.'

'You'll never pay for a cab again,' said William.

'I look a lot like her. And we have other . . . things in common. I've never told anyone this before – I didn't even realize it myself until I met you – I've been struggling to keep my body and mind in control, as if I could prevent an aneurism by force of will. Sex is all about abandon, and I simply couldn't allow myself to do it. I was subconsciously sabotaging myself. Preventing myself from letting go of . . . whatever one has to let go of to have good sex.'

'And this struggle has been going on for eight years?' he asked.

She nodded. How had she not noticed that her sex life died right after Anise did? For all her super sensitivity, Emma thought, she could be awfully dense.

William said, 'Her death really screwed you up.'

'Yeah, but I was screwed up already,' she said.

'My mom died too. Have I told you that?'

He had, at the rose garden, to an old lady. But had he, when Emma was herself? She said, 'You mentioned something.'

They sat together in silence for a while.

'My arm is falling asleep,' he said finally.

She stood up. 'I'm going to splash my face, freshen up. You can turn on the TV. Check your email. Make calls. Just please don't leave.'

'I'm not going anywhere,' he said, kissing her tenderly. 'And I will check my email, if you're sure you don't mind.'

She booted up the iMac on her desk for him and went in back. She had never showered and shaved more quickly and thoroughly. She wanted every inch of her body to smell like lavender. Emma felt high from the hot water, the scents. The ever-changing moods – anxiety, relief, joy, sadness, contentment, in a span of fifteen minutes – had the effect of a designer drug. She was euphoric.

After toweling off, Emma anointed her skin with moisturizer and slipped on a black rayon scoop-necked nightgown. Sexy and sweet. She also put on a pair of black fuzzy slippers. Fluffing her wet waves as best she could, Emma flounced into the living room.

William was at her desk. She looked at him with gratitude and joy. He looked at her with anger – not the lust and warmth she was expecting.

'Where did you get these?' he asked.

He held up the three portraits Victor took of Daphne. The air went out of her lungs.

'Who took them?' he asked.

'No one you know,' she said.

He turned the pictures over and saw Victor's sticker. William read, 'Victor Armour. Ann Jingo's new boyfriend.'

'What a coincidence!' said Emma.

'I've had these images in my head for days,' said William. 'I've spent most of today painting this one.' He held up the red picture of Daphne as a flame. 'Do you know who the woman is in this picture?'

'A model?' she asked.

'It's Daphne Wittfield. The woman I just hired to do the advertising for ArtSpeak.'

'She must be a friend of Victor's.'

'Victor, who is, according to Ann, a close friend of yours.'

'Another coincidence!' said Emma.

'Explain to me how a photograph dated seven days ago could be the exact image that popped into my head three days ago. I thought this image belonged to me.'

'Do images belong to anyone, really?' asked Emma rhetorically.

'Yes. They do,' said William. 'These belong to Victor Armour. They have his sticker on them. What I want to know is: why do you have prints? How did the pictures get into my head? And what do you and Daphne Wittfield have to do with each other?'

Feeling rather foolish now in her nightgown, Emma opened her mouth to lie and paused. She'd been lying and hiding and disguising herself for their entire relationship. If they were to go forward – and Emma put herself out on the thin limb of admitting she wanted that – William had to know everything about her. The telegraphopathy, The Good Witch, Inc. Her connection to Daphne.

So Emma told him. She started at the top, and kept going until she'd hit bottom. Throughout the telling, William listened, asking relevant questions, showing nary a hint of anger or betrayal or hurt.

When Emma finished, she said, 'That's it. The truth. No more lies between us.'

'Daphne said she was in love with me?' he asked. 'I'm shocked to hear it.'

'I only take on clients with the purest intentions.'

'Oh, her intentions were pure,' said William. 'But they weren't about love. Fifteen thousand is a drop in the bucket of the ArtSpeak ad budget. You say she art-directed these shots?'

'Victor and Daphne collaborated.'

'Does Ann know about all this?'

'None of it,' she said.

'May I keep this one?' William held up the red photo of Daphne.

'Take,' said Emma.

'So let me get the timeline straight here,' he said. 'You slept with me on the same day Daphne paid you off?' Emma nodded. 'How could you betray your client like that?'

'She betrayed me,' said Emma, knowing for sure now that Daphne used her to get the ArtSpeak job.

'Daphne paid you in full, with a bonus,' he said. 'She

kept up her end. Your ethical lines are a bit blurry, Emma.'

She felt panic rise in her throat. 'If you look at it logically, all of my choices make perfect sense.'

'Leaving me in the hotel room yesterday,' he said. 'What was the sense in that?'

'I was jealous and confused,' she said. 'It was rude and thoughtless and I'm sorry.'

'Are you lying now?'

'Don't be an asshole,' she said.

'You're not a Good Witch,' he said. 'You thrive on deceit. You say everyone is out to swindle you, but you're the one tricking other people for a living. Have you ever considered the feelings of the men you manipulate? I can tell you, as one of your simple-minded dupes, I don't like it at all. And what of your clients? Women you lure into a false sense of hope with your sneakery. And then you absolve yourself of responsibility when the relationship falls apart? This is using your power for good?'

'The greatest good,' she mumbled.

'You're lying to yourself,' he said.

'Dozens of my clients have gotten married. I still get Christmas cards from some of them. And,' she added, '*sneakery* is not a word.'

He said, 'I really liked that old lady in the rose garden. I even bought myself a dozen red roses the next day to remind me of her – you. But that was a lie, too. You and I haven't shared a single honest moment.'

'Yesterday in the hotel room,' she said, daring to move closer to him to see if he would resist. She reached out her hand.

'Don't touch me,' he said.

Emma drew her hand back, scalded by the rebuke. 'What about our connection?' she asked.

'I'm breaking it,' he said, and then he walked out of the door.

He'd been searching for someone he didn't want to flee from, just as she'd been searching for someone who wouldn't flee from her. As his footsteps in the hallway collided like steel balls in her ears, Emma realized that she honestly loved him – and that he honestly despised her.

She flopped on the couch in her sexy black cutie-pie outfit. She'd bought roses the day after their garden talk, too. To remind her of him. He'd told her that night he went berserk when lied to. She had fair warning, but she couldn't stop piling on the bullshit.

Emma would have found it amusing (were it not so miserable) that she'd been paranoid (what she accused Jeff of being) about being cheated (her bugaboo), when all the while she'd been cheating other people left and right (make that wrong): her targets, her clients, William. She'd cheated herself, certainly. What's more, her ethical lines had been deemed blurry.

'Great!' she said. 'Now I have to rethink my whole fucking existence.'

All at once, Emma got a throbbing head, a roiling stomach, stabbing back pain, and a dull ache in the center of her being – one that couldn't be cured with an over-the-counter remedy. She took whatever she could find in her medicine cabinet, got in bed, and tried to sleep, her slippery smooth thighs rubbing together, reminding her of what William would not be touching tonight or ever again.

23

'You look bad,' said Deirdre at Oeuf the next morning, Friday, Halloween Eve. 'I was going to say "different", like you got laid or something. But then I saw you up close.'

'Coffee, black. Eggs, charred. Toast, burnt,' said Emma, hiding in her biggest, blackest sunglasses, hair in a tight ponytail, black turtleneck and black trousers.

'Don't *tell* me,' said the waitress, playfully holding out her hand. 'Give me a hit.'

'No more hits,' said Emma. 'I'm rethinking my whole fucking existence.'

The waitress retracted her arm, miffed. 'This is a family restaurant,' she said. 'Watch your language.'

Emma glanced around the place and at its three gay couples and two single middle-aged female diners. 'Have you seen Victor?' she asked. He was already fifteen minutes late. And she'd had the decency of showing up early, meaning ten minutes late.

'Nope,' said Deirdre.

Emma's appetite had left her along with William Dearborn last night. 'I'll wait.'

She didn't have to wait long. Two minutes later, Victor strolled in. He was also in black up to his mandible, as if they'd called each other. He saw Emma and said, 'You look positively morose.' To Deirdre, he said, 'And you are gorgeous. I'll have the usual. Eggcept, make it sausage instead of bacon.'

'That *is* the usual,' said Deirdre.

'You have an eggceptional memory.'

'Do something with her,' said the waitress, pointing her pencil at Emma. 'She's frightening the customers.'

'Okay, what's up?' asked Victor, now settled in his chair, his arms folded on the table in front of him. 'You look different, by the way.'

'Is what we do wrong? Are we making impossible promises to the clients and duping the men?'

'A crisis of consciousness?' he asked. 'That is so unlike you, Emma.'

'Have I been lying to everyone – including myself?' she asked.

Victor shook his head. 'We dupe the men. We make promises to the women. And sometimes the duping and promising turns into a lasting love both parties are grateful for. Sometimes it doesn't. The men are no worse for the effort. And the women are out money they can afford to spend ten times over – and do, at Barney's – any day of the week. Your intentions are honest. You work hard. You have no reason to question yourself.'

'There is one reason,' she said. 'William Dearborn

called me a bad witch and accused me of sneakery. In hindsight, I see that it wasn't a good idea to tell him about Daphne's case.'

'Why the hell did you do that?' said Victor, shocked she'd break confidentiality.

'I had to,' she moaned. 'We had sex. It was great, and that freaked me out. Flailing in confusion, I was honest with him. And let me just say, the truth is *not* all it's cracked up to be. I should have stuck with anorgasmia.'

Victor's eyes, meanwhile, had bugged. '*You had sex with William Dearborn?*' he whispered reverently. 'Was he amazing? Can I touch the hand that touched his . . . wait a minute. You had sex – like a normal person? Dearborn didn't run away screaming? And what is "sneakery"? Is that like buggery? Those mad Englishmen. They have all those mysterious words.'

Emma shook her head, then dropped it into her hands. 'William is only part English. He's a barmy half-Brit. The rest of him is sane, stubborn American,' she said. 'He found your photographs of Daphne in my desk. I had to explain. He liked the pictures, by the way.'

Victor squealed. 'I've just died,' he said. 'Tell me his exact words.'

'He said, "They're good."'

'Was it the composition or the technique?'

'He liked the art direction.'

'Did you tell him I did it?'

'I said you and Daphne collaborated,' she said. Seeing his fallen face, she added, 'You did collaborate!'

'I hate your truth kick,' he groused.

Deirdre appeared with their plates. Emma looked

down at her breakfast. As requested, the toast was blackened. Hard, dry, overheated, tasteless, useless, and unappetizing.

I am that toast, she thought.

The eggs looked okay, but Emma wasn't hungry anyway. Victor, meanwhile, could have a steel girder lodged in his head and still manage to eat.

Emma took a sip of her hot, black coffee. Then she said, 'I have enough cash for a couple months to think things over. I need a change. I might shut down The Good Witch, Inc. Try to find a normal job.'

Victor said, 'Remember the success stories.'

'The women of New York will be better off without me,' said Emma, removing her glasses to rub her eyes. 'I'll think of something to do. Besides hand holding.'

'But that's what you do best,' said Victor, taking hers. 'I hate seeing you like this. Dearborn is wrong. You do help people. His ego was dented, and he took it out on you. And that pisses me off. Who does he think he is? Dearborn is a fucking idiot! He was lucky to be in the same room with you. You're more gifted than ten of him. I'm starting to question everything I've thought about that shithead. He's a fraud. A sham!'

Victor's phone rang. He answered. 'Hello? Yes? *Yes, sir!* Yes, sir! I'm flattered. I'm honored. Yes. One hour. I can't tell you what this means to me. Yes, okay. Bye, and thanks!' He hung up, eyes aglow.

Emma said, 'Speaking of the fucking idiot, fraud, sham?'

Victor stared moonily at the phone. 'It was him,' he said. 'William Dearborn. He's doing an art book. He needs to hire an art director. Emma! He wants to talk to me about it!'

Emma asked, 'Did he mention a publisher?'

'Ransom House,' said Victor.

So Hoff had gotten his book deal with William after all. When had he managed that?

'I've got to go,' said Victor, leaving a ten on the table. 'I have to be at Dearborn International in one hour.'

'You'll be wonderful, Victor,' said Emma. 'As long as you don't make any puns.'

'My puns are my charm,' he said. 'You'll be okay?'

'No,' pouted Emma.

Victor said, 'Ann's probably heard the whole story by now. Which means she knows I obscured the truth a bit.'

'Will she be angry?' asked Emma.

'Probably. But she's forgiving, and I didn't lie to her about *me*. I lied to her about *you*.'

'I cause indirect deceit,' moaned Emma.

'Why don't you go to the bank and count all your new money?' he suggested. 'That'll cheer you up.'

A bright idea. 'I will,' she said.

'What do you mean the check's been cancelled?' asked Emma, ripping off her sunglasses.

'According to my screen,' said Mr Cannery, bow tie yellow today, 'The check was cancelled at nine o'clock this morning, before it cleared. But for depositing a cancelled check, we will have to deduct sixty dollars from your account for processing.'

'But you said that you hadn't processed the check,' said Emma, in a rage.

'We'd only just begun,' said Mr Cannery.

Emma groaned. 'Now that song will be stuck in my head for days. *Thanks a lot.*'

'I'm very sorry to have to tell you this, Ms Hutch. But you're overdrawn again. You have only three days before the next mortgage payment is due. Bet you're glad for the extra day now.'

Emma got the feeling Mr Cannery, who got off on the green stuff, also got off on a customer falling into the red. 'Can I get a short-term loan?' she asked.

He shook his head gravely. 'We could give you an annuity, but you'd have to turn over your property to us. And since, forgive me for saying so, it's likely we'll take possession in the next few days anyway, I doubt anyone here would bother doing the paperwork.'

Emma's amber eyes blazed with fury. Mr Cannery leaned back in his chair and held up the elbow of self-defense. 'I'm just the messenger,' he said defensively.

She stormed out of the bank and flipped open her cell phone. She frantically dialed Daphne's work number.

'Ms Wittfield is not here,' said Natasha. 'She's in Times Square overseeing the billboard unveiling.'

'What billboard?'

As if reading from a press release, Natasha said, 'Twenty stories, two hundred feet high, the biggest billboard in history, of Marcie Skimmer for SlimBurn diet pills. The unveiling is at noon. But I wouldn't go if I were you.'

'Lunchtime crowds?'

'Ms Wittfield got a call first thing this morning from William Dearborn. He fired her. Ms Wittfield blames you, and she's been cursing your name and spitting on the carpet,' she said. 'Which I have to clean up. And let me tell you, my mother didn't scrub toilets for eighteen hours a day so I could grow up to blot spittle.'

'She didn't,' said Emma of Natasha's mother.

'That's right. She didn't. Mom is a marketing VP at NBC. I spit on the carpet and curse her for refusing to get me a job there. I'm five months out of college and stuck dabbing a carpet with tissue paper because of something you did. But I'm grateful to you, Emma Hutch, for reminding me of the huge advances black people have made in America today.'

'Where'd you go to college?' asked Emma, agreeing that Natasha was meant for better things.

'Columbia,' said Natasha.

'What was your major?'

'Bitter irony,' she said and hung up.

Natasha must have graduated with top honors.

Despite Natasha's warning, Emma had to find Daphne. There was the small chance that William merely fired Daphne and didn't reveal Emma's breach of confidentiality. In which case Emma could plead for a small part of her fee. The situation was hopeless, but Emma had to try. No other choice.

Times Square was a long slog from the Village. Two miles. But she had an hour and didn't want to pay for a cab. She started walking.

As she hoofed, she imagined Daphne's expression when William said, 'You're fired.' She couldn't help smiling. She would have loved to hear the whole conversation. She heard William's voice. Saw his face. Touched his face. Licked his face. She pictured him on the phone, naked as usual, sitting in an executive desk chair, feet propped on his desk, saying, 'And one more thing, Daphne. I never wanted you. There is only one woman I want.' He hung up, looked at Emma, breaking the fourth wall, and shouted, 'You'd better apologize, or I might not forgive you.'

Honk. A white stretch limo pulled up alongside her. The back door opened, and Sherman Hollow, Esq., Marcie's lawyer and adviser, stepped out.

'Pleasure to see you again,' he remarked, strolling alongside her. The limo cruised along, keeping pace with the walkers. This was her third limo rendezvous in a week. Her neighbors must be getting suspicious.

'I changed my mind about the twenty thousand,' said Emma.

'Twenty thousand?' he asked.

'What you offered me for info on Daphne Wittfield.'

'That offer is off the table. If you please,' he said, gesturing toward the limo. She hesitated. He begged softly, 'You've got to get in there. I can't be alone with them for another second.'

Curious, Emma peered inside the limo door.

Sprawled on the commodious backseat, Marcie looked strangely plebeian. Her platinum hair flat and unbrushed, she wore a plain white T-shirt, a pair of cargo pants, and sneakers. No makeup that Emma could see, but then again, most of her face was eclipsed by the large dreadlocked head of sculptor Alfie Delado, also in a white T-shirt, cargo pants, and sneakers. They were sucking each other's tonsils.

'They've been like this for two days. And I've had to

listen to it,' whispered Sherman. 'Marcie insisted I sit in a chair outside Mr Delado's Brooklyn hovel – on a decrepit landing – in case I was needed.'

'Needed for what?'

'Food,' he said scornfully. 'I also had to arrange a clothing delivery from Old Navy.' He spat out the last two words with disgust.

'Emma!' trilled Marcie suddenly.

The two lovers disentangled.

Emma waved at them. 'I see you found each other.'

'We have to be in Times Square in an hour for my billboard unveiling,' said Marcie. 'Want to come?'

'You bet I do!' said Emma, getting in. Sherman joined her on the bench facing Alfie and Marcie. 'I was headed that way myself.'

Alfie held out his hand. They shook. He said, 'I have you to thank for sending Marcie to me?'

'Don't thank me,' said Emma.

'We do,' said Marcie. 'Without you, we never would have met.'

'But you had met,' said Emma. 'At Alfie's art exhibit.'

'How do you know that?' asked the blond. Emma stammered. She'd been in disguise that night, of course. Thankfully, Marcie cut in. 'It doesn't matter. I wasn't open to Alfie then. That was the old Marcie. The superficial, money- and appearance-obsessed Marcie. The one who didn't understand anything. But now I do. Thanks to Alfie.'

The limo set a slow course uptown. Facing backward was making Emma slightly sick. She said, 'What, exactly, is your new understanding?'

Sherman scoffed. Couldn't help it. Marcie glared at him and said, 'I understand that everything my life used to be about wasn't real. Fashion. Jewelry. Fame. Money. None of it is real.'

Emma would love to disagree. Money *was* real. As real as eviction and homelessness.

'Neither is religion,' said Alfie, blasphemer sculptor. 'Or physical beauty.'

The same beauty he was apparently transfixed by in Marcie's fresh-scrubbed face. Emma preferred her this way, natural, approachable. She looked like any (dumb-foundingly) pretty girl on the street.

Alfie said, 'Marcie can't help being beautiful. But true beauty comes from inside.'

At that, Marcie opened her lips for Alfie, all the better to appreciate her inner loveliness. He responded with fervor, and the two started making out again. They seemed oblivious of their spectators.

Emma looked at Sherman. He said, 'Two days.'

Marcie came up for air around 14th Street. 'I admit, I sought out Alfie for the wrong reasons.' She gave Emma a knowing stare. 'I admit, at first, I wasn't attracted to him.' They laughed nostalgically, remembering the earlier hours of their relationship. 'But then we started talking. And I started to think about what I was doing with my life. The influence I have on people, on women. Gaining and losing weight for money is wrong. To be the reason women take diet pills . . . Did you know that the active ingredient in SlimBurn is some tree bark that thousands of acres of rain forest are destroyed for each year? I didn't. Alfie showed me how to research on the web. Did you know that fourteen people have overdosed on SlimBurn? The pills aren't even FTA approved.'

'FDA, Marcie,' said Alfie.

'You see?' she said. 'He corrects me. He wants me to learn. The men I knew before would just nod and tug on my g-string. It was like they weren't even listening to what I said. This love is real. And I'm going to prove it to Alfie and the world.'

Sherman droned, 'As your lawyer, I advise you not to do anything that'll jeopardize your contract with SlimBurn. They can sue, Marcie.'

'They won't,' said Alfie.

'What do you know?'

'Don't you want them to sue, Sherman?' asked Marcie sharply. 'You can head the legal defense team. Surely, you went to Harvard Law School for that!'

Emma asked, 'So what's the plan?'

'Alfie has a brilliant idea for a new collection of sculptures,' said Marcie.

'The theme is how major corporations suppress feminine power and identity,' said Alfie.

'Corporate logos with breasts attached?' asked Emma.

'No,' said Alfie. 'Clitorises.'

Marcie said, 'There's a press conference in Times Square today. At the unveiling of my billboard. I'm going to give a speech that will knock them dead. Will you stay and watch?'

'Definitely.'

'Daphne'll be there,' said Marcie.

'Nervous to see her?' asked Emma, who was.

'Can I tell you a secret?'

'If you dare. I haven't been very trustworthy of late,' muttered Emma.

'Daphne and I have a competitive friendship,' said Marcie. 'I've stolen one or two of her boyfriends. And she . . . well, the jealousy between us goes deep. Alfie has made me realize that I should end the friendship. I'm through with her. Today will sever our connection forever.'

'Do you have your index cards ready?' asked Alfie.

Marcie patted a cargo pants pocket. 'Right here.'

Sherman said, 'We're on 42nd Street.'

'Emma, will you stand by me?' asked Marcie. 'For emotional support?'

'If you want,' she said. 'But you've got Sherman and Alfie.'

'I'll be right next to you the entire time,' promised Alfie.

Sherman said, 'Permission to speak freely, Marcie.'

'Granted.'

'You've known this man for two days,' started Sherman. 'You've been working on this ad campaign for a year. With another year left in the extremely lucrative contract.'

'You see?' said Marcie to Emma. 'Another man who thinks I'm a moron.'

Sherman said, 'Has it occurred to you that Mr Delado might be using you? That he's an opportunist, seeking publicity for his own purposes, and once you've done all you can for him, he'll move on to use someone else?'

Emma expected Alfie to defend himself. But he merely smiled serenely at Sherman while holding Marcie's hand. She said, 'I know you're trying to protect me, Sherman, and I appreciate it. But you can't understand. You weren't in bed with us.'

'I was close enough,' muttered Sherman.

Emma wondered if sex could be that transformative. Was it possible that two days in bed with a man could completely change one's outlook, goals, perspective? Perhaps it wasn't so inconceivable if the woman was, like Marcie, a deep, empty well that desperately needed to be filled. Emma thought of sex with William. How he'd shown her colors, made her look different (everyone noticed). The leap from 'looking different' to 'a different way of looking' was small. Only three words. Perhaps Emma, too, was a deep, empty well, thirsty and dry?

She'd been in bed with William for one hour. Imagine what he could do to her in two days. It was useless theorizing, Emma chided herself. He'd never come near her again.

The limo pulled to stop. Sherman dialed his cell phone. 'We're here,' he said into it. 'No, Marcie wants to stay in the limo until it's time to go on stage. We're parked underneath the grandstand. No, Ms Wittfield. Absolutely not. Marcie will leave the vicinity immediately otherwise. Okay, then.'

He hung up. 'We can wait here. Daphne will call me five minutes before you're supposed to speak. Someone will wait outside the limo to escort you up. She asked me twice if you've practiced the speech she wrote for you.'

'How much longer?' asked Marcie.

'Twenty minutes,' said Sherman.

'I'm getting nervous,' she said.

'You need a distraction,' suggested Alfie. He cupped her perfect chin, raised her mouth to meet his, and then kissed her. Emma watched, not repulsed, but in awe of the beauty of it. Marcie's face, tilted just so, and Alfie's lips, which were red and full. With his dreadlocks pushed back, his profile was sublime, with a prominent nose and strong jaw. Emma hadn't noticed how handsome he was before. Perhaps sex was transformative for men, too.

Emma wished she could be William's mirror. To see him as he saw himself.

Sherman said, 'I need air.' He stepped out, and Emma followed him. She could use air, too. As soon as her boots hit pavement, she got a skin prickle. Daphne was near. She could smell her, even in the miasma of Times Square odor. Boiled hot dogs, roasted pralines, cigarette smoke, burning light bulbs, horses, peppermint gum, paint, wet cement, newsprint, hurried bodies, anticipation, dread, excitement, fear. Broadway was business as usual.

Emma looked up, up, on the riser. There was Daphne, twenty feet away, atop the grandstand, seating reporters and photographers in metal chairs. The stage itself was built on scaffolding against the uptown side of One Times Square, the sole building on the tiny island of pavement where Broadway and Seventh Avenue intersect at 42nd Street. Above the stage, twenty stories high on the side of the building, hung a white sheet covering the billboard with its historically huge Marcie. A single breast would span two stories.

Police circled the stage, some on horseback. Emma waited until one was giving directions to a tourist and then slipped by, walking quickly but casually toward the stairs that would take her to the top of the stage. She emerged onto the platform and practically tripped over Daphne at the top of the stairs.

'Out of my way,' said her former client.

Emma followed her back down. 'We have to talk,' she said.

'Not now,' said Daphne. 'I have nothing to say to you.'

'You canceled my check!'

At the bottom again, Daphne plowed into the doors of One Times Square and barked instructions at a couple of guys with walkie-talkies. Something about ropes and pulleys and a live broadcast on New York One.

'Are you still here?' growled Daphne, speeding back up the stairs to the stage. 'I don't owe you anything.'

'But you got what you wanted,' said Emma, breathing heavily behind her.

Daphne stopped, spun around, and pushed Emma against the metal railing of the stairs. 'William Dearborn called me this morning and fired me. So I didn't get what I wanted.'

'Did he give a reason?' asked Emma, trying to sound shocked and horrified.

'He said he didn't trust me,' answered Daphne. 'That he'd had a vision. Of me, prying into his brain with a crowbar. He said this vision "popped" into his head. Out of nowhere. As if it'd been put there. By magic.'

Emma said, 'Sounds like he's having a nervous breakdown. He should seek help.'

'Perhaps that's what I'll tell my bosses when they want to know why Crusher Advertising lost a twenty million dollar account,' said Daphne.

Twenty million? William hadn't been exaggerating when he'd called Daphne's fifteen thousand dollar payout a drop in the bucket. It was less than a drop. A droplet.

'Okay, forget about the bonus,' said Emma. 'I'll swing by your office later, pick up a check for five thousand.'

Daphne dug her fingers into Emma's shoulders. 'You'll get nothing from me and like it.'

'I can work on Dearborn some more. I can fix things,' said Emma. She could beg William to rehire Daphne.

But the blond didn't want to hear it. 'Being fired by William Dearborn is the worst thing that ever happened to me.'

'This can't be the absolute worst,' said Emma. 'What about that time you killed a guy?'

Daphne had the lightning reflexes of a leopard. She didn't hesitate for a second before slapping Emma across the face.

Emma rubbed her cheek and said, 'I guess a reference is out of the question.'

Daphne, crazy eyed, would have thrown Emma off the stage stairs, but a cowering techie behind them said, 'Ms Wittfield? We go live in five minutes.'

The advertising dynamo instantly forgot Emma. Daphne screamed at the techie to 'get the fucking talent'. He zoomed down the stairs. Daphne hurried back up, prowled the stage, barked orders left and right, made twenty underlings jump this high.

Marcie, Alfie and Sherman ascended the stairs, the techie prodding them along.

When Daphne saw Marcie, she shrieked, 'What are you wearing? Where's the Prada gown?'

'It didn't fit,' said Marcie. 'Too tight. Besides, no ordinary woman could wear that gown. I didn't want to make ordinary women feel bad about themselves.'

'Who gives a shit about ordinary women?' roared Daphne.

The techie counted down. 'We go live in four, three, two . . .'

'Greetings from the crossroads of the world,' boomed a man at center stage into a microphone. 'I'm Upton Synergy, president of SlimBurn Energy Pills and Herbal Remedies. I'm honored to unveil the largest billboard in Times Square history. Marcie Skimmer is the world's most beautiful, glamorous woman, and we're proud she's had so much success using our product. As have other women all over the country. So far, we've sold ten million units in North America this year! America loves SlimBurn! And America loves Marcie Skimmer! So without further ado, I present DreamBody by SlimBurn!'

He fumbled clumsily with a remote switch, and then the white sheet rolled upward, revealing the billboard from the bottom up. First we saw Marcie's bare feet, then her shins, then her slim thighs, then the jeweled bikini crotch, her flat washboard belly, her rounded tits in the jeweled bra top, her elegant arms, her bony shoulders, her lanky neck, and, finally, her Barbie doll face, with puffy platinum hair on top. One slender arm rested on her jutting hip, one hand fluttering at her collarbone. Her eyes were round and big as manhole covers. From where Emma was standing, directly underneath the billboard, Marcie's legs appeared to be all of twenty stories long.

The crowd cheered the gargantuan nearly-naked woman. Marcie herself was speechless. Alfie whispered something in her ear. The president of SlimBurn was waving her over to say a few words.

'Here goes everything,' said Marcie.

Alfie at her side, the mannequin took the microphone. She said, 'Hello, New York.' Camera flashes popped, clicked, spun. Marcie wasn't flustered. She was a pro.

'I have some people to thank,' she said, smiling. 'This is my fiancé, Alfie Delado. He's an artist with a sculpture exhibit at the Brooklyn Museum of Art. He's been an inspiration to me, and I hope I can be his muse.'

They kissed neatly. The cameras flashed a wall of light. When they stopped, Marcie reached into her cargo pants pocket, and pulled out her notes.

'I'm going to read a short statement now. As most of you know, I gained fifty pounds last year. And I recently dropped the weight in three months.'

Marcie paused. Alfie rubbed her back. Emma glanced over at Sheldon whose eyes were closed, as if he couldn't bear to look. Daphne's eyes, however, were unblinking, locked on Marcie.

'It is true that I gained fifty pounds. And it's true that I lost it,' said the spokesmodel. 'But the rest of the story is a lie. The image on this billboard is a lie. And the people who created the ads are liars, including myself.'

Daphne let out an anguished whimper.

'You might have heard my weight gain last year was the result of a depression. Not true. As per my agreement with Crusher Advertising and SlimBurn, I checked into a Swiss hospital where I received intravenous lipids and glucose – ten thousand calories a day – for eight weeks. I came back to New York, as planned, to pose for the original ad campaign – the now-famous series of magazine and TV ads featuring me as a cow and a parade float. I'm sure many of you can't believe a model would willingly put on that much weight. I did it for money. Crusher Advertising brokered the deal with SlimBurn to pay me five million dollars to follow their two-year plan to the letter, with the promise that, when it was all over, I'd be more famous than ever.'

The crowd was hushed. Times Square, quiet. Emma had never heard such silence. Marcie continued. 'When the time came to lose the weight, Crusher Advertising sent me to a remote Catskills spa. I had every intention of using the pills, exercising and eating sensibly. But the weight didn't come off. At least, not quickly enough. That's when a decision was made that will torment me for the rest of my life.'

'One more word and she's dead,' said Daphne under her breath.

Marcie was rolling. Nothing could have stopped her. 'A team of plastic surgeons from Europe was brought to the spa,' she said into the microphone. 'They put me on a weekly liposuction schedule. On Monday, I'd have the procedure. For the rest of the week, I was bedridden in pain. I was forced to take ice baths and was bound in constriction wraps to reduce swelling. I had ten liposuctions in total. Six of those surgeries required general anesthesia. In recovery once, I overheard a nurse at the spa say my "diet" cost fifteen thousand dollars per pound. That's $750,000 total.

'Mr Upton Synergy – the man having a coronary over there . . .' Marcie paused for laughter. Then she continued: 'Just kidding. He's fine. Anyway, he says that ordinary women can lose weight if they buy a forty dollar bottle of pills. I'm supposed to be living proof of that. But the truth is, an ordinary woman will never look like *that* – she pointed behind her to the billboard – 'unless she spends three months in a remote spa with a team of plastic surgeons. The truth is, I'm living proof that these pills are worthless. Every woman who's bought SlimBurn pills in the last year has been the victim of a multi-million dollar swindle.'

And that was when Upton Synergy really did have a coronary. The president of SlimBurn grabbed his chest, emitted a wounded yelp, and fell out of his chair onto the stage floor. The cameraman from New York One rushed over, filmed a close-up of Synergy's face as it turned purple. Police and ambulance sirens roared from all directions. In a minute, EMS workers stomped up the stage stairs, bowling over journalists along the way. They began CPR on the fallen president.

Photographers swarmed Marcie and Alfie. Sherman fought his way into the tight cluster. Emma was knocked to the side by techies and reporters, everyone scrambling like headless chickens. The chaos overwhelmed Emma's senses. She had to get out of there.

She fought her way to the stairs. Coming up alongside, Alfie was pulling Marcie down the steps, Sherman at her rear. Alfie yelled, 'Come on!' to Emma.

Elbows flying, Alfie knew how to bulldoze through a crowd. Marcie's driver was waiting at the bottom of the stairs, limo door open to catch them. The four piled in and locked up. The driver hustled around to his seat, and they were off.

Marcie looked scared but excited. She said, 'That was

incredible! I can't believe I did it! Did anyone see Daphne's face? How did she react?'

'I'm sure she was impressed by your bravery,' said Emma.

'She was livid,' said Sherman.

Alfie said, 'You changed the world today, Marcie.'

He might be right about that, thought Emma. Perhaps the model's bold confession would start a hot new trend: accountability.

Emma thought about something Marcie said on stage – that the billboard image was a lie, and that the creators were liars. The evening they met, Daphne said that she and Emma were in the same business: image making. That was true, to a point. Emma sent images for love, to create joy, as any artist would. Daphne was also an artist – a con artist. There was no joy in what she did. She promoted self-hate, if one wanted to be philosophical about our fat-obsessed culture. The biggest difference between what Emma and Daphne did was intent. Emma might manipulate, but she didn't defraud. She used real images of real women. She represented the truth, even if she used deception to do it. Emma was satisfied by this logic. Soul satisfied. And, surprisingly enough, she had Marcie to thank for her revelation.

William was wrong about me, she thought. *I am a good witch*.

Meanwhile, Marcie was still talking. 'I didn't get to say the part about the giveaway.' To Emma, she said, 'I want to reimburse the women who bought SlimBurn pills because of me. A dollar a bottle, until I run out of money. It's the best I can do. Alfie's idea.'

Emma raised her eyebrows at the artist. Alfie shrugged and said, 'You've got to stay hungry.'

'Which is true in art – and dieting,' conceded Emma.

Marcie said, 'Only one problem. How can I possibly organize something so huge? If only I knew about a not-for-profit charitable organization that could set this up. Sherman, can you look into that?'

'It just so happens,' said the Good Witch to Sherman Hollow, Esq., 'I know the vice president of a charitable organization with all the infrastructure in place to handle that kind of monetary distribution.'

'You don't say,' monotoned Sherman.

'I can call her right now, if you'd like,' said Emma, already dialing Susan Knight at the Verity Foundation.

'I definitely didn't go to Harvard Law School to give money away,' Sherman said scornfully before pressing Emma's cell phone to his cheek.

24

Twenty minutes later, Emma was receiving instruction from Hoffman Centry.

'Say, "I'm impressed,"' he prompted. 'Say, "Your office is huge! I had no idea you were so important."'

'I never judge a man by the size of his . . . desk,' said Emma. 'You know what it means, anyway, if a man has a big desk?'

'Overcompensating?' he asked.

'Big desk, big . . . files,' said Emma. 'But he's probably overcompensating, too. Not you, though.' She winked exaggeratedly.

Hoff blushed. 'What do you think: should we tell Susan about our one night of thwarted passion?'

'Why not?' she said. 'I'm on a truth binge.'

'Does this mean I really do have big . . . files?' he asked.

'Honestly, Hoff, I don't have all that much of a basis for comparison,' said Emma. Although, she could tell him right now, truthfully, that William Dearborn had him beat by at least two hanging folders.

Emma had asked Marcie to drop her at Ransom House. It was close enough to Times Square, on East 49th Street. The Good Witch was going begging. Her soul might be satisfied, but she still had worldly realities to deal with. She'd been against borrowing before, loath to ask others for assistance. But the time had come to pop her bubble and seek help. To humble herself, and share her problems with the people who cared about her. She knew Hoff had family money. Surely, he could spare ten thousand. Or five thousand. She'd be thrilled with two thousand.

So she'd come to Ransom House. The contrast between her chilly reception at Crusher and the warm welcome at Ransom was like night and day. Hoff dashed to greet her at the elevators (she'd been announced by lobby security), and escorted her to his corner office, introducing her to colleagues along the way as 'one of my best friends'.

Now they were alone in his, yes, very large and impressive office. 'Susan called me about Marcie Skimmer's cash giveaway plan while you were on the way up in the elevator,' he said.

'She's got you on speed dial already?' said Emma.

'You realize what a high-profile case like this will do for the Verity Foundation.'

'I guess they'll get to keep on not making a profit for another decade,' said Emma.

'Susan owes you,' said Hoff.

'I owed her,' said Emma.

'In the past few days, you've found her a fiancé, a star client, and helped her purge an ex-boyfriend. I think she owes you,' said Hoff. 'There's a popular clothing store named Old Navy – have you heard of it?'

Emma laughed. 'Maybe once or twice.'

'Old Navy is going to offer Marcie Skimmer an endorsement deal. Apparently, she was wearing their cargo pants at the press conference today.'

'When did this happen?' asked Emma.

'I'm not sure it has yet,' he said. 'I saw it on a news crawl on FFN.'

'That girl is as bouncy as a ball,' said Emma. 'And that's not a fat joke.'

Hoff stroked his chin and mused, 'I wonder if Marcie would be interested in writing her memoirs.'

Emma groaned. 'I bet you wonder. As does every other book editor in New York.'

'We are a depressingly predictable bunch,' said Hoff.

The Good Witch grinned at him in his cashmere jacket. She was a sucker for his dash-it-all humility. 'I'll make sure Marcie talks to you first,' she said. 'My gift to you. But only because I like you.'

'And here's my gift to you,' he said, tossing a manila envelope across the desk to her.

'Is it ten thousand dollars?' she asked, astounded at his prescience.

'Ten thousand dollars?' he asked. 'Do you need money?'

'So what's in the folder then?' she asked. 'And what if I do?'

'It's my file on Seymour Lankey,' said Hoff.

'What if I do?' she repeated. 'Need a loan?'

Hoff took a deep breath. 'You understand the difference between old money and the nouveau riche?'

She said, 'Old money never spends principal.'

'Precisely,' he said. 'Except, sometimes, that's not always possible. And a bad investment here, a damaging settlement there, a drunken uncle with a gambling addiction. Old money magically, tragically, turns into the nouveau poor.'

'But you have the Gramercy Park apartment. The Danish modern furniture. That cashmere jacket.'

'I inherited the furniture, spend every penny I make to maintain my apartment with just enough left over for the occasional extravagance,' he said, stroking his lapel. 'I love cashmere. I have two dozen pairs of cashmere socks.'

Emma had seen them in his underwear drawer. 'Maybe you should keep the cashmere fetish to yourself – until after the wedding. And the compulsive showering. Man, you get weirder by the minute.' And she liked him more by the minute.

'You've done so much for me,' he said. 'I wish I could help you.'

'We'll just have to get that Riptron reward money,' she decided.

That comment made him check his watch. 'Oh, we have to hurry,' he said suddenly. 'Bring the folder. You can read it on the way.' Hoff took Emma by the elbow and led her back out through the labyrinth of cubicles and down the elevator to the building's underground garage.

Hoff gave a ticket to the attendant, who returned with a hell of a car – an iris Mercedes coupe.

'If we leave now, we can beat the traffic on the Merritt,' said Hoff. 'It'll take an hour and a half to get there. We'll have a brief visit and then return to the city for a celebratory dinner. I haven't driven the new company car yet. I'm really looking forward to this.'

Hoff held open the passenger side door for Emma. She climbed in and snuggled against the black leather seat. The interior was pristine. Still smelled new. Hoff adjusted the driver's seat five different ways and checked the rear view mirrors.

'We're going in style,' said Emma. 'But where?'

'To the Glatting Correctional Facility. I've scheduled us a fifteen-minute audience with Seymour Lankey,' said Hoff. 'I'll have to insist you buckle your seat belt.'

'I'm the kind of girl you can take anywhere,' said Emma. 'The opera. A park picnic. *A federal prison*.'

Hoff laughed, put the car in gear and stepped on the juice.

The Glatting Correctional Facility was a campus of three separate buildings connected with razor wire and a ten-foot-high fence. A uniformed guard sat in a tower with a machine gun on his hip.

To get inside the prison, Hoff had to state his name into a camera by a steel-plated sliding door. It opened with a metallic creak. A uniformed cop stepped forward and frisked them thoroughly. They were directed through a metal detector and X-ray machine. Then through two doors of bulletproof glass into another holding area. Several dozen other people were waiting there. Hoff and Emma took seats on red plastic chairs. Dreary but not dingy, the room's yellow wallpaper was relatively clean. The linoleum floor wasn't fatally scuffed. She stared at it, like everyone else in the room, until she and Hoff were called ten minutes later.

They were instructed to go through another set of metal detectors and into another room, this one set up with long wooden tables and chairs. Emma and Hoff were escorted to the last table in the back row and told, again, to wait. Their visit with the most reviled man in modern corporate history was imminent.

Emma had been in a police station before (yesterday). But she'd never been in a prison. Granted, this institution was no Oz (as in, the HBO show). Nearly all the visitors were Caucasian, as were the handcuffed prisoners who'd just entered the room.

Hoff leaned over and whispered to Emma, 'Glatting houses about 350 inmates. All of them white-collar criminals.'

So these crooks steal with a pencil instead of a gun. That tidbit didn't quell her anxiety. Club Fed or not, Emma was rattled by the slam of metal doors, the bleach fumes, the too-vibrant orange jumpsuits on the prisoners. Her sensitive senses were starting to chafe. Emma leaned toward Hoff and asked, 'Do we have a plan?'

'Yes,' he said. 'It's called "Seat of the Pants".'

Emma nodded. 'I was going to suggest "Wing and a Prayer", but I like yours better.'

'I've been here once before,' said Hoff. 'They brought out Lankey last.'

And that was where Emma found him – the last link on the chain gang. Lankey was shorter than she'd expected, but otherwise, he looked like his photos in *The New York Times*. A studied scowl, a double chin, bald on top with gray hair on the sides, pointy ears. His eyes were watery and blue. Old man eyes.

'*Smoke and Mirrors* comes out, officially, on Sunday,' said Hoff. 'I brought a copy for him. He hasn't seen the cover yet.'

He took a first-bound book out of his shoulder bag. The cover was a close-up of Lankey's face. His expression was earnest, steady. 'I hope he approves,' said the anxious editor. 'He doesn't like me very much.'

'How can you tell?'

'He once called me "Fancy Pants".'

'Do you think he'll like me better?' she asked, wondering why he'd brought her along.

'I have no doubt,' said Hoff. 'Emma, if you please, unbutton your sweater a bit. And take off your sunglasses. And let down your hair.'

'I could sit spread-eagle on the table with my hand in my underwear,' she suggested.

'Shhh. Here he comes,' said Hoff, standing.

A guard – tall, beefy, brown crew cut with a goatee and a tattoo of a cougar on his neck – escorted America's iconic corporate criminal to the table.

'Who is this?' Seymour Lankey asked the guard.

'Your four o'clock,' said the guard, grinning.

'This isn't who I was expecting.'

The guard seemed disturbed. 'Let me see what's going on,' he said to Seymour. 'Talk to these people in the meantime.'

Seymour sat. He turned toward Hoff and Emma, confused and annoyed, but something else too. Emma sniffed for clues. She thought she smelled fear.

'What're you looking at?' he asked her.

'Nothing much,' she said out of habit.

But Seymour liked it. 'You should see me in my formal jumpsuit, young lady.'

Hoff said, 'Mr Lankey. You may not remember me. I'm Hoffman Centry. Your editor at Ransom House.'

Seymour took a closer look at Hoff. 'Yes, Mr Centry. Sorry I didn't recognize you. I was thrown by the black eye, missing tooth and gashed cheek.'

Hoff said, 'Hazards of the job. I have a copy of *Smoke and Mirrors*. Hot off the presses. We release on November first. Day after tomorrow.'

The criminal received the book gratefully. He examined the cover photo and seemed pleased. 'I like it. It looks just like me, doesn't it?'

'Oh, yes,' said Emma. 'Very flattering.'

'I want this photo plastered all over the world.'

'Well, we release in North America on the first, but we won't put out foreign editions for another month,' corrected Hoff. 'We've sold rights to most of Europe, Japan, Australia . . .'

'You could've just mailed the book,' said Seymour. 'I appreciate your professionalism, Mr Centry, coming all the way out here. And you – whoever you are – you have a stunningly beautiful face. God knows I appreciate that. But I'm going to have to ask the two of you to leave. I'm expecting another guest, and they only let one party in at a time.'

He was dismissing them. And they'd come bearing gifts. Emma felt a salty and sour taste on her tongue. This man had stolen her money. And he was treating her like a nuisance. She thought about the nuisance of losing her apartment because of him.

Hoff said, 'Before we go, I have one quick question . . .'

'No time, Fancy Pants. Door's that way,' said Lankey.

And that was when Emma saw red. He could steal her money. He could be rude to her. But he couldn't insult her friend. 'Jeff Bragg isn't coming,' she said with sadistic glee. 'So you have a few minutes for us.'

Hoff blanched. Seymour said, 'I don't know anyone named Jeff Bragg.' Lankey was a good liar, but that was to be expected.

Emma said, 'No? He told me you knew each other well. He's sorry he can't come today. He's probably on the beach by now. Sitting in the sun, drinking a daiquiri. Grand Cayman is beautiful this time of year. Any time of year.'

Seymour ground his teeth. The motion of his jaw was so violent Emma felt the friction in her own mouth. He said, 'Phone. Now. Cell phone.'

Hoff said, 'We were told not to give you any electronic . . .'

'Give me a fucking cell phone!' Seymour demanded, slamming his cuffed wrists on the table. The beefy tattooed guard had reentered the room and was watching them closely from the periphery.

Emma said, 'He can't stab us with a phone,' and gave Seymour hers. The convict dialed a number, fumbling in the cuffs. He finished and hit send.

Hoff's briefcase, with Bragg's phone inside it, started to ring.

Seymour pushed end. Hoff's briefcase went silent. Seymour hit redial. Hoff's briefcase rang again. He pushed end.

The poster boy of corporate greed returned the phone to Emma. Then he leaned across the table. His eyes weren't quite so watery when he was royally pissed off. 'Are you fucking with me, Centry?' he asked. 'Because if you are, I'll fuck you back so long and so hard, there'll be nothing left but the painful memory.' He turned toward Emma. 'You, too,' he added.

Then he scooped up his copy of *Smoke and Mirrors* and yelled, 'Watts!'

The tattooed guard rushed to his side. 'Yes, sir?'

'Get me out of here.'

The guard whisked Seymour away. The two walked close enough for Seymour to whisper in his ear. Emma pricked up her super hearing and caught a few phrases. 'Change of plans.' 'A slight delay.'

She turned back toward Hoff. He was shaking, his skin drained of color, except for the purple bruises and the red cut.

Emma said, 'He's much shorter than I thought.'

'What do you think you were doing?' he asked, compulsively stroking his cashmere lapel.

'Seat of Pants?'

'Would you consider what he said to me an overt threat?' asked Hoff.

'I'd call it an idle threat,' said Emma.

Another guard told them their time was up. Emma was surprised that her legs were shaking when she stood. The two interlopers were led out of the visitation room. They retraced their steps and eventually escaped to freedom on the other side of the steel-plated sliding door.

Safely settled in the Mercedes, Emma let her shoulders relax. Hoff turned the ignition key. 'He's locked in prison for ten years,' she said. 'What could he possibly do?'

'He could hire someone,' said Hoff.

'He's broke,' she said. 'Or, at the very least, he can't access his money. That's what Jeff Bragg was for.'

Hoff said, 'In ten years, when he gets out, I'm moving to South America.' He negotiated the car out of the prison parking lot and back onto the Merritt. It was slow going. Friday afternoon traffic.

'If we can prove he stole the money, he'll face new charges. He'll never get out of jail,' said Emma. She put her head against the cushy rest and closed her eyes. She thought of her first close look at Jeff Bragg, at Bull on Water Street. He'd seemed like a creep, but not a criminal. She'd sized him up as a harmless accountant. But his manner, his bravura, his suit were all parts of a perfect disguise – what he wore and how he acted to appear normal. To seem like a regular guy. No wonder Susan had been fooled. Jeff had a flawless anti-costume costume. And Emma knew costumes. She was the Queen of Costumes.

Emma's eyelids snapped up. She turned to Hoff, who was cursing the traffic.

'I know what "the big day" is,' she said.

Hoff kept his eyes on the road and said, 'Go ahead.'

'It's the day Seymour was to escape from prison.'

Hoff blurted, 'That's impossible!'

Emma said, 'Seymour's four o'clock was supposed to be Jeff Bragg. We know this. Jeff was supposed to come with proof that he'd arranged the wire transfer from Seymour's offshore account to the other bank account number he'd given to you. But who gets the money – and why?'

'Lankey needed the money to escape?' asked Hoff. 'A bribe? I did find it odd how chummy Lankey was with that tattooed guard.'

'Tattoo takes a bribe and gets Lankey out of Glatting – and out of the country,' she said.

'To Mexico, for plastic surgery. The authorities will be hunting for the man *on the book cover,*' said Hoff, getting excited. 'He specifically asked if the photo looked like him. The world would be searching for a face that no longer existed.'

'Without the wire transfer, Lankey can't pay off the guard,' said Emma. 'And now, he thinks Jeff Bragg has double crossed him and kept the money for himself.'

'Thanks to you,' said Hoff. 'But we still don't know the password.'

'Sure we do,' said Emma. ' "The big day" is the day of the planned prison escape.'

'Which is when?'

Emma said, 'After the bribe . . .'

'Today,' said Hoff.

'. . . and before the book comes out . . .'

'Day after tomorrow.'

'Which leaves one day in between. Tomorrow.'

'The password is "tomorrow"?'

'No,' she said, frustrated. 'What is tomorrow?'

'The day that never comes?' asked Hoff, philosophically.

'Tomorrow is *Halloween,*' said the Good Witch. 'My

favorite holiday. When ghouls, goblins, and corporate criminals are free to roam the Earth.'

Emma dialed her cell phone and waited for someone to pick up.

A man asked, 'Hello. You've reached the Grand Cayman National Bank.'

'I'd like to check the balance of my account,' said Emma, her heart thundering in her ribs.

'We're calling the Feds,' said Susan, henceforth the Good Snitch, when Emma called her from the car.

'No way. They'll trick and cheat.'

'Isn't that "trick or cheat"?' asked Hoff.

'Just watch the road,' said Emma. Into the phone, she said, 'We are transferring this money into my checking account. I'm the one who's lost her life savings because of Seymour Lankey. I'm the one who solved the password mystery. I'm taking control of this money. I need it. I deserve it. Some of it. A little tiny crumb of it. And that is final.'

Hoff said, 'You can't just wire six hundred million dollars into your checking account.'

'Why the hell not?' asked Emma. 'And it's not six hundred million. It's $600,000,011.'

'It would be stealing,' said Hoff.

'I'm not going to keep it,' said Emma. 'I just want to hold it.'

'Come to Verity before you do anything and we'll talk more,' said Susan on the phone.

'We can talk all night,' said Emma. 'But I'm not going to change my mind.'

An hour later, Emma and Hoff dropped off the car at Ransom House and took a taxi to the Verity Foundation downtown. As soon as they opened the office door, government agents swarmed all over them. Emma was questioned for hours by various members of the FBI, IRS, and SEC. She steadfastly demanded an IOU for her share of the reward. The federal agents were not amused.

Emma cursed Susan's name. Repeatedly. She swore she'd never forgive her. But later that night, Susan brought her a roast turkey sandwich with chopped liver from the Second Avenue Deli and Emma forgave her anyway. The Good Snitch apologized, explained over and over again that she'd been working with some of these agents for a year on the Riptron class action suit. That the money recovery had to be done legally. That there were twelve thousand other small investors who'd been fleeced.

Emma buckled and agreed to embrace Susan's way. As the night wore on, the agents informed Emma and Hoff that Lankey had been questioned in his cell about the bribe, etc. and denied everything, as did Barney Watts, the prison guard Seymour spent nearly all of his time with. The agents hadn't gotten a lead on that second bank account number. The upshot: without Jeff Bragg's testimony, the government agents couldn't confirm the prison escape plan or the GCNB account holder (the account had a number, but, alas, not a name).

At one o'clock in the morning – Halloween morning –

the agents told Emma she was free to go. Since Verity was so close to Waverly, Susan and Hoff walked her home.

Along the way, Emma asked, 'Do we get the reward or not?'

'Not unless they can prove the account is Lankey's,' said Susan, woefully.

'Ironically, the man you fear most is the only one who can give you what you want,' said Hoff.

'What does William Dearborn have to do with this?' Emma asked, miffed.

Susan waited a beat and said, 'He meant Jeff Bragg.'

'Oh,' said Emma.

Hoff rubbed Emma on the back but said nothing, bless him.

The couple decided to stop up at Emma's apartment for a quick drink. Despite their fatigue, none of them were quite ready to go their separate ways. All three collapsed on Emma's white couch, legs outstretched, feet plopped on her white shag carpet.

'I'd offer pot and beer,' said the host. 'But I'm out.'

'I'll settle for a clean bathroom,' said Susan, hauling herself up to use Emma's.

Hoff said, 'We'll sleep at your place tonight?'

Susan lived on Franklin, not too far away. 'I can't wait for you to see it,' she said and left down the short hallway to the bathroom.

When she was gone, Hoff whispered to Emma, 'How's her apartment?'

Emma grinned. Hoffman 'Danish Modern' Centry was in for a shock. She asked him, 'On a scale of one to ten, how do you rate pine-veneer furniture from Ikea?'

A piercing scream. It came from the bedroom. Emma and Hoff sprang off the couch and hurried toward it.

Susan, meanwhile, was running toward the living room, and the three collided in the hallway, bounced off each other and the walls, and landed in a tangle on the floor.

'It's Jeff Bragg!' Susan shrieked. 'He's in the bed!'

'We can take him,' said Emma, detangling herself. The accountant had made a bad miscalculation. They were three against one (unless he had the gun with him, making it three against two).

Hoff said, 'Let's call the police.'

'I've had enough of police for one day,' said Emma, angrily. And she was pissed. At Lankey, the government agents, William, Daphne, Mr Cannery, Susan (a little still), her mother for dying, her father for splitting New York, herself for years of seeking vicarious pleasures when she should have been grabbing her own. Well, Emma would get a thrill now. She reached in the hall closet and gripped the aluminum baseball bat she kept for precisely such an occasion. Thwacking it against her palm, Emma crept into her bedroom, Hoff and Susan on tiptoes behind her.

Sure enough, there was a body under the covers. Just the top of his head, the brown hair, was visible. Amazingly, despite the screaming, he hadn't moved. Maybe he was dead. Maybe Seymour Lankey had had him killed and dumped there as a warning to Emma.

Emma nudged the body with the bat.

It moved.

Emma shrieked, setting off Susan and Hoff. The figure on the bed moved again. He pulled down the covers, opened his eyes. Upon seeing the trio standing over him and the big bat high over Emma's head, he shrieked, too.

'Victor!' screamed Emma.

The photographer, arms protectively over his head, said, 'Emma, what the hell are you doing? Oh, wait.' He reached into his ears and took out yellow, foamy plugs. 'Put down that bat!'

Emma lowered the bat and said, 'You scared the shit out of me!'

'I scared the shit out of *you*?' he answered, yelling. 'What about me? You're going to have to change your sheets now.'

Emma laughed with relief and plopped down on the corner of the bed. Hoff and Susan were still blinking and shaking, arms wrapped around each other.

Victor said, 'I let myself in.' To the couple, he added, 'I'm Victor Armour. Emma's friend. Platonic. I have a key.'

Hoff offered his hand. Victor shook it. 'Hoffman Centry. I believe we were introduced before. This is my fiancée, Susan Knight.'

Victor smiled. 'Susan and I have already met.' He'd taken her nearly naked portraits only last year.

She said, 'Victor. Of course. Hello.'

Turning to Hoff, Vic said, 'Of course I know you, Hoffman. From Emma. You're the editor on William Dearborn's art book, right? He's hired me to be the art director on the project.'

'Has he?' asked Hoff.

'Liam told me he hadn't finalized your deal yet. But he's excited about it and wants to get started anyway. Liam has real vision.'

'He's a major talent,' said Hoff.

'To tell you the truth, Hoffman,' said Victor, 'I have a huge man-crush on him.'

After a beat, Hoff said, 'To tell you the truth, Victor, I have a huge man-crush on him, too!'

And that was it. Victor got out of bed – thankfully, he was wearing sweat pants and a T-shirt – and he and Hoff started prattling like fishwives about their book project. Emma and Susan went into the kitchen and found the bottle of Bailey's. They poured some over ice and took their drinks to the couch.

'Shall we toast?' asked Susan.

'To the five thousand calories we are about to consume,' said Emma.

'Cheers.'

The women drank in silence. After a minute, the men wandered into the living room.

Victor was saying, 'Yeah, and Emma got to fuck him!'

Hoff said, 'I know! She's so lucky!'

Susan said, 'You fucked William Dearborn?'

'I'm so lucky,' said Emma.

'Are you going to do it again?' asked Susan.

'I'm too tired to talk about it,' she said, meaning it. 'Can everyone go home now? I don't mean to be rude. On second thoughts, I do mean to be rude.'

Hoff and Susan could take a hint. They left. Victor stayed. They took the bottle of Bailey's into the bedroom and lay down with it between them.

'Ann dumped me,' he said.

'Because you lied to her?' she asked. He nodded. 'You told her you did it to protect me and my client?'

'Yeah, except she found out that Daphne was the client,'

he said. 'She remembered gossiping to me about her alleged manslaughter. She said, "All that time, you pretended as if you didn't know her, but you'd photographed her naked."'

'As if that means you know a person,' said Emma.

'Exactly!' agreed Victor. 'So the afternoon started badly. But Liam was great. He loves those shots of Daphne. He painted one, you know. I took a Polaroid of it. Wanna see?'

'No,' said Emma.

'Trust me,' he said, reaching into his bag at the foot of the bed. 'You want to see this.'

Emma dared to look at the Polaroid. William had painted the flame portrait with thick impressionist dabs, globs of acrylic, presenting the shape of a woman's body and the palette of heat and fire. But the subject did not have Daphne's face.

'You recognize her?' asked Victor.

How could she not? The painted lady had the same face Emma saw in the mirror every morning. 'Did he mention me?' she asked.

'He was all business,' said Victor. 'Very fun, but nothing personal.'

'I blew it with him,' she said, putting her head on Victor's chest. He pulled her in tight. The closeness was good. Comfy and cozy. Emma's pulse didn't quicken. The temperature of her skin did not rise. Victor smelled like baby powder.

He said, 'Here we are again. Both of us alone.'

'But together,' she added.

'Maybe that's our destiny,' he said. 'To grow old and withered at each other's side.'

'You make it sound so good,' she said. 'Wait, I've got an idea.' She sat up, excited. 'It'll cure our sadness, if temporarily.'

'Have sex?' he asked.

'I said *cure*, not *spur*,' clarified Emma. 'Let's throw a Halloween party, at your studio to watch the parade.'

Victor snorted. 'You HATE parties.'

'I do hate parties,' she agreed. 'But I'm on the verge of losing my apartment and my business. So change is clearly in order. If I'm to find a new place to live and a job, I have to widen my circle of acquaintances. Besides that, Halloween is my favorite holiday.'

Victor wasn't buying it. 'You don't have another reason tucked up in your sneakery little mind, do you?'

Nearly every time she'd seen William, they'd been at a party. Not that she'd invite him. But maybe someone else would. 'Do you want to do this or not?' she asked Victor, who loved parties.

'Why my place?'

'It's bigger, you've got a terrace over Sixth Avenue to watch the parade. And it's a mess already.'

'I like this idea,' said Victor, getting into it. 'I'll roll out the costume racks and set up a backdrop. I can take pictures. Naughty pictures.'

'Goes without saying,' agreed Emma. 'Think how distracted we'll be, planning and inviting and chopping vegetables.'

'Fuck vegetables,' he said. 'Hey, I don't mean right this minute, Emma. Where are you going?'

'I want to show you something,' said Emma. She'd gotten out of bed and was rummaging in her closet.

He said, 'I've seen everything in there.'

'Wait for it,' she said, dragging a bulky box out from underneath her boot pile. She dropped it on the bed, and flipped off the top. Emma removed a fancy gown, white, sparkly, with tulle and a sequined bodice.

'It was a gift from my mother. When I started the business,' said Emma, showing Victor the Lucite crown and wand that went with it. Holding the dress against her chest, she said, 'It's a custom-made replica of the gown Billie Burke wore in *The Wizard of Oz*.'

Victor looked at her blankly. 'Who is Billie Burke?'

'She played Glinda,' said Emma. 'Giver of the ruby slippers? "You had the power all along"? Bronze hair? Lived in a bubble. For Christ's sake, Victor! Glinda was the Good Witch.'

'Ohhhh,' he said. 'Now I get it.'

Emma said, 'Help me put this on.'

Dutifully, Victor shifted through the layers of tulle and crinoline to find the side zipper. He dropped the dress over Emma's head. It fit, barely. There was just enough room to breathe. He placed the crown on top of her waves and fanned her hair to curve into the neckline of the dress.

'You've never worn it?' asked Victor. 'Bloody shame. If I looked that good in a dress, I'd never take it off.'

'I put it on only once before. For Mom, the night she gave it to me.' Emma looked at herself in the mirror, remembering how excited Anise was to give her the gift. She died less than two years later.

Victor said, 'You look sensational. Your mom would be crying right now if she could see you.'

Emma started crying instead.

'Curse my glib tongue,' said Victor, hugging her.

'It's the same old shit,' said Emma, wiping her tears. 'The legacy.'

He sighed. 'How many times have you had your brain scanned?'

'Eight.'

'How many doctors have told you that brain aneurisms are not hereditary?'

'Five.'

'From this day forward, I want you to think of this gown as the *only* gift your mother gave you,' said Victor. 'Forget about her powers, which, by the way, I always thought were bogus. She could guess weight and age? When someone got laid? She had *feelings*? Every woman has *feelings*. Every woman has powers. Your mom was insightful, observant, and optimistic. She wasn't gifted.'

'Then why can I do what I do?' asked Emma to Victor for the 3,499th time. 'Why am I different?'

He said, '*Why* isn't the right question.'

'So what is?'

'How about, "Is there any food in the house?" Or, "How can I make my guest more comfortable?" Or, "Who should I invite to my party?" Anything but *why*. Give *why* a fucking rest.'

'Okay,' she said, drying her cheeks.

'Really?'

'Yes.' She turned back toward the mirror. 'This gown is Mom's gift, her only legacy to me. Nothing else.'

Emma stared at her reflection. She liked what she saw, was amazed the gown still fit. She twirled, watching the tulle sway with her movement. She imagined William was on the other side of the mirror, sitting in a chair with a drink, looking at the glass like a TV. A twinge took her heart, a flutter. *He can see me*, she thought. *He's watching right now*.

'You okay?' asked Victor. 'You're zoning out.'

'I think I just got a *feeling*,' said Emma.

'See? You are like every other woman,' he said.

'I'll wear this dress at my wedding,' Emma declared. For the first time in a long time, Emma let herself believe she'd live to see the day.

'Tonight, eightish,' said Emma.

'Okay if I bring Chloe?' asked Armand Chicora.

'You're still together?'

'I'm her boyfriend slash bodyguard,' he said. 'It's a full time position.'

'You quit the hospital?' asked Emma.

'Their loss,' he said. 'I've already done more for Chloe than I was allowed to do for any of my patients. Besides, I have to be with her around the clock. Human existence is fragile. She could die at any moment.' He said it so casually, Emma had to laugh. He added, 'If it wasn't for you, Emma, I never would have met Chloe. I wouldn't have been at the hotel to save her life. Chloe Sevigny is alive today, thanks to you.'

'Think of all the indie movies that would go unmade,' said Emma. 'Of the clothing designers who'd be muse deprived.'

'I'm serious,' said Armand.

* * *

'Tonight, eightish. And bring whomever you want.'

'What's so great about this parade?' asked Sherman Hollow, Esq. 'It's just a bunch of queers dancing in the streets, high on ecstasy, wearing idiotic costumes, if they're not completely naked.'

'Exactly!' said Emma. 'You coming?'

'Do I have to wear a costume?' he asked.

'Why don't you come as a lawyer who didn't go to Harvard to watch half a million gay men dance naked in the street?'

'I could do that,' he said. 'Or come as the Wolfman.'

'Tonight, eightish. Costumes preferred, but not required.'

'It's a good view?' asked Natasha of Crusher Advertising. 'Because I want to see everything.'

'My friend's building is on Sixth,' said Emma. 'He's got a terrace that hangs over the avenue. You won't miss a thing.'

'Will there be any single guys?'

Emma thought of William. 'Why else would I throw a party?' she asked. 'Natasha, if you don't mind, could you give Daphne a message for me? Tell her she was right to cancel the check. I don't deserve the money.'

'I would tell her. But she no longer works here.'

'She got fired?'

Natasha said, 'Fired? Ceramic bowls get fired. Daphne Wittfield has been excommunicated from Crusher Advertising. She no longer exists. She is like a dead person. I've been reassigned to another exec, a thirty-year-old white boy who must've been raised by a mean black nanny. He's terrified of me.'

'And you'll use your black power for good?' asked Emma.

'What the hell are you talking about?' asked Natasha. 'My mother didn't scrub toilets so I would go easy on the man.'

'But she didn't.'

'That's what I *just said*.'

'Tonight, eightish. Can you and Susan bring some food?' asked Emma. 'Victor insists that we serve only fun-size candy bars. And what's so fun about a teeny-tiny Snickers? A fun-size Snickers should be three feet long.'

Hoff said, 'What about drinks?'

'Victor will allow only a hard cider punch. Mulled.'

'I'll order a few sandwich platters and a couple of cases of beer,' said Hoff. 'And you'll reimburse me.'

'Absolutely,' said Emma, counting down to her last dollar. 'And, maybe, grab a few boxes of Clementines. And a case of wine. Also, if possible, some olives for martinis. Plus vodka. And vermouth. And some chips. Dip. Salsa. Oh, and wear a costume.'

Hoff said, 'Why don't I come as the caterer?'

'Or you could come as the sexiest man at the party, who also happens to be a genius editor, stupendous friend, stylish, charming, articulate . . . did I say sexy?'

'You said sexiest,' said Hoff. 'Does that means William Dearborn isn't invited?'

'He's not on my list, no.'

'Has it occurred to you that everyone you know is better off since you met William? That, in the last nine days, you've changed lives, created couples, inspired art, boosted careers, and, in Marcie Skimmer's case, possibly saved her very soul?'

'Daphne's not better off,' said Emma.

'Who is Daphne?' asked Hoff.

'Tonight. Eightish. Costume. Friends.'

'I work until nine,' said Deirdre at Oeuf. Emma could hear the plates clattering in the background.

'So come at nine.'

'But I have to go home and get on my costume first.'

Emma sighed. 'So come at ten.'

'Guess what my costume is,' prompted Deirdre.

'Laura Bush.'

'Noooo.'

'Minnie Mouse.'

'Wrong again,' said Deirdre.

Emma said, 'A pain in the ass?'

'See you at ten,' said the Oeuficious waitress. 'Closer to ten fifteen.'

'Tonight. Eight or nine. Bring Alfie. Congrats on the Old Navy thing, by the way.'

'It's been a whirlwind,' said Marcie. 'Will Daphne be coming tonight?'

'No,' said Emma. 'She'd rather die than see me again.'

'Or me.'

'Considering what she did to you, you should be glad to be rid of her.'

'I hope I am,' said Marcie cryptically. And then, chirpily, 'See you later!'

* * *

'It's tonight. Eightish. At Victor's.'

'Didn't Victor tell you? We broke up,' said Ann Jingo.

'So?' said Emma.

'Breaking up means you no longer see the person you broke up with.'

'I didn't realize you were so conventional,' said Emma.

'I won't be lied to,' said Ann.

'Oh, for Christ's sake, he's sorry,' said Emma dismissively. 'What do you want from him? Blood? And, if so, does it have to be human?'

'I'm never going to forgive Victor,' said Ann.

'Right,' said Emma. 'So I'll see you tonight.'

Ann said, 'Hold on one second.'

Phone muffled. Emma listened as hard as she could, and picked up murmurings – English accented murmurings. Emma imagined William standing in front of Ann's desk in his skinny suit, bangs hanging, smiling, eyes alive, thoughts hatching. Then she pictured him completely naked, the dusting of chest hair, package jiggling from laughter.

'You there?' asked Ann, suddenly back on the phone. 'Liam just told me that Alfie Delado sold the Penis Christ sculpture to Paris Hilton for fifty thousand dollars. He's gone now, down the hall. Do you, uh, have a message for him?'

Did he have a message for her? 'I've got to go,' said Emma.

Victor and Emma worked for hours decorating his studio. At a discount warehouse store they came across a crate of battery-powered motorized ghosts that glided back and forth on a cable and made tormented, creepy sounds. The hosts wired the cables all over the studio, and, after flicking a dozen 'on' switches, the loft was overrun with gliding, moaning nylon ghosts.

'Do they sound scary – or sick?' asked Victor.

'They sound like they need a drink,' said Emma, taking a sample of hard mulled cider.

'How many people did you invite?' he asked, pouring a package of fun-size Mounds into a crystal bowl.

'About ten. I told everyone to bring a friend.'

'I sent a mass email,' said Victor. 'I haven't had a chance to check the RSVPs, though.' He powered up his iBook and clicked to the evite page. 'Oh, shit,' he said.

'No one's coming?'

'Everyone's coming!' he said. 'And they're all bringing five friends. The RSVP total says two hundred!'

'We're going to need more Mounds,' said Emma.

The two hosts ran out to the corner deli and bought every last package of candy they could find. It would never be enough.

At eight on the nose, the first wave of guests arrived. Victor introduced Emma to his photographer friends, and their friends, and their friend's friends, but she'd remember them only as the A-Team, the Justice League, the Powderpuff Girls, and the Seven Samurai. Amazingly, her party anxiety hadn't showed up. She made a point of keeping the music low and the lights dim. *So far, so good*, she breathed.

By eight-thirty, the party was packed. The famous Greenwich Village Halloween Parade was also under way. Sixth Avenue was crammed with floats and revelers on foot. The throng wasn't composed solely of gay men, of course. Emma spotted costumed families (her fave: Frankenstein's monster, his bride, and two little Igors), singles, couples, gangs of friends, seniors to teenagers. The ad hoc theme this year seemed to be classic horror: monsters, vampires, ghouls, hunchbacks, mummies, ghosts, masks with eyes falling out, head wounds, stab wounds, spilling brains – the good, old-fashioned gore Emma grew up on and was fortified by like spinach and fresh air. In her Glinda the Good Witch gown, Emma felt like a confection, way too sweet.

'You look good enough to eat,' said a Hillary Clinton in a blond wig, taupe blazer, and velour headband.

Emma said, 'She gave up the headband in 2001.'

'I'm First Lady Clinton,' said Natasha. 'Not Senator Clinton.'

'You look exactly like her!' said Emma. 'If she were twenty-two years old. And black.'

'She is black,' said Natasha. 'America's first black First Lady.'

Emma laughed but had to stop when all the oxygen in the loft was sucked into the elevator shaft as it lifted Marcie, Alfie, and Sherman into the studio.

Marcie's arrival (in the broader sense – and Emma hated to use the word 'broad' in connection to Marcie) was punctuated by her costume. She'd come as Marilyn Monroe, an obvious choice perhaps, but she was a stunner. Dreadlocked Alfie, head-to-toe in red, green, and gold, accessorized with a cigar-sized joint, appeared to be a white Bob Marley.

Emma pointed out Sherman. 'You see that guy over

by the elevator dressed as the Wolfman?' she asked Natasha.

'The shrimp in pelts?'

'That shrimp didn't go to Harvard to fall unexpectedly in love with the first black First Lady whose mother didn't scrub toilets to see her daughter hook up with a rich, white entertainment attorney with offices on Park Avenue.'

'She didn't,' agreed Natasha. 'You know, I've always been attracted to hirsute men.'

Even if they were prematurely balding? 'Keep that under your wig,' whispered Emma. 'Come, let me introduce you to your new boyfriend.'

She'd only just brought Natasha over to Sherman when Marcie grabbed Emma by the wand and pulled her aside.

'We need to talk. I'm worried about Alfie,' Marcie said breathily. 'He's in moral danger.'

'Aren't we all?'

'Someone wants to kill you too?'

Probably, thought Emma: 'Do you mean *mortal* danger?'

'What did I say?' asked Marcie.

'Let's find a quieter place to talk.'

Emma was daunted by having to push through the crowd, but it turned out she needn't have worried. The people parted for Marcie as if she were Moses and they were the Red Sea. The two women found privacy on Victor's bed behind a Japanese screen in the back of the loft.

Emma fluffed out her tulle and watched Marcie sit gracefully beside her on the bed, cross her endless legs, and look at her host from under thick, black eyelashes. For a moment, Emma was speechless.

Marcie asked, 'You think I can pull off Marilyn?'

'If you can't, no one can,' said Emma.

Marcie smiled and said, 'I might manage to achieve iconic status on my own.'

'What a relief that will be.'

'You have no idea,' said Marcie. Then she sighed heavily, sexily. Emma fingered her wand.

'I'm afraid of Daphne,' said Marcie.

'Me, too.'

'I'm afraid she's going to kill Alfie.'

A nylon ghost flew over their heads, moaning.

Emma said, 'Does that sound scary, or sick?'

'You know Daphne and I were roommates in college,' said Marcie. 'When we graduated, we got an apartment together. We were both broke. Daphne was in business school at Fordham and I was trying to get modeling jobs, but I was always either too old or too fat. We talked about becoming stars all the time. But neither of us could get a break.

'We survived on dates,' she continued. 'Dates for dinner. Dates to pay the phone bill. Dates for movies. I might have gotten a few more dates than she did. I might have stolen a few of hers, too.'

Emma didn't need intuition – or super vision – to see where this was going. She said, 'The rumor that Daphne killed a guy.'

Marcie nodded. 'Steve Wren. Daphne met him at a party. She brought him home. She went into her bedroom to change. I found him alone, on the couch. I'd been rejected by an agency that day, and I needed a boost. You understand, right?'

Not in the slightest. 'Go on,' said Emma.

'Daphne caught us. She says I shoved her first. I remember it differently. Years of mutual resentment came out in the fight. We were punching and scratching. Hair pulling. Steve tried to stop us. He was pushed back, tripped on the rug, and landed face first on the corner of the glass coffee table. We called 911, but it was too late.'

A ghost whirred above, its tormented cry low and slow.

'That ghost needs new batteries,' said Marcie.

Emma said, 'I heard that the police found Daphne alone with the guy. She claimed self-defense.'

'We not only killed him, we killed his reputation,' said Marcie. 'Daphne looked more beat up than I did, which worked for the self-defense story. She said, "I'll get this one," like she was picking up the check at dinner, and told me to leave. That was five years ago, and she's been holding it over me ever since. She uses our secret like' – she glanced at Emma's accessory – 'like a magic wand. She waves it, and I do whatever she wants. I've gone out with men so she'd get jobs and promotions. I've agreed to her schemes, like the SlimBurn ads. It's almost like Steve Wren's death was part of her master plan to get control over me.' Then, almost reverently, she added, 'Daphne is an excellent long-term planner.'

'Both of you got to the top of your professions. She must have done something right,' said Emma.

'But I dumped her yesterday,' said Marcie. 'She'll want payback. Alfie is my world, so I assume she'd go after him. I've seen first hand how cold-blooded she can be.'

'Why did you want to know who Daphne hired me for?' asked Emma.

Marcie shrugged. 'That old jealousy, I guess.' The two women had been needling and tormenting each other for years as if their lives depended on it, thought Emma. Maybe they did.

Emma said, 'You should confess, about the accident.'

'I know,' said Marcie. 'Alfie needs to know.'

'I meant to the police.'

'Well, that would be taking the soul cleansing a little too far.'

The host's ears pricked up. Despite the party noises, Emma heard someone calling her name.

Marcie said, 'I need you to help me protect Alfie.'

'I will. Whatever I can do. He wasn't the man Daphne wanted, you know,' said Emma. 'I tricked you about that.'

'On a subconscious level, you knew what you were doing to send me to him,' said Marcie.

'EmMMMA! Where the devil are you?' shouted the voice again. Hoff.

Marcie heard it too. 'Shall we?'

The two women returned to the party. The hostess found Hoff quickly enough. 'You look beautiful,' said Satan himself, with horns. And a forked tail. 'The food is on the table. I have a receipt.'

'Susan is an angel?' asked Emma.

'She's also dressed up like one,' said Hoff. 'Let's go find her.'

The party had grown in the five minutes Emma and Marcie had been talking. The crowd was a swelling, pulsing animal in black. It seemed like the parade had run a detour through Victor's loft. Emma's gown was cumbersome, and she had difficulty penetrating the crowd.

She started to get that antsy, 'must leave now' feeling. Holding Hoff's hand, she scanned the swarm of vampires, ring wraiths, elves, hobbits, aliens, and wizards for Victor as an ogre ('I'll be an ogre-night sensation!' he bragged while doing his makeup), and noticed, out of the corner of her naked eye, someone dressed in a brown Beatles suit, a skinny tie, and long, brown bangs.

She froze on the spot.

Hoff squinted in the same direction. 'That's not him. It's a William Dearborn costume. I've seen three already.'

'Let's go on the balcony,' she said to Hoff. 'I need air.'

They pushed their way outside and onto the loft's wrap-around terrace. Three flights up, they were high enough to see the scope of the parade and close enough for detail. Emma and Hoff leaned over the terrace's waist-high ledge to watch the parade marchers and floats on Sixth Avenue below.

'There's Susan,' said Hoff.

Across the terrace, on the non-viewing side, Susan was divine in her white robes, halo, and wings. She was talking to a hideous beast (Victor) and a woman dressed as a daisy, neck-to-toes in green, with a circle of white petals around her yellow painted face.

Victor, in lime-colored face paint, leaned over to kiss this delicate flower, transferring a splotch of green onto her yellow, and vice versa.

'Ann,' said Emma as they approached. 'I'm so glad you could make it.'

'How dare you invite Ann behind my back!' said Victor, smiling.

Ann said, 'As if this party wasn't a big excuse for Emma to call me.'

'That's ridiculous,' he said.

'I knew you'd resort to some kind of stunt to get me back here,' said Ann. 'I was counting on it.'

Victor said, 'The party was Emma's idea.'

'Oh,' said Ann. 'So the lure was for someone else.' Ann was searching Emma's eyes. The Good Witch looked away.

Victor asked, 'What lure?'

'Poor Victor. Is all this going ogre your head?' asked Ann, grinning.

'Good one,' he said. 'I love it when you pun, Daisy. It makes me want to pluck you.'

'Patience, dear,' said Ann. 'Don't be ogre eager.'

Meanwhile, Hoff and Susan, devil and angel, were straightening each other's costumes with the love and comfort of an old married couple.

There was only so much romantic happiness Emma could stand to watch. She wondered suddenly if the party had been a bad idea. Emma contemplated escaping to her place where she could be safe and alone. And she would have tried it, but Queen Elizabeth, Captain Picard, and Martha Stewart blocked the terrace door. She could escape by jumping over the balcony, but then again, she'd go splat on the sidewalk.

Mata Hari came up to her and said, 'You look so pretty!'

'You look freezing!' said Emma. 'It's fifty degrees out here.'

Deirdre patted her exposed belly. 'I've got body fat to keep me warm.'

Emma could see that. Deirdre's costume consisted of a

silver bikini, diaphanous genie pants, a few veils of the same light fabric tucked into her bra straps, and ample love handles.

'Check out that hot Blacula over there,' said Deirdre, pointing. 'Maybe I'll let him suck my blood.'

'Costumes bring out your frisky side?' asked Emma.

The waitress/spy nodded. 'Grown-ups get so few opportunities to break out,' said Deirdre, and she headed over to Blacula.

Emma looked down at her gown. This was one costume of many for her. The disguises she'd used just this week: Emeril, Bettie Paige, the old crone, the doorperson, the Jersey dyke. Unlike Deirdre, who used her costume to show a hidden side of herself, Emma wore disguises to hide all of herself. Maybe if she stopped hiding in disguises (including her everyday all black, all the time), she'd be able to break out too.

'If only,' she said out loud.

'If only what?' asked the man who appeared at her side.

She barely glanced at him. 'Another William Dearborn.'

'Yes, I noticed three of me here,' he said. 'But I'm the most authentic.'

Emma's amber eyes widened. 'It is you,' she said. 'What are you doing here?'

'I was invited,' he said haughtily. 'And I'd like to watch the parade. If you'll excuse me.' He gently nudged her aside and walked over to the ledge.

William turned his back to her, watching the parade go by. Emma crept up behind him (hard to do when swishing with tulle and crinoline) and tried to think of an image to send him, something soft and sweet. She touched him gently on the back of his neck, thought of Cloudy the cat, and closed her eyes.

A second or two later, he took her hand from his neck. He didn't give it back. 'Your fingers are cold,' he said. 'And if you don't apologize, I might not forgive you.'

Another echo from her daydreams. 'I'm sorry. You know how much. And if you don't accept my apology,' she said, waving her wand, 'I'll turn you into a plumber.'

'Please do,' he said. 'My garbage disposal broke this morning.'

'You have a garbage disposal?' asked Emma covetously.

'Liam. My man! Thanks for coming!' shouted Victor. He and Ann were waving from across the terrace.

'Liam!' said Marcie, darting over. 'I'm glad you made it. Have you seen Alfie?'

'Not yet,' said William.

Emma said to him, 'Guests were encouraged to wear costumes, you know.'

William said, 'I've come as a narcissistic bastard who can't always control his temper.'

'Good costume,' said Marcie. 'Now help me find Alfie. He didn't think you were going to show.'

The model linked arms with William and Emma. The three of them walked back inside. As soon as she was next to William, Emma no longer wanted to escape. Or be alone.

As quickly as it grew, the crowd had mercifully thinned. Victor's mulled hard cider punch bowl was empty. So were the sandwich platters Hoff presumably brought. Emma saw one lonely egg salad on a mini-bagel and grabbed it for herself.

'Will the real William Dearborn please stand up,' she

heard Hoff say. She turned to see Satan shaking hands with Dearborn, as if they were making a deal for his soul. 'I'm thrilled you made it,' said Hoff. 'I didn't think you'd accept a last-minute invitation.'

'Happy to be here,' said William, taking a beer from Hoff.

'I'd like you to meet my fiancée, Susan Knight,' said Hoff.

William took her angelic hand and kissed it. 'Susan and I are well acquainted. We've had a wonderful time together.'

'We sure did,' said Susan.

'Of course, that afternoon at the hotel,' said Hoff. 'I was a bit out of it on Vicodin that day.'

'The party where Chloe Sevigny nearly choked,' said Emma.

'I got a call from her today,' said William.

'She's supposed to be here,' said Emma.

'I know. She invited me, too.'

So her fish had taken the party bait. How could he not? It'd been offered six different times. 'Your phone must have been ringing off the hook today,' said Emma.

'I got some calls,' he said, smiling weakly at her. 'From everyone but the one person I'd most hoped to hear from.' She swallowed some egg salad. William handed her the beer to wash it down. 'I like your gown,' he added. 'Billie Burke, right?'

Hoff said, 'I wonder if Chloe Sevigny would like to write her memoirs.'

'Go ask her,' said Susan. 'She's over there. Victor is photographing her.'

Sure enough, where Victor had set up a backdrop, Chloe sat on a stool in leather chaps and a cowboy hat and nothing else (!). *Thwap*. Flash pop. Victor snapped her picture. Ann and Armand were watching the shoot. Armand was dressed in a black suit with a wire attached to his ear. He was sweeping the party with his eyes, and then they connected with Emma's. She waved.

Lumbering over (black was slimming, but not shortening), Armand greeted his host and his former patient tenderly.

''Sup,' he said.

Hoff shook his hand. 'You look well,' he said genially.

'You too,' said Armand. 'The swelling has really gone down.'

Emma said, 'How's the fight against death going?'

'Constant struggle,' said Armand. 'You of all people must feel it tonight, Emma.'

'Feel what?'

'Bad spirits.'

Emma said, 'If you're referring to the cider, I had nothing to do with it.'

Armand touched his ear wire. 'Chloe wants me.' He made eye contact with each in the circle and said, 'Be on high alert. All of you.' And then he lumbered off.

Marcie, who'd flitted off somewhere, returned. 'I can't find Alfie anywhere,' she said, agitated.

A ghost sputtered by overhead, barely choking out a moan. Hoff said, 'Emma, I think it's time you gave up the ghost.'

To Marcie, who was increasingly upset, Emma said, 'I'm sure Alfie's here somewhere.'

'He's not,' she insisted. 'He's gone,' and then she started to cry.

Only Emma knew that when Marcie said 'gone', she didn't mean 'out on a beer run'. The Good Witch started to formulate a search plan. Turned out she didn't have to.

'Hey, Marcie!' called Alfie, trying to get her attention from the other side of the loft, his dreadlocks bouncing as he jumped to be seen over the crowd.

'See? He's fine,' said Emma. His reappearance would, hopefully, allow Emma to turn her attention back to William. She'd said she was sorry, but he hadn't officially accepted. Until she heard him say so, she'd feel lopsided, unbalanced. She needed him to straighten her out.

Alfie had pushed his way over to their little group, 'I've got a big surprise for you, Marcie,' he said. 'Liam. Dude.' Alfie thudded his chest with the side of his fist in greeting.

William thudded his chest in return and held up a peace sign. Marcie said, 'Where have you been?'

'I went to pick up a present for you,' said Alfie. 'Are you ready?'

'I was worried about you,' said Marcie. And then, 'A present? *For me?*'

Alfie kissed her poreless forehead. 'The most important thing in life – my life, anyway – is to keep my relationships pure. Family, friends, people I work with.'

'You work?' asked William.

'In the spirit of purity,' Alfie continued, 'I tracked down someone you've had a hard time with and invited her here so the two of you can forgive each other and move on without baggage. And here she is!'

As if reaching into a grab bag, Alfie stuck his arm

into the revelers behind him and dragged a woman into view.

It was the Wicked Witch of the West, Glinda's evil nemesis. Pointy black hat, black flowing robes, green painted face, a hooked prosthetic nose, and a chin wart with a single hair growing out of it.

Marcie asked, 'What is this? Where's my present?'

The Bad Witch cackled. 'Forgotten me already?' she asked.

'Daphne?' Marcie whispered.

'That's right,' said the manslaughtering, liposucking, unemployed person. 'I've come to make good.'

Marcie quavered, 'I don't know what you're talking about.'

'This has been in the works for a long, long time.'

Daphne stood between Emma and Alfie. Only Emma could see Daphne reach into the folds of her robe with a menacing green-lipped grin. She withdrew something long and thin. A flash of shiny metal caught Emma's eye.

'She's got a knife!' screamed Emma, lunging at Daphne and throwing her to the ground. Emma had the weight advantage, but Daphne had the muscles. The Evil Witch rolled on top of Emma, crushing her crinoline and slamming her on the floor.

Victor's voice rose above the fray. 'Hold it!' he shouted.

The two women froze. Victor clicked. *Thwap*. Flash pop.

'Got it,' said Victor.

Emma recovered more quickly and slapped Daphne, her palm sliding across the face makeup, leaving a glop of it on Daphne's shoulder. Daphne retaliated by grabbing

Emma's hair and yanking it hard. Emma saw stars. Planets. The moon with William's face on it.

Alfie and William pulled Daphne off. Marcie was screaming dramatically (she should take some acting jobs, thought Emma). Hoff and Susan helped Emma to her feet, finding her crown and wand. The party had gone quiet and everyone was staring at Emma's chest. She looked down to see that her glorious gown, her mother's legacy, was torn in front, her lacy white bra visible for all to see.

Hoff said, 'Yet again, Emma showcasing her assets.'

Victor said, 'Hold it!' *Thwap*. 'Got it.'

Emma tucked the torn panel into the top of her bra to cover herself. 'I'm trying to save a life,' she said, 'not give a free peep show.' She walked over to Daphne, who was still restrained by Alfie and William, and reached inside her robe.

'This could be hot,' said Victor, aiming his camera again.

Daphne screamed, 'Get away from me.'

'You won't melt,' said Emma. Inside the black robes, Emma felt around and made contact. Slowly, she withdrew a hard metal object.

Marcie said, 'That's a funny looking knife.'

'It's a nameplate,' said Daphne, shrugging free of Alfie and William. 'A nameplate for my new desk, at my new job.'

Emma examined the twelve-inch flat hunk of metal that, indeed, wasn't a knife. 'Daphne Wittfield, Producer,' she read. On the lower left hand corner was the Bravo network logo.

Daphne righted her wig/pointy hat combo and then snatched the nameplate back from Emma. 'I got the call from Bravo within minutes of the SlimBurn press conference. They like my "success or die trying" attitude and offered me the job of producing a TV show. A reality show. And guess who they want to be the star.'

'This is really flattering,' said Emma. 'But I'm more of a behind the scenes . . .'

Daphne hissed at her. She turned her attention to the model and said, 'They want you, Marcie. And Alfie. The two of you.'

'My own TV show?' Marcie whispered.

'It's what we've always planned, what we've dreamed of,' said Daphne. 'Cameras on you – and Alfie – around the clock.'

'Oh my God!' cried Marcie. 'I can't believe it!'

Alfie said, 'I'm not sure about this.'

'But *darling*,' said Marcie, back in seductive mode. 'Your art will be seen by millions. Think of the multitudes we can reach with our message of peace and love! Where is Sherman? I need him here. Sherman! Has anyone seen a Wolfman?'

'He's in the lobby,' said Alfie, 'making out with some black chick in a blond wig.'

Natasha and Sherman. Another match! Emma had done it again. *Damn, I'm good*, she thought.

Marcie said, 'To the lobby.'

Marcie, Daphne, and Alfie walked toward the elevator in a tight cluster, discussing the logistics of their new venture. Marcie seemed to forget her fear of Daphne completely. Emma imagined Daphne's face when she discovered her former assistant making out with Marcie's legal adviser.

William took Emma's hand and said, 'Come outside with me.'

She let herself be led to the terrace and right up to the ledge. Several yards away, Deirdre as Mata Hari was flirting with a Blacula in his cape and tux.

Emma looked down at the parade. The FDNY float was just going by, two dozen firemen dressed as dalmatians upon it. 'Daphne is capable of anything. Should I be worried about Marcie?' she asked.

William said, 'For all your vision, Emma, you can be blind as a bat. Daphne and Marcie are linked. They're destined to be together, for better or, more likely, for worse.'

'I'm not blind. I can see just fine. Super fine. And I can *feel*. Only recently I've discovered my sixth sense.'

'You see naked people?' he asked, waggling his eyebrows.

'I have intuition. Run of the mill, apparently. But still palpable.'

'And what does your intuition tell you about me?' he asked.

'It says you could have come up with a better costume.'

'What does it say about why I'm here?' he asked.

'You wanted to see me?' she ventured.

'I sure didn't come for the food,' he said. 'What did I want to tell you, when I saw you?'

'That you forgive me.'

'I forgave you ten minutes after I left your apartment last night,' he said. 'I wanted you again when I saw you on stage at Marcie's press conference. And I fell back in love with you tonight while you were tangling on the floor with

Daphne.' He touched Emma's cheek with his bare hand. 'And now I'm full of regret.'

'About what?' she asked.

'That I haven't seen all of your free peep shows.'

'You forgive me, and you love me,' said Emma, seeking confirmation.

'That hour we spent in bed. There's no going back after something like that.'

'Imagine what two hours in bed would be like.'

'We don't have to imagine anymore,' he said, inching toward her. 'If we kiss, we might spontaneously combust.'

She smiled. 'The risk to reward ratio is in our favor.'

'Try to keep your eyes open,' he said and planted one on her.

The conflagration behind her eyes. The urge to close them was powerful, but William kept his eyes open too. They watched each other kiss. Emma wrestled for control of her rising temperature.

He pulled back and said, 'I'm sweating.'

'Me, too,' she said.

'Kissing you is like taking a sauna.'

'We'll have to keep a glass of water next to the bed.'

'Make it a pitcher,' he said.

Crash. The sound of glass breaking. Emma and William instinctively turned toward it.

A woman in a lobster costume was on the ground, a broken beer bottle next to her. A man as a clam was at her side. He was upbraiding another man in a black hoodie and a ski mask.

William's muscles tightened. 'Step behind me, Emma.'

The hooded man spotted her and lifted his arm. In his hand, he held a gun.

The lobster screamed. So did the clam.

'Connie Quivers,' said the Hood, pulling off his ski mask.

'Jeff Bragg,' said Emma from behind William.

William asked, 'Connie Quivers?'

Emma said, 'It's my porn star name. In case match-making didn't work out.'

A crowd gathered on the balcony behind Jeff. 'Get back,' he said in an eerily calm voice. To Emma: 'Seymour Lankey got a message to me from prison today. He thinks I've cheated him. He's sworn to send me to hell,' said Jeff. 'But I'll go happily knowing you got there first.'

William spun and threw Emma to the ground. A gun blast. The crowd erupted, pushing, screaming, scrambling for cover. Emma realized she was intact and tried to scramble to her feet but got caught in her crinoline. Through a forest of legs, she thought she saw Armand Chicora pinning Jeff on the ground, one foot on the gun arm, a knee on his spine. Blacula had another gun drawn and trained on Jeff. Dozens of people had rushed to the balcony railing and were looking over.

Emma didn't see William anywhere. He'd been standing right next to her. Hoff appeared and lifted Emma to her feet. He said, 'Are you all right?'

'Where's William?' she asked.

Hoff said, 'He went over.'

'*What?*' she shrieked and lunged for the ledge.

Peering down three stories, Emma saw the man who loved her. Her breath caught and then she started crying.

E mma ran off the balcony, through the loft, down the fire stairs, and out onto Sixth Avenue. She pushed aside a man dressed like a Roman gladiator to scale the side of the float/pick-up truck William had landed on. It wasn't easy in her gown. Half of the tulle ripped off when she heaved herself onto the flatbed.

There lay William Dearborn, on his back, atop a mountain of yellow T-shirts.

Emma cried, 'William! Say something!'

He groaned and said, 'I did a double gainer with a twist. Did you see?'

The gladiator said, 'I'd give it a ten.'

William sat up and rubbed the back of his head. He said, 'What did I land on?' He pulled a T-shirt loose from the pile. 'Jews for Jesus?'

'I knew I liked those shirts,' said Emma, sobbing with relief.

'Emma?' asked the gladiator. 'Is that you?'

'Martin,' she said. 'Consider me converted.'

'Really?' he asked.

'No,' she said. 'But I'll make a donation with William's money.'

Hoff yelled down from the balcony. William waved up at him. The crowd on the balcony cheered.

Emma said, 'I guess I was wrong.'

William said, 'About what?'

'Jesus does save.'

'He saves big time,' said Martin. 'And with the Jews, he pays wholesale.'

'You will tell me who that gunman was and why he wanted to meet you in hell?' asked William.

'It's a long story. It might take all night.'

'Then tell me tomorrow,' he said, eyeing her exposed bra. 'We've got other plans for tonight.'

William stood up, wincing a little, and waved at the parade-goers who'd gathered around the pick-up truck. The crowd on the terrace started throwing fun-size Snickers bars at the Jews for Jesus truck. For a moment in time on Waverly Place, the sky rained chocolate.

Paramedics were climbing onto the truck now. Emma was told to get down and give them room to make sure William hadn't broken anything, even a fingernail.

Emma's attention turned toward a commotion at the front door of Victor's building. Armand and Blacula exited with Jeff Bragg in handcuffs. A spill of people followed behind them, including an ogre, a daisy, an angel, and the devil. Blacula had removed his widow's peak wig and fake teeth, and Emma could see his face more clearly.

'Detective Marsh,' she said. 'You crashed my party?'

'I was on covert surveillance,' he said. 'Best night of my life. I met a girl – and got my man.'

'Ms Hutch, is that you?' asked a man with a blue bow tie who'd run out of Citibank to see what all the commotion was about.

'Mr Cannery!' she said. 'I'm flat broke. Take away my apartment. Put me in debtors' prison. I don't care.' She was still sobbing with relief that William was okay. The T-shirts had broken William's fall; his fall had broken something inside Emma. Like an explosion of the mind, a violent burst in her brain, Emma saw the light. She would not hesitate again. Or wait, worry, or hide, as long as William was at her side. She'd face the sad ending if she had to. But hopefully, she'd be spared.

Mr Cannery said, 'My God, is that William Dearborn?' The banker started twitching, as if he'd suddenly seen all the money in the world. Emma supposed the sight of William might be the equivalent.

'That's him, all right. And he's my boyfriend!' Emma announced giddily and proudly before turning her attention back to the action.

She watched Armand help Detective Marsh shove Jeff into one of the police cars that had zoomed in from every direction. The New York One news van also materialized. Emma overheard Detective Marsh explain to another cop what'd happened on the terrace. 'And at the critical moment,' he said, 'this big man here grabbed Bragg's arm, causing him to misfire.' Detective Marsh looked up at Armand Chicora. 'If it hadn't been for you, William Dearborn might've been shot.'

The ex-orderly said, 'I knew something was going to happen.'

'You're a hero,' said Detective Marsh.

Emma gave Armand a hug. William had been helped down from the flatbed by the paramedics and was making his way over. The gentle giant turned to receive him. The artist smiled gratefully at Armand, and the two men shook hands.

Thwap. Victor took the photo that would appear on the front page of newspapers around the world the next morning.

Martin, meanwhile, was standing next to his pick-up truck, telling his side of the story to a couple of cops. Emma noted that his Roman skirt showed a lot of leg.

She rushed over to him and said, 'What are you doing over here? Put on a T-shirt and get in front of those news cameras.'

'Emma, I can't,' he protested.

'You're on a quest, remember? You've got conviction. Prove it. Put on a fucking T-shirt and tell New York that your truck saved William Dearborn from being splattered all over Sixth Avenue.'

'But my costume,' said Martin. 'My legs are showing.'

Emma groaned. She climbed up the side of the truck – again – and grabbed a T-shirt. She forced Martin's head into it, and pushed him toward the New York One van.

He said, 'Wait. I need to tell you something important first.'

Emma said, 'Stay away from accountants with guns?'

Martin said, 'Two seconds before your friend landed in the flatbed – and I mean, two seconds – the truck stalled and stopped.'

'Why?' she asked.

'I don't know.'

'You popped the clutch?'

'It's an automatic.'

'Dead battery?'

He shook his head. 'Brand new.'

Emma said, 'So you think it was . . .'

Martin held up his hand. 'Maybe it was divine intervention. Maybe it was something else.'

'Magic,' she said.

Martin shrugged, smoothed down his T-shirt, and headed over to the news van.

28

October again. The first day of Emma's favorite month of the year.

'Hit me,' said Deirdre at Oeuf, reaching out her hand.

Emma said, 'I'm trying out a new skill. Put your hand down and look at me.' She stared into Deirdre's eyes and thought hard about breakfast.

'Eggs Florentine, sauce on the side?' asked the waitress. 'You can send without touching now?'

Emma said. 'My brand new eggstraordinary trick.'

'Don't brag,' said William, next to her at the table. 'It's immodest. You should let me do that for you.' He inhaled before telling Deirdre, 'Emma can now send messages without touching. She's figured out how to retain complete control of her skin temperature during moments of physical defenselessness. And she's been an avid student of the erotic arts.'

'Okay, stop there,' said Deirdre.

'She's eggsquisite,' continued William, 'at one particular skill. I call it the Big Gulp.'

Deirdre said, 'Tone it down. This is a family restaurant. I don't care if you are the owner.'

'She's very bossy,' said William to his girlfriend.

'That's what happens when you date a cop,' said Emma.

About eight months ago, when William and Emma's relationship was three months old, the barmy half-Brit decided he loved Waverly Place more than any other block in New York and that he wanted to buy it. Not for lack of trying, William wasn't able to purchase an entire city street. But he did succeed at acquiring Emma's building, Victor's building, the neighboring storefronts (a bong shop and a Greek diner), and Oeuf, a sale that was over easy. His ownership of Emma's building did not, however, include her apartment. Even though William had lent her the money to keep it out of Citibank's clutches all those months ago, he called the apartment 'hers'. She called it 'theirs'.

Victor, seated at William's right, said, 'I'd like to lodge a complaint with the landlord too. Liam, you have got to do something about the crime scene tourists. I can't get in or out of my own building. The neighbors blame me.'

'So hire a goon to watch the door, and I'll put him on the payroll.'

The photographer said, 'I would if I had time.'

Since his famous photo of William and Armand shaking hands appeared in newspapers around the globe, Victor'd been working his arse off. Editorial, advertising, portfolios, travel brochures. Victor continued to shoot portraits for The Better Witch, Inc. The work was quicker and easier for him, though, now that they'd stopped doing the staged sexy setting and costuming. It was William's idea to try straightforward smiling portraits. Counterintuitively, the subtle approach was more effective. The targeted men were asking out Emma's clients, on average, four days sooner than before, and the relationships lasted longer too. Her 'long term' to 'short term' ratio was up. And business was booming. Emma paid back William's loan within three months.

She asked Victor, 'Where are you off to next?'

'Hawaii,' he said. 'A new hotel is opening, and they want me to shoot pictures for their press kit.'

'How long will you be away?' asked William.

Victor laughed. 'In other words, how long will Ann be cranky?'

'Cranky?' said William. 'Try a raving, frothing, hateful bitch.'

'She's always so sweet on the phone to me,' mused Victor.

'Maybe if you married her, she'd feel better about your trips,' suggested Emma, not for the first time.

'Marcie and Alfie got married,' countered Victor. 'And look how that turned out.'

'Happily ever after doesn't draw the ratings like infidelity and divorce,' said William.

'Hoff and Susan are happy,' said Emma. 'And Sherman and Natasha.'

'Who are Sherman and Natasha?' asked Victor.

'Don't change the subject,' said Emma.

Victor said, 'I'll propose to Ann exactly three minutes after you and William get engaged.'

Emma said, 'Chicken.'

'Look who's talking,' said Victor. 'You're both chicken.'

William said, 'We're not chicken. We're busy. ArtSpeak 2.0 launches next month. The book comes out at Christmas. Emma is still embroiled in the Lankey/Bragg criminal investigation.'

Victor asked, 'Any update on the reward?'

Emma shook her head. 'Susan says a three-year delay is typical, so it's another two years at least before I see a penny. And, even then, legal fees will eat thirty percent of it. The government will take thirty percent. I'll be left with a mere forty percent.'

'Forty percent of two million is still eight hundred thousand,' said Victor.

'Like I haven't done the math,' said Emma.

Vic's cell phone rang. 'Hi, Ann,' he said into it. To Emma and William, he said, 'Cover my coffee?'

They nodded and Victor got up from his chair and left the restaurant.

Emma and William ate a leisurely breakfast and then left Oeuf hand in hand, just as they had nearly every morning for the last eleven months. Some nights, when William had meetings the next day, they slept at his midtown office residence. When he was entertaining friends or business partners, they stayed at 'their' suite at the Tribeca Grand. On the many nights Emma posed for William, they slept on the bed in his Greene Street studio. But usually they stayed at Emma's white apartment, their one-bedroom slice of heaven.

They strolled along Waverly, toward Washington Square, taking their time, enjoying the autumn air. William said, 'You know, I have a mysterious power of my own.'

'Really?' she asked.

'I can make people walk into lampposts,' he said. 'Watch.'

A young woman came toward them from the other direction. William rumpled his trademark bangs. When the woman got close enough, he stared at her. When she was right alongside, William winked. Her mouth dropped and her eyes bugged. She gawked openly at William and then – smack – she walked right into a lamppost.

Emma nodded. 'Very impressive.'

He said, 'Better than anything you can do.'

'I can match that,' she said.

'Prove it,' he countered.

They'd entered the park and were nearing the rings of the fountain at the center. Emma found her pigeon and led William toward her. She said, 'Okay. See that woman with the cornrows and the blue sweatshirt?'

'What about her?'

'With my incredible powers, I'm going to make her scream and then collapse on the ground.'

'I can hardly wait,' he said.

As they rounded the fountain ring and got closer, the woman looked up and said, 'Palm reading, twenty dollars.'

Emma smiled broadly at her and cocked her head discreetly at William.

The palmist took a few minutes to register what she was seeing. Then she screamed dramatically and fell on the pavement, her arms splayed out in front of her. Stenciled on her sleeve were the words 'Above Average'.

William said, 'Quite a show! I'd say well above average.'

Recovering almost instantly from her shock, the palmist sprang to her feet and started yelling, 'I've got the sight!'

Ring. Cell phone. William's. He took a quick call. 'We have to go. There's a surprise waiting for you in your apartment,' he told Emma. 'Just dropped off by my head of security.'

'You have Armand making deliveries?' tisked Emma.

'Trust me. This was a fragile package. Handle with care.'

William hurried Emma along. When they left the park, Above Average was still ranting at the fountain.

Back at Emma's building, they practically ran down the seventh floor hallway. Grinning with anticipation, Emma pushed open her apartment door and scanned the living room. Nothing.

William said, 'In the bedroom.'

Emma went in back. On the bed was a large box with a red ribbon. She untied it and removed the lid.

A furry little face popped out.

William said, 'I can't count how many times you've put images of a certain cat into my head. Black, with gold eyes.'

'This kitty is white,' said Emma, scooping it into her arms. 'With green eyes.'

'White furniture, white cat,' said fastidious William. 'You don't want black hair everywhere.'

Emma hugged the tiny animal to her cheek. 'It's been decades since I had a pet. I honestly never thought I'd have another.'

'So you don't want the cat?' asked William.

'No!' she said. 'I do. I want this cat. I need this cat. I can't live without it.'

He seemed relieved and sat on the edge of the bed. 'What shall we name her?'

'How about Martin?' she said.

'It's a girl,' he said. 'I was thinking more along the lines of "Mrs Emma Dearborn's Cat".'

'Cat? Not very original,' said Emma.

'You prefer Martin?' he asked. 'Fine. What about the Mrs Emma Dearborn part?'

'Mrs Emma Dearborn's Martin?' she asked, perplexed.

'No, I meant . . . you know what I meant,' he said.

Emma laughed. 'You want to make me the Betrothed Witch. A hitched Hutch.'

'Eggsactly,' said William.

She kissed him gently. 'Most men give a ring to propose.'

'Do they?' he asked, kissing her back.

'I've had visions of our wedding,' she said. 'I know just what to wear.'

'Glad that's settled,' he said, easing back on the bed. 'Now put that pussy in the box and take off your pants.'

A sweaty, sex-drenched hour later, the two lay naked, glistening, and breathing hard.

Emma said, 'We should call Victor. Tell him who's chicken.'

'Speaking of chickens, and eggs,' said William, 'I think we've just now solved the age-old dilemma.'

'We have?' asked Emma, snuggling against him.

'Unless I'm mistaken,' he said, grinning, 'witch came first.'

NINA KILLHAM

Mounting Desire

Jack Carter and Molly Desire are just housemates. There could never be anything between them – they're far too different. **Aren't they?**

Jack, a successful romance writer, is looking for his soul mate. Molly, a fully paid-up sexaholic, views having to lodge in Jack's house as a necessary but very temporary evil.

For a while, it looks as though they're the exception to the oldest rule in the book: **the one that says opposites attract**. But then Molly takes to writing her own instantly successful steamy romances, and Jack is furious. As the sparks start to fly, it appears there's a whole lot more to their relationship than meets the eye. But could it be that two such different housemates could really be . . . soul mates?

'Truly a book to be devoured with relish' Jennifer Crusie, author of *Faking It* and *Fast Woman*

0 7553 3277 6

little
black
dress

SWAN ADAMSON

My Three Husbands

What's a girl to do when husbands just keep lining up?

Meet Venus Gilroy: twenty-five, carefree, irresistible, and with a nasty habit of getting hitched to the wrong guy.

Husband No 1: would have been a winner, if it hadn't been for the forgery and embezzlement charges.

Husband No 2: sometimes a girl has to realise – meeting a husband in a strip bar will never end well.

Husband No 3: is the real deal. Isn't he? Surely sexy, rugged, *principled* Tremaynne is finally the right one for Venus?

With her insane mother, not to mention her two gay dads, plus porn-video-store-owner boss, all weighing in with advice, it's time for Venus to learn for herself – how you know that Mr Right . . . doesn't turn out to be Mr Wrong.

0 7553 3364 0

little
black
dress

You can buy any of these other **Little Black Dress** titles from your bookshop or *direct from the publisher*.

FREE P&P AND UK DELIVERY
(Overseas and Ireland £3.50 per book)

Daisy's Back in Town	Rachel Gibson	£3.99
Sex, Lies and Online Dating	Rachel Gibson	£3.99
I'm In No Mood for Love	Rachel Gibson	£3.99
The Bachelorette Party	Karen McCullah Lutz	£3.99
My Three Husbands	Swan Adamson	£3.99
Step on It, Cupid	Lorelei Mathias	£3.99
Mounting Desire	Nina Killham	£3.99
He Loves Lucy	Susan Donovan	£3.99
Spirit Willing, Flesh Weak	Julie Cohen	£3.99
Decent Exposure	Phillipa Ashley	£3.99
She'll Take It	Mary Carter	£3.99

TO ORDER SIMPLY CALL THIS NUMBER

01235 400 414

or visit our website: www.madaboutbooks.com

Prices and availability subject to change without notice